The Picture
of Contented
New Wealth

First published by O Books, 2009
O Books is an imprint of John Hunt Publishing Ltd., The Bothy, Deershot Lodge, Park Lane, Ropley,
Hants, SO24 0BE, UK
office1@o-books.net
www.o-books.net

Distribution in:	South Africa
	Stephan Phillips (pty) Ltd
UK and Europe	Email: orders@stephanphillips.com
Orca Book Services	Tel: 27 21 4489839 Telefax: 27 21 4479879
orders@orcabookservices.co.uk	
Tel: 01202 665432 Fax: 01202 666219	Text copyright Tariq Goddard 2008
Int. code (44)	
	Design: Stuart Davies
USA and Canada	
NBN	ISBN: 978 1 84694 270 9
custserv@nbnbooks.com	
Tel: 1 800 462 6420 Fax: 1 800 338 4550	All rights reserved. Except for brief quotations
	in critical articles or reviews, no part of this
Australia and New Zealand	book may be reproduced in any manner without
Brumby Books	prior written permission from the publishers.
sales@brumbybooks.com.au	
Tel: 61 3 9761 5535 Fax: 61 3 9761 7095	The rights of Tariq Goddard as author have
	been asserted in accordance with the
Far East (offices in Singapore, Thailand,	Copyright, Designs and Patents Act 1988.
Hong Kong, Taiwan)	
Pansing Distribution Pte Ltd	
kemal@pansing.com	A CIP catalogue record for this book is available
Tel: 65 6319 9939 Fax: 65 6462 5761	from the British Library.

Printed by Digital Book Print

The Picture
of Contented
New Wealth

Tariq Goddard

BOOKS

Winchester, UK
Washington, USA

Tariq Goddard was born in London in 1975. He read Philosophy at King's College London, and Continental Philosophy at The University of Warwick and The University of Surrey. In 2002 his first novel, 'Homage to Firing Squad' was nominated for the Whitbread (Costa) Prize and the Wodehouse-Bollinger Comic Writing Award. He was included as one of Waterstones "Faces of the Future", and the novel, whose film rights were sold, was listed as one of the Observer's Four debuts of the year. In 2003 his second novel, 'Dynamo' was cited as one of the ten best sports novels of all time by Observer Sport's Magazine. 'The Morning Rides Behind Us', his third novel was released in 2005 and short-listed for the Commonwealth Prize for Fiction. He lives with his wife on a farm in Wiltshire where he is writing his new novel, 'The Message'.

Acclaim for Tariq Goddard

FOR 'HOMAGE TO A FIRING SQUAD

Cerebral, powerful and accomplished **The Face**

A pacy, poised and undeniably exciting debut...a teat bleakly humorous, well written adventure **Boyd Tonkin, Independent**

A clever mix of humour and horror and sadness and life and death...a surreal book that juggles humour with horror as it journeys deep into the night **John King**

Goddard's highly impressive debut mixes a black comic tone reminiscent of Quentin Tarantino and Graham Greene, a cracking good read **Mail on Sunday**

Goddard's eye is for irony and disaster, a potent thriller, driven by unravelling the neuroses of his characters as much as by uncovering the politics behind their predicament **Observer**

Frank sex and bloody and farcical violence, serious, readable and unpredictable **The Big Issue**

A highly polished debut, bullets fly through the air, knives flash silver in the moonlight **Daily Mail**

Bravura quality, a dazzling debut, half farce half atrocity **James Collard, Saturday Times Magazine**

Beautifully choreographed, plotted with the minimum of fuss...dark with excellent seasoning **Spain Magazine**

Well rounded, sophisticated, evocative and darkly humorous, full of fear, excitement and futility **The Morning Star**

Auspicious and audacious, a triumph of philosophical enquiry with earthy gory action **Independent on Sunday**

Impressive, each character is drawn with humour and subtlety...a fine balance between comedy and tragedy, pathos and slapstick **The Times**

A nasty and carnage ridden pastiche **The Guardian**

FOR DYNAMO

A tremendous story of everyday life in a place of tremendous unrest **ES Magazine**

A thoroughly entertaining story of drinking and women, colourful, lively and enjoyable **The Times**

Laugh out aloud, an acute grasp of subtlety and irony, one of our finest young novelists **Arena**

Crisp, colourful, lively and enjoyable **The Guardian**

Riveting, authentic and very down and dirty... essential reading **David Shukman, Daily Mail**

Original, clever and accomplished, a wonderful premise for a novel, which he pulls of with a flourish, a smart, engaging novel from a refreshingly unusual voice in British Fiction **Martyn Bedford, The New Statesman**

STAR CHOICE- irresistible and original **Bookseller Magazine**

A compulsive, headlong narrative, profound psychological sense, the conclusion is surprising and masterly **Uncut**

Sheer excitement that matches Elmore Leonard in hyperbole and humour. Characters slip into the readers heart **Sunday Times**

Frictionlessly combines the individual and universal, both an aria and hooligan holler to the human spirit **Time Out**

A colourful and pensive novel full of eccentricity and desperate humour...Dynamo's closing moments grip like a vice **Sunday Herald**

A fascinating story told with tension, pace and humour **Daren King, Scotland on Sunday**

Very little football occurs in Dynamo, yet it remains as transfixing as a Maradona run and as surprising and wonderful as Wales beating Italy. Dynamo like football itself, is an affirmation and exageration of life **Niall Griffiths**

Four stars, a brilliant and offbeat comedy spun out of a bizarre true story **South China Morning Post**

FOR THE MORNING RIDES BEHIND US

An exuberant narrative that turns on the fresh possibilities of tenderness...simply rumbustious **James Urquhart, Independent**

Valiant, full of anecdotes maxims and bravado **Time Out**

The politics of the time are portrayed with a simple gusto, it sparkles with a depth of language and ideas but retains buoyancy, it's also very funny and playful...a universal and entertaining novel about England, freedom, fear and existential malaise **Richard Cabut, The Daily Telegraph**

It's tone is dark, getting darker, a remarkable portrayal of friendship and frustration, grimly funny rolling with narrative energy **Arena**

It strives to explain post war society, the endeavour of which is exhilarating **Sunday Telegraph**

Large minded and deserving of a wide readership. It is hard to believe that there is a more promising novelist under the age of 30 working in Britain today **Andrew Biswell, Scotland on Sunday**

A pacy and intelligent tale that has won him friends in high places, full of whip cracking prose and characters that bounce of the page **Romford Recorder**

A story of heroes who fell to earth, akin to Dennis Potter, stunning set pieces handled with gusto and poignancy... redemptive and genuinely moving **The Scotsman**

For Emma

What is constant is not an invariable quantity of suffering,
but its progress towards hell

Theodor Adorno

Prologue

Not all houses are built to be lived in. The paths that lead to them do not lead to other places; they are seldom found on maps or listed in directories, and were it not for the curiosity of a world watched by strange gods, they would not exist at all.

At night their owners, who fear the dark, talk in raised voices to rid themselves of their shared misgiving that they are the inhabitants of a dead body, the smell of which has grown too strong to ignore.

Yet the decision to live in such a place engenders a binding loyalty to one's choice, casting a spell where there would otherwise be the willing admission of a mistake. Stubbornly the owners persist in treating these places as mere buildings, explaining away the rot and the other more troubling aspects of their homes, as aberrations that will be addressed in the fullness of time. With reckless haste they spread their lives and associations through rooms betrothed to other, earlier memories, making themselves comfortable when they ought to have remembered their ancestors' loathing of the unknown.

Tyger Tyger House, unlike so many buildings of its kind, had never stood empty for long; its successive owners having arrived in the expectation of being the first to experience transcendence there, the superficial unlikelihood of doing so part of their new project's charm. The house had struck them all as a presence; the squinting turrets growing upwards like a pair of deformed heads, the paltry moat a canvas for their unrealisable expectations; the property's very loneliness proof of the subtle individuality of their perception.

Dr Graves-Maurice had bought Tyger Tyger at the turn of the last century seeking a second career as a watercolour artist. Schoolmaster Motley had followed him thinking that the house's seclusion would aid him in his ambition to become a male

Bronte; and Maureen Crompton, more modestly, thought that the country air would save her ailing health. Others had followed in the belief that they had simply purchased a sound investment.

They were all wrong. The house was there for itself; biding its time for the arrival of the thing it had been built for. One after another, its various owners parted with their money, lost sight of their initial purpose and waited for whatever it was they feared most to happen, never sure that it would but never forgetting that it might.

Alone amongst them all, Brigit Conti knew that she had chosen the house in which she might die, but would never grow old in. Its old walls Saxon in inspiration, its site, she guessed, very like the beginning of evil.

Taking a deep breath, she turned to her husband of six months, felt the comfort of his hand on her pregnant belly and said, "Yes, I like it here, Dad can pay, I feel at home, I want to stay."

Book One

Chapter One

Southern England, the 1980s

The sleeping body yawned gently, its arms causing a ripple against the expertly constructed bedding which bound them.

'Snug,' said the older woman to her daughter, 'though some might see it as a little tight. Pleasant to hear her so quiet.'

'Are you sure she can't hear us?' asked the younger one, wedging the last of the hospital corners in over the springs.

'Not with what the Doctor gave her, the poor dear.'

'She's pretty in a way, but thin, no tits,' said the younger, emboldened by her mother's assurance.

On the bed their employer sighed dreamily, her long brown hair wrapped around a face that weighed more towards definition than substance. Taut flaps of skin stretched over a fleshless profile, a once striking woman suffering, like the house she lay in, from subtle neglect.

Quietly the younger of the two servants reset the digital clock, its modern appearance swallowed in the antique surroundings. 'The batteries never last and the electricity's no good in here. Give me a wind-up any day.'

'I thought your generation liked reading the numbers?'

'I do when they tell the time right. It doesn't matter what I do with this one, it's all over the place.' As she talked, the girl, a well-built twenty year-old, pulled at the chandelier earring that dangled from her ear lobe, the compliment to the bouffant side parting worn to commemorate a recent Royal wedding. In her orange socks, bobble flecked leggings and pixie boots, she made for an unlikely domestic help. In contrast, her mother was dressed like a cook of thirty years before; a white cloth hat sat over her long nose and mirthless eyes, humanised slightly by a turquoise eyeliner.

'Funny, I thought *he'd* be the difficult one to begin with,' said the old woman, 'what with her father splashing out for everything I took our Mr Conti for a bit of a ponce. And then there was his not being interested in the country, rushing back to town all the time, but he turned out all right, for a want away.'

'She was all right too, to start with, right quiet and shy and that. And kind. Well, it's all change for our madam here,' said her daughter, kicking a pair of crutches under the bed, 'if he thought he married a shy one he was in for a shock. To think she couldn't even say boo to a mouse,' she added cruelly, 'living here's bought the spunk out, when she's awake... never known a grown woman to sleep so much, or need it.'

'The rich can do as they like,' her mother muttered. 'On all that medicine and those pills, she needs a bit of hard work to make her really tired. Even then there'd still be her old man in Africa to bail her out, should it go the way of the pear. A proper relationship with work and pleasure is what those two lack.'

Her daughter drew the long green curtains. 'Mister hasn't even said which room he wants tonight. Least they're not all as big and ugly as this. I'd hate to sleep here myself, it's too *something*.'

Although the room they were cleaning was airier than most, it had the same deficiency of natural light that dogged the whole building, the irregular shape and new annexes cancelling out the original design so that the views closed in on themselves protectively. The one painting of Tyger Tyger, hidden in a box room, depicted a shrinking structure surrounded by outgrowths and bent extensions, the impression of a house trapped within the house rising through its base.

'What about the one up above, for her brother when he comes. Shall I unlock it?'

'No,' her mother answered curtly, 'don't go in.'

'Is it one of the rooms he wants locked?'

'He didn't say anything, though he would do if he knew what I do. It smells, you see, always has done, no matter how long you leave the window open. We'll put her brother in the one next to it, with the stuffed eagle in. He'll like that, coming from where he does.'

Her daughter nodded and replaced the water by the bed with a fresh jug. As she did so she heard whispered, so quickly as to verge on a hiss, 'Judith, pour some sugar on me.'

'Mrs Conti?'

Both woman stared at the bed but the speaker was fast asleep, if indeed she had been awake, her request hopeful sleep talk or, the older one mused, her way of keeping them guessing.

*

'We never thought we'd be the sort of people who'd send their child to a private school…'

'*Public* school,' her husband corrected her.

'Public school,' his wife repeated gratefully, 'as me and Ashley never went to one ourselves.'

Hartley Conti smiled as though surprised by the revelation, the early evening sun blazing through the stained glass windows of his office with the dying force of a lost cause.

'Mrs Hatter, if you'd told me ten years ago as I paraded around in a Maoist smock, that a decade later I'd be employed by a preparatory school as a public schools advisor, *I'd* have probably thought you were pulling my leg.'

The proud couple smiled, pleased to be included in this circle of the elect, their son sitting with his legs crossed in imitation of someone far older, indifferent or perhaps scared of this new turn in life's trajectory.

'As I was saying,' Conti continued, 'Billingham enjoys a well deserved reputation for sport and a high entry rate to the armed forces, particularly the army…'

Mrs Hatter twitched slightly, her small nose betraying something of the improbable attraction between her and her husband, a flat-topped curio of a man who reminded Conti of why he no longer went to football matches. How, Conti asked himself, had these people ever found the money to subsidise the community of delusion that afforded him a living?

'Mr Conti, I ought to level with you, I'm not investing in my son's education for him to end up practising close order drill with the Devon and Dorset Regiment in West Germany. If we wanted Enoch to be a soldier I'd have let him go to the local comprehensive.' Mr Hatter squinted meaningfully to dispel any notions of an inferiority complex and wondered whether he should add something about growing up in a council house and never taking the good things in life for granted.

'Which is why I don't think Billingham would be the right school for Martin, Mr Hatter,' Conti gently adjusted his pitch, 'schools like Billingham can be a little too big and old fashioned, a child can feel lost on his first day and experience trouble settling in. All that can wait until University, it's best to take each challenge as it comes, and not be rushed in to one you're not ready for.'

Mrs Hatter's pretty head bobbed up and down in agreement, there was something charming about such an attractive woman taking the trouble to care about what was, Conti felt, a matter of little importance. Education, in his opinion, had always been overrated.

'Have either of you ever thought of Claysmug, one of the more pupil orientated schools? It's not in any of the brochures you were sent but it's in a lovely part of the country where Martin would be free to find his feet, in his own time...'

Claysmug was a minor public school where an old friend of Conti's taught auto-engineering, the headmaster, otherwise known as the Midnight Badger, having recently been dismissed for a nocturnal tour of a first year dormitory.

'How do its fees compare to the other place?' asked Mr Hatter.

'Very favourably, being a smaller school it costs less to run.'

'That sounds nice,' said Mrs Hatter, her hand stroking the back of her son's neck, 'but we will miss you Martin...'

Conti watched the Hatters drift from his office with the mechanical thrill of a boy entering the next level of Space Invaders, his eyes following Mrs Hatter's tiny bottom so closely that he wondered whether he had seen her turn round, smile and pat it, or whether this sort of hallucination was common in men of calculation. Though professing to have nothing in common with yuppies, modelling his look on the method actors of the 1950s, Conti guessed that with his useful side profile, and handsomely fitted suit, he could easily pass for the era's zeitgeist.

Ever since he had read "a shilling life will give you all the facts" and watched the waves at his artist's retreat break and vanish like so many pages of unwritten text, he knew that he would never make the leap from being a man who had a lot to say for himself to one who could write a book. His political beliefs had not helped, conditional as they were on a lot of things he knew were never going to happen, happening, so that the choice between renouncing them and being taken seriously, or retaining them and continuing as a joke, had not been difficult to make. Convincing himself that maturity meant mixed feelings, and an imperfect life was preferable to an impossible one, he left his job at the night school and embraced the spirit of the times, which in his case meant advising others on where to send their children to school.

Conti knew that there were other decisions he could have made, but since they would all have been equally unimportant, in terms of motivation and outcome, he had settled for a mastery of surfaces and a regular income. Without particularly liking his life, Conti found that he was strangely satisfied with it and did not believe that anything about it would ever change, the hammer and anvil of history having ground to a halt at a moment most propitious to him.

Conti was soon to learn that he had predicated his life on a mistaken assumption. Since moving his young family to Tyger Tyger House, an awful consequentiality had replaced the arbitrary course of the past decade, bringing what he understood to be his innocence to an end.

'Hartley, I've a couple of messages for you,' his secretary Melissa Stack stood at the door connecting her office to his, a converted priest hole if the school historian was to be believed, 'from Doctor Bliss and Martin, your brother in law.' She adjusted a shoulder pad and nibbled the end of her ball point pen, in a way that might have been sexy, had she done it by mistake.

Conti smiled wanly, his cerulean blue eyes and reluctant handsomeness making him look every inch the confused SS officer Stack had fallen in love with over a decade earlier. Through an exchange of Christmas cards Conti had learnt of the collapse of her marriage and her availability for work. When they had met, Conti saw this really was all he would want her for, Stack's once perfect figure blighted by disappointment, chocolate biscuits and Buckfast wine. Painfully he accepted that the face, which had helped get him through the past fifteen years, no longer existed. Conti had always sought continuity in his life and regretted that Stack had broken off their relationship once it became clear that it could not develop without their sleeping together. The break had allowed him to idolise her, whereas the reality was that she had chosen a second-rate husband, whom she felt superior to and could blame for all the underachievement that still lay ahead.

Staring into her face was like being shown a completely different view of life, where happiness, having already been postponed indefinitely, was at last officially replaced by a gratitude that things were not worse. This, and the deep lines of lonely cynicism that marked her eyes, ought to have meant that in purely neutral terms, Stack was bad for business, but in those mediated by tender sympathy, which Conti found to his surprise plenty of his clients possessed, her face was a prize asset. She had been his secretary for over two years now and he had finally come to rely on her like the underwear he had forgotten he had put on.

'The Doctor asked if you could drop in and see him on your way home. Also Martin will be arriving a week early...'

'You mean next week?' Conti stood up; his well-built body a tribute to the school's exercise amenities.

'No, tonight, his train gets in at eight and he'll need picking up because he doesn't know how to get to your house by cab. I told him most taxis would know but I think he wanted to see you first... They seemed like an okay couple didn't they?'

Conti, who often had trouble distinguishing his own thoughts from Stack's voice, replied, 'I wish people would interrupt me a bit more so I'd know what they were thinking... but they were, they bit.'

Stack smiled indulgently, 'Well, I'll see you in the morning then. Goodbye.'

The forecourt, surrounded by an Old Priory, was full of choristers playing their concluding games of the day. Conti was amused at the purely haphazard way in which the pupils elected new leaders, and how the most feted boy in each year switched with random alacrity, competition for these spots having hardened since his day, or so he felt. Though admired for his height, humour and the fact that he was not a teacher, Conti experienced no real closeness to these children, disliking the ways in which they already resembled their parents, and how wealth was the fastest way any of them knew of settling an argument. And yet Conti, like the boys, was happiest when he thought that he had got away with something.

'Mr Conti,' called a pupil he could not recognise, coming off his skateboard, 'my father doesn't have a secretary, he has a *sex*etary…'

A smaller boy smiled, not understanding the joke.

'Ah, but would *you* know what to do about it, would you Haskell?' announced the night master on duty, Mr Squeers, rhetorically. He was at the front of a line of pupils waiting for their names to be ticked, before leaving for their parent's Volvo for home. 'At your age I didn't even know what a secretary was, let alone what was up one's skirt…' A ripple of controlled laughter rolled through the line. 'Did *you* Mr Conti?'

'No, I was probably still at the stage of wondering what a rubber Johnny was for…' replied Conti, conscious of his role in an adult double act. Without ever having been able to fathom why, Conti felt uncomfortable around Maurice Squeers, and consequently distrusted him. Sunset was always the contaminated hour that he seemed to bump into the skinny bachelor, the master's eyes leering suggestively at him as he invariably asked after his wife.

"And how is the lovely Mrs Conti, we don't seem to see so much of her these days, in fact, it must be getting on for nearly a year now… since she looked so lovely on Sports Day, if I remember. She has a figure an athlete would be proud of, a much better one than most of these lads…' Squeers allowed the words to tail off into a facial innuendo…

'Thank you for asking, she's fine,' replied Conti without conviction. The birds had stopped singing, and even the boys had momentarily gone quiet, a cold patch forming between the two men, as Squeers ran a finger down the diagonal stripes of his polythene tie.

'Will she be coming on the sponsored walk this year, it's for Save the Children again, I believe.'

'No, her legs are still playing up, she's having to spend quite a lot of time in bed.'

Squeers winked obligingly, to remind Conti that they both

enjoyed a special relationship with the opposite sex. In his day, Squeers had enjoyed a reputation as a libertine who never repeated a joke or slept with the same woman twice, but age had given his wit and libido a decidedly creepy air, and Conti had never confused his sneering contempt for the tic Squeers passed it off as. There was something distasteful in the way Squeers possessed the confidence of a man who supposed he could supplant the partner a woman had loved all her life, for the sake of a night of passion with him. Conti had no trouble accepting Stack's view that whereas he was a good man who had fallen, Squeers was a bad one who had no trouble accepting himself as such.

'A whole year now... Mr Conti, inform her from me that absence makes the heart grow fonder.'

'Time flies,' Conti replied without turning round, his soul already immersed in the brilliant red doom of a Hampshire sunset.

Dr Bliss had always thought of himself as a professional who could get a job done with the minimum amount of fuss, the medical school nickname of "sceptic Ed" encapsulating his no-thrills approach to phenomena. His heroes were not dashing leading men whose deeds won them beautiful spouses, rather their earnest, no-nonsense sidekicks who modestly held things together. Perhaps this is why old Doctor Wyatt had given him Brigit Conti as a patient, his arthritic hands shaking as he said, 'I think you'd be better at dealing with this sort of thing, sore throats and chicken pox are more my line now...'

Bliss's reputation for unflappable calm, and his rudimentary knowledge of psychoanalysis, so useful in dealing with "awkward patients" in the past, were of no use to him that afternoon, and he was half way through pouring his second whisky when his receptionist announced the arrival of Hartley Conti at the surgery.

Hastily, Bliss hid the glass and washed his mouth out at the sink, taking care not to wet his oversized calculator watch, bought on a ferry from Le Havre. Puffing his cheeks out, he ran a hand through his straw thin hair and straightened the bow tie he still affected to wear. Every time he had met Conti, he had felt the limitations of his own personal aesthetic, Conti not only standing a good foot taller than him, but so immaculately turned out that Bliss imagined him caring more for a set of clothes, than being on the correct side of an argument, an attitude that secretly fascinated him.

'How did you find my wife?' asked Conti without sitting down. He was wearing a light knee length coat that gave him the air of an impatient businessman caught between meetings.

Bliss hesitated, 'How do *you* find your wife...'

He blushed, immediately recognising his mistake, languorous intellectual probing did not suit him. What he wanted to say was that Conti seemed very alone. Smiling cautiously he began again, 'I'm sorry, please have a seat, it's just that your wife is a very enigmatic character, there's no other way I can think of putting it, which is why I ask you your opinion.'

Conti smiled warmly, 'She is?'

'I would say so, yes,' Bliss replied, his hand running down the length of his beard.

'Well I guess that's one word you could use for her, "enigmatic"... "difficult" is the one I thought you were going to come up with!'

Bliss laughed good humouredly and made a pretence of going through his notes. 'Since Dr Wyatt first saw her at Easter, has she in the intervening time changed at all, or taken a turn for the... less well? Please do sit down. And by the way, I'm sorry Dr Wyatt wasn't able to offer you more...'

'Don't worry about it.' Conti glanced round the room and took his seat, an orange plastic cone that bent under his weight. 'Any change? Yes. Before, Brigit spent some of the day in bed and we shared a room, now she spends pretty much the entire day in her bedroom which I no longer share with her, so yes, there has been change.'

Conti was not feeling particularly helpful, having decided after Dr Wyatt that patronising his local surgery was a country convention rather like visiting a vet's. 'Anyway, what are we talking about here, a medical change or her personality?'

Politely ignoring the question, Bliss continued, 'You understand, I am under oath, but I really did struggle to get anywhere concrete with Mrs Conti this afternoon. Women do react to the country in different ways, don't they? Ones that weren't brought up here originally, I mean. Some are unhappy because they've given up careers. Others find all the... isolation that comes with living here rather lonely...'

'It was her decision and her father's money that sealed the move. I'd have sooner stayed in London, nice as it is here, I'm a city boy. She's here because she wants to be.'

'Even so...'

'Look, I understand the connection between morale and mental health, and I appreciate you taking an open minded approach, but are you able to tell me what's wrong? If it's her nerves then what kind of problem is it, schizophrenia, or some kind of split personality thing?'

'Possibly...' Bliss pulled the cap off a marker pen. 'She mentioned very bad headaches, and intense mood swings.'

'But it isn't just a *mood* thing is it? I've noticed at times she looks like she's come back from a skiing holiday that's gone wrong, a sunburnt face and her lips are chapped, is there a physical reason for that, a skin disease, or do you really believe she could have willed it on herself through depression, which I admit she's prone to? It looks too severe to me to be psychosomatically induced. And she's complained about hair loss too, and her bones.'

Bliss put the cap back on the pen. 'Nothing, there's definitely nothing medically wrong with her at all, and,' he added with defeated finality, 'as far as I can tell, there never has been. The symptoms you're describing would *have* to have been psychosomatically induced. There's no other way she could have ended up with them, unless she picked up something undetectable on her travels...'

'Then what about all the pills Wyatt's been prescribing her, what were they for?' asked Conti.

'A misdiagnosis I think. Wyatt thought that she was experiencing mild hysteria and depression because of her failure to adjust to... English life. He said that she gasped when she was trying to speak, like there were certain words she couldn't physically say, and had an excitable manner that could be linked to exhaustion. I have continued with the medication he was prescribing but I don't think it'll get to the bottom of anything.'

'She was born and bought up in London. That hardly makes her a foreigner.'

'Quite, I quite agree with you. He was on the wrong tack. At the time I did wonder whether what she really needed was someone to talk to. In fact, I'm of the opinion that the antidepressants he prescribed probably exacerbated her condition...'

'Condition? You just said that there was nothing wrong with her.'

'Nothing *physically* wrong that we could detect... Look, I'll be as frank with you as I can, Mr Conti, I believe that your wife is in need, maybe urgent, of some form of psychiatric help...'

'And you don't consider that a medical problem?'

'Not one that I can treat, and contrary to what Dr Wyatt told you, one that won't blow over in the fullness of time or get better by itself. I'm sorry.'

'So you're telling me she'll continue to mentally degenerate if left untreated?'

'Almost certainly,' Bliss swallowed hard, surprised at his candour, 'in as much as you can ever be sure of these things,' he qualified weakly.

Conti fastened his eyes on a poster of a giant set of false teeth, wondering briefly what it was doing there. 'Why?' he said, 'what did she say to you this afternoon to make you so sure of that?'

Ruffled by Conti's persistence, Bliss said, 'Please, Mr Conti, I would sympathise with you if you thought I was making a mountain out of this but surely you must know her day to day moods better than I...'

Conti raised his fists. Then he smiled, 'Go on, I'm not going to take any offence.'

Bliss shuddered slightly. 'It was terribly *strange,'* he said, 'I've never come across anything like it.'

Conti tapped Bliss's leg and pointed to the half hidden whisky bottle sticking out of his bag.

Bliss nodded.

'She was lewd,' said Bliss and drained his whisky in one. 'I've met her before and found her perfectly charming. It's why I asked you about change... I was surprised at what she came out with.'

'You needn't spare my feelings,' Conti replied. His face was flat and without the lightness he was able to squeeze from most situations, 'I know that listening to her can be like hearing a perfectly indexed A to Z of pornography, without a single category or word omitted.'

'She advised me, amongst other things, "to not grope her", and to get out of her "minkle" – not that I had thought of getting into it in the first place,' Bliss added quickly.

'I'm sorry,' said Conti.

'It wasn't just that though, I mean, what I feel is,' Bliss stared at Conti as if for inspiration, 'this unnerving strangeness. The smell in her room for instance, it was quite strong, even through the disinfectant.'

'Though she was completely clean, physically? I take it that you *do* mean her rather than the room?'

'Perhaps it was just me, neither of the servants seemed to notice it...'

Conti shook his head, 'No, you're right. There have been mornings when I walk in,' he said weighing each word 'when that room *stinks* like a cross between a farmyard and an abattoir. It's impossible to be in there without speculating about what combinations of filth could produce such a stench. I find myself checking her bed for clods of shit, and dousing the place with aftershave as though it were a good luck charm. But we clean it, and bathe her, all the time.'

'Is that what led you to sleep in separate rooms?'

'It could have been, but no, it wasn't. Brigit was the one who asked me to move her to a room in a different part of the house so that she "could be in the light".'

'Natural light, you mean?'

'No. She has these places all over the house, places of "the light"... I don't know what there is to say about them except that they're the parts of the house I like least.'

'So it wasn't... no, I think I see,' Bliss paused, keen to conceal the distasteful curiosity in his voice. 'You said it was never your decision to buy Tyger Tyger House, was it?'

'I told you. It was her inner conviction to move there.'

'But not yours?'

Conti laughed self-consciously. 'Me? I keep my light on at night.'

'Mrs Archer gave me this note,' Bliss handed Conti a folded sheet of A4 paper.

Conti scratched his neck. 'You've read it?'

'I admit I tried to. She found it under your wife's bed. It's apparently her handwriting.'

'You ought to remember my wife wrote a doctoral dissertation in philosophy,' said Conti, looking at the page with sullen distaste, 'perhaps it'd be easier if I summarized its highlights aloud.'

He cleared his throat and held the paper to the light.

"Whilst making love he likes to call it dirty names to emphasise it's recreational, sadistic and pleasurable overtones at the expense of any possible meaning our lovemaking may have. But this is the sex we love the best... he's afraid of becoming lost...needs the self restoration after orgasmic relief..."

'No,' said Conti staring at the page, 'It's not me she's writing about...me or anybody. It's the site of her problems she's addressing. Ever since I've known her she's been seeing shrinks to discuss this kind of stuff. She only stopped last summer.'

'So there might be a connection?'

Conti glanced at his watch.

Bliss raised his hand, his heart fluttering like an eagle trapped in a shawl. 'Of course this is between just us.'

'Brigit and I have an angry, argumentative kind of sex life, which followed the pattern of our relationship, but as she got ill – or whatever we've agreed to call it – our lovemaking did too.'

'Because she was finding sex physically painful?'

'No, because she realised I was distracted and thinking of other women. Big deal you might say. But she would, I don't know how, successfully guess who I was thinking of and then try and "become" them while we made love.'

'Maybe you told her?'

'No. She would guess and then will herself into their persona and ask me to look at her, but when I did she was... unrecognisable. I wasn't myself either. It was like someone else was having her in my place. I was replaced by another kind of energy, a thing I wanted nothing to do with, that had its own desires. Something else had come between us.'

'And you say your wife...'

'She didn't really seem to mind. We argued about it, though as you can imagine, I wasn't in a very strong position.'

'An extreme form of love play perhaps, animal passion?'

'No. I know the difference between a randy woman breathing down my neck and what Brigit's become…'

'Have you considered going back with her to see a psychiatrist, Mr Conti?' Bliss interrupted. 'Maybe I could recommend you one, if it'd help?'

He waited for Conti to reply, his cheeks flushed with excitement, 'After all, I have examined you both, in a way. Perhaps I could be of use…'

'Dr Bliss, my wife was in therapy for three years, three times a week with Harley Street specialists of every stripe. I don't know if it ever worked, but what I do know is that by the time we moved, she had made complete mincemeat of them all. She's an intelligent and formidable woman, even when she's ill. The use that you and Wyatt had was that as local men I thought you wouldn't threaten Brigit, or at least, she wouldn't want to compete or play games with you. But that doesn't seem to be the case.'

'Nonetheless, we can't just give up… She mentioned feeling suicidal, perhaps she feels stigmatised by her depression.'

'No more psychiatrists.' Conti was emphatic.

'But Mr Conti, modern medicine and science have ways of explaining perversity. I'm sure if you were talking to the right kind of expert…'

'Thank you,' Conti stood up, cutting him short, 'but I think it'd probably be a backward step. I want to say, it's easy to feel a long way away from people here, that your problems are entirely your own business and no one else cares, so thanks, I appreciate you at least taking ours seriously.'

Bliss scratched the edge of the table, eager to disguise the distasteful aspect of his interest. 'I have an old colleague in Southampton who helps run a woman's group and yoga class, perhaps your…'

'Thank you.' Conti offered his hand.

Bliss looked momentarily askew as though afraid of touching it. Conti withdrew the hand slowly, his secrets hidden in the darkness of what he had chosen to reveal.

Once Conti had left, Bliss glanced again at Brigit's note and grudgingly concluded that he was no longer made of the same stuff as "sceptic Ed", his medical school alter ego. This was the longest he had talked to Conti and he had liked him. Rather than allowing himself to be tantalised vicariously, he ought to have mentioned the stories he had heard concerning Tyger Tyger House, however ridiculous he believed them to be, or the strange treatments Doctor Wyatt had been forced to prescribe several of its previous inhabitants. But instead of embracing his role as a middle class professional, Bliss had become the boy who joins the audience to gawp at the tight rope walker, or worse still, the local who plays dumb. What mattered most as he heard Conti's car pull away, was that at least he was not the outsider who had disturbed the natural order, for there was no promise of safety in that.

Yet he had not earned his nickname for nothing. Those student years of putting down astrologers, pot heads and Christians had made him who he was; a trusted member of the community precisely *because* he stood above it. The Contis were probably just another couple undergoing a marital tragedy, the husband too proud to let outsiders in, the wife too angry. Bliss turned the note over and re- read the rhyme scribbled along its back, starting to feel queasy as he did so:

Cunning and art she did not lack
But aye his whistle would fetch her back
O, I shall go in to a hare
With sorrow and sighing and care,
And I shall go in the Devil's name
Haste me unto my husband's house

Husband, take heed of a black cat
That was never baulked of mouse or rat
For I'll crack thy bones
Thus shalt thou be fetched hame.

He put down the note and wiped his mouth, suddenly afraid that he was being watched by something he could not see. Outside, the 8.05 to Waterloo whooshed past rattling the flimsy frame of the surgery, its noise for once failing to reassure him. Turning the lamp off, Bliss pressed his face to the window, incapable of seeing past the eyes trapped in their own reflection.

He was lucky that he could get to sleep at night without thinking of making love to women who were not his wife, lucky that he did not cry for his missing beliefs, and lucky that he did not live in Tyger Tyger House. These were Conti's affronts, not his.

He reached into his trouser pocket for his keys. They were not there, or in his other pocket or blazer. This was not unusual but tonight it frightened him, because he felt they had been moved by something that wanted to show him it was there.

Deep in his guts, the taste of whisky and the pickled onion sandwich he had eaten at lunch rose forcefully; an aroma of rotting vineyards filling his mouth, followed by a sensation like the scattering of burning hail. Clutching his chest, Bliss staggered out of his office; called for the receptionist and sank down to his knees.

There was no one there but he was not alone.

Steadily and methodically, Bliss began to wretch over the deserted waiting room floor, first in spurts, and then in a long uninterrupted flow, until the last remnants of "sceptic Ed's" unbelief had been sated at last.

*

Conti could not understand how an area could be nondescript and foreboding at the same time, but the old Roman road connecting the Cathedral city to the brewery town was both. Plain chalk fields stuck behind 1930s bungalows comprised the first part of the journey, grander versions of the same style of housing displacing them as the road broke into blandly ordered country, the view rescued by a watery mist, lending it the feel of a cut-price Atlantis. Above it all, the grey sky felt confined, no larger than the petty concerns it floated over, the neatly trimmed hedges and newsagents dotted below like trapped clutter no one had bothered to move.

Perhaps, thought Conti, his family had not gone far enough, tripping headforemost into the horizon that lay west of Bournemouth, preferable to this tidy ideal, its aspirations reflecting a cosmic banality that made him dizzy. The extremes here, embedded in every signpost and driveway, were of a different kind from the sort he was used to, an enemy he was surrounded by, but had decided not to fight.

Carelessly, Conti turned off a roundabout onto the newly constructed dual carriageway, built through a hill with equipment purchased for the Channel Tunnel. Without thinking, he jumped gears and overtook a wobbly Citroen, slowing down again. In spite of a natural inclination to speed, he was never in a hurry to get home, his heart always sinking when he reached this point of the road.

Conti had only known his wife through love, not as a separate person to be evaluated on neutral terms. From the very first it had been suggested by some that the woman he married was a little peculiar. Brigit, in more than one sense, had always used English as a second language, her first being an enigmatic silence. They had met at Art school and her way of looking at Conti, as though the secrets of the universe were cast across his face, awakened the hope that she could see things he could not, the small matter of her relationship with his best friend quickly overcome with a flurry of apologies.

Intimacy with the mysterious waif drew Conti into a world where other people's opinions did not matter, Brigit's recalcitrant idea of herself rendering her an unknown quantity capable of surprising him in ways girls rarely had. Not knowing what was going to happen next fulfilled Conti's idea of a bohemian love affair, and if Brigit were prickly, or needed second-guessing, she at least provided him with the energy that being with her required. The taciturn moods, secrecy, and inability to explain herself were all traits that would vanish in time, if indeed they needed to, for as far as Conti was concerned these "abnormalities" only added to her appeal.

Remembering that he had to pick his brother-in-law up from the station, Conti pulled off the main road into a narrow lane. Overhead a solitary bird chirped in time to the rhythm of the dual carriageway, its voice lost under the accelerating drone of traffic. It was important for him to think rationally, to ignore his suspicions of what had caused his wife's difficulties and concentrate on the facts. Too often he had thought of their problems as unique when it might have been more helpful to isolate what they had in common with other dysfunctional couples.

And yet struggle as he might, the pieces did not come together. Marriage undeniably changed a person, but not as much as it had changed Brigit. For the first year she treated him as before, or rather, as other people treated him, at his own estimation.

Since boyhood Conti had existed as a kept man, friends buying him things because they expected to, in return for him being very generous with himself. Flattery made him easy to like, neither challenging others or himself, scared that they all had something to lose if he did.

As if this were a pattern to emulate, Brigit let Conti take her buying power and adoration for granted, her father's immense wealth rescuing them from bohemia so that a life of comfort was assured. Since then Conti had asked few questions of life, a desire to survive in style displacing all else, even his wife's disillusionment that grew exponentially with their social status. Had this led to the ugly changes in her, culminating in the doctor's visit, or was there something else?

Brigit could still see what he could not. He knew that she was looking out, but that he could not see inside, if ever he could. Stopping the car, Conti scrambled in the glove compartment for a cigarette, found one, and pulling the filter tip off, lit it. The mist was turning black on the road ahead. He inhaled and spat out the end, the tobacco tasting rotten and noxious, his stomach lined with a slippery apprehension of what reason could not endure.

Chapter Two

Brigit Conti had often wondered whether she was really alive, but that was before she could see through walls.

Unfortunately her extra sensory gifts came at a price. The voices were quiet today but from the garden she could feel her son dig up the corpse of his cat. The sixth time since it was hurriedly buried, and in the basement she could smell Chantal, their au-pair, wriggle into the panties her husband had removed with his teeth the night before. Clutching the sheets to her face Brigit emitted the low moan of a tearless grief, droning on like a heifer until her bedding was thoroughly soaked in urine.

Dimly, through the impulse to suffocate herself, Brigit remembered that she had not always been like this, that the bad breath, bedsores and incontinence were the strange consequences of being lied to by an *atmosphere* that had promised so much.

It had come to her one afternoon near the beginning of spring and it had been deliciously fast. She was sitting cross-legged in the garden, bored after a morning of walking round the house. These indoor excursions were an attempt to break Tyger Tyger down into small and conjoining sections, so as to reduce the sense of its enormity and be less scared of its size. Sleepily she had watched the cat ambush flakes of dandelion petal while a plane passed overhead, the gentle hum of its engines rumbling like an empty stomach. The house and garden were peaceful in the bright noonday light. Without consciously meaning to, she lay flat, her arms outstretched in a cross and not protectively hunched over her chest as they usually were when she slept. Like a vanishing insight before bed, a sudden itch in her leg forewarned her of the approach of something, but she was too drowsy to acknowledge it, and by then, she reflected, it was already too late to prevent what followed. She heard a cow grunt and a thundering pressure, like her childhood nightmare of becoming a ball crushed by a noisy landscape, begin to pound behind her ears. Uncannily, Brigit could see a woman whom she recognised as herself asleep on the grass, but there were cold fingers inside her pulling her another way towards a new and weird realisation.

Say yes, it said, say yes.

The world, which for so long had consisted of a handful of shades, was becoming a carousel. She *knew* it was happening, that she was truly alive and the knowledge she was waiting for was here. It was incredible how close Brigit had always been to "it", as close as night-time was to day but different, as if the sun had risen instead of the moon to heat a void. One by one her senses were turning animal and she could hear insects welcome her initiation amongst their kind. The thrill grew more extreme in its purity as Brigit ceased to experience herself as a limitation and laughed as she had never done before. She had wasted years trapped in a single perspective, lacking the courage to propel herself forward into endless *becoming* where she could be *many* and feel *more*. 'I'm here,' she heard herself shout, 'I'm here!'

But in the centre of her euphoria Brigit sensed her joy recoil under the iron conditions of its possibility. Its spirit mediated by the dark laws of an earlier concept.

It was not the return of meaning, or even a life-denying quali-fication, she now noticed, but a *thing* revealing itself to her, as fascinating as what she had hoped for, although not what she had anticipated. On close inspection the lights she saw were not luminous, or the colours varied.

Instead, she could see the dark opposite of everything emerge slowly, rotting flowers, soiled household waste, brown grass and a bestiary of insects. It was enough to think of laughter or hope to induce their reverse and destroy the memory of them. What remained of her excitement was a hypnotic interest that would not allow her to pull away, its cold fingers travelling through her with impunity.

'Come,' she heard it say, 'come to the kingdom.'

A trade-off had occurred. Life was clearer but stained by a foul presence that made the clarity possible. Brigit felt tricked. She had not become the multiplicity she had dreamed of on acid-trips, rather, she was merely one of many ruled by *One*. Its voice reminded her of an Eye she had seen in her sleep as a child, when it had been impossible to dream of anything without the Eye opening. 'I remember you,' she cried, 'go away!'

'Come in.'

Desperately Brigit tried to reach out to common sense but it was no good. Her third person image of herself had leaked away, and if she sought it she found the Eye in its place, or worse, a feeling of complete solitude.

The garden was growing darker and, clutching a thistle, she closed her palm over its bristles, never so aware of the beautiful connection between the natural world and evil. To her surprise she felt no pain, and more disconcertingly, no fear. Staring at the vanishing dot that was the sun, so inadequate for a world that needed it, Brigit felt a lost history unravel, its memory her own.

She had often wondered why her friends were wicked compared to her, but if *it* had chosen her before she was born then those around her would have had to be corrupt precisely for this purpose. The notion of "good" for Brigit had only ever been a warning against her destiny, its power preventative. Whereas evil's lure over her was primal. Perhaps this was why evil had never frightened her before, it had been careful not to when it wanted her so much.

Tyger Tyger was her place of worship, the church where her new master had waited for her to come to him. Here fascination had finally prevailed over caution and she and the carousel were united, spinning out of the solemn reach of sanity into the Eye that had always watched her. This was not a Kingdom of love. There were no people, just patterns, noise and everlasting loneliness, a machinic caricature of life ruled by the Eye that she saw whenever she closed her own.

Brigit's glorious world of difference had gone, swallowed by a dreadful no-thing that was not, her urge to speak of its arrival cruelly forbidden for it wanted no one else to know. The terrifying isolation of Brigit's ordeal was thus sealed, her new master at once omnipotent but so far as the world was aware, undeclared.

Whether hours or merely minutes had passed, Brigit did not know, for her reality and the one she had previously occupied were never to meet again.

When Mrs Archer, the house keeper found her on the compost heap staring serenely at the stars, her first reaction was to cross her fingers and thank Jesus that her own soul was too docile to arouse the interest of forces that would devour it.

'Mrs Conti, what are you doing out here! Come in at once.'

Brigit, whose skin had tightened, making her appear unnaturally young, replied, 'Why? Is it wrong to enjoy the grounds of my own home?'

For a moment Mrs Archer looked puzzled, as if trying to take in the significance if this remark, before asking, 'Mrs Conti...are you all right?'

'I am perfect.'

It was the answer Mrs Archer had dreaded the most. 'One can only save a ship that knows it's in distress,' she muttered, smothering Brigit in a rug and hauling her off the decomposing pile of manure. As the weeks passed, this ritual was repeated many times, Mrs Archer becoming used to, but steadily more unsettled by her mistress's deranged pilgrimage.

For Brigit that first night dwelt in her like a swarm of locusts that had sucked out her best. Scornfully she hissed at the person transformed forever, at that woman's naïve beauty, simplicity and health.

Clots of vomit rose and sank in her throat, the words of her father, the Banker, still so apt. 'Keep everything hazy in your mind now Brigit, and you will have all eternity wherein to amuse yourself in the peculiar kind of clarity hell affords.'

Clutching a sooty lump of chalk, Brigit began to mark her sheet with Roman numerals, the surreal quality of her waking life a reminder of the nightmare she had yet to escape.

Some miles away, her brother, Martin "the mighty trunk" Botha-Hall waited to be collected from the local railway station, his cricket bag the only reminder of a former life as Captain of his country's Test side. Unlike his team-mates, Martin considered sport, especially cricket, to be a big nothing, and life too, with only money, prostitutes and consumer goods interesting him for their own sake. Pride, as an idea let alone in practice, made him chaff, as did glory, stealth, and the desire to excel in one's craft, this last notion perhaps the most puzzling of all. If there was one general idea he found agreeable, it was giving up before he began to try. He was, in every sense, a man used to living a double life.

Surprisingly, none of these reservations had prevented other cricketers from accepting him as one of the boys, largely because the truth about Martin was not found at the base of his personality, near his heart or in the way he played, but hidden round the middle of his misleadingly ordinary manner. With his hair brushed flat in a side parting, sloped shoulders and earthy one liners, Martin had never displayed the intelligence the dressing room would have felt threatened by, or in a different man, respect. Instead, his team-mates thought of him with the endearing condescension reserved for the fat boy given first prize in an eating contest. Once the Last Test had started, Martin was the obvious fifth choice Captain, after numbers one and three had been injured out, and two and four had departed for early holidays.

Without much fuss he had accepted the honour, winking for

the benefit of the old lags lest anyone thought his head might be turned by promotion. Few people detected the slight change in manner, the way his jokes had grown more bitter as it took a pint less for him to turn morose, or the self-pitying tone he used to run himself down. His pre-match talk was short, and team building was restricted to a drunken water pistol fight, evidence of the laid-back mood in the camp, or so journalists were told. On the morning of the Test the ground had been three quarters full, a good attendance for a series already lost, and having won the toss Martin had opted to bat first, his face swollen with uncharacteristic impatience.

Martin pinched the sides of his bag, now mercifully free of bat and whites; the pockets stuffed instead with used fifty-pound notes, his reward for throwing his last three innings of the Test. Of the two leather jackets the Malaysian bookmaker had included as a bonus for his "convincing acting", the first had been lost at the hotel and the other left on the plane when Martin, reacting to a girl's laughter, realised that red leather did not suit him. It had always been a feature of his game that he had a tendency to put on weight, his stomach looking all right when he stood up, but not so good when he sat down, adding to his conspicuousness when wearing "fashionable togs".

Half-heartedly Martin scanned the small roundabout at the bottom of the hill, mildly relieved that his brother in-law was still nowhere to be seen. The pea green station fairly well summed up what he disliked about England, its office closed and its shabby walls decorated like the notice board of an abandoned Post Office. This was the country his sister had embraced, rejecting the frontier avarice that had launched the wagon trains of their forefathers into the Dark Continent.

Blankly he separated a testicle from his thigh and stared down at his newly acquired plimsolls, which had already collected the thin crust of a day's use. The fact of it was that in Africa he was a marked man, no more at home there than he was here. Since he had left school, cricket, much as it bored him, had preserved his boyhood, and the decision to abandon it was a form of revenge against its stifling familiarity.

His catastrophic clumsiness in both innings, to say nothing of earlier dropped catches and bungled throws, had not had the effect he feared, that of his being found out, for he had always been a slightly erratic performer, rather he had been criticised for playing like a girl and the press had stripped him of his nickname, "the mighty trunk". The following day's sports pages had developed a new and unwelcome narrative that Martin, usually indifferent to criticism from the fourth estate, was badly affected by. Young men were coming through, and Martin represented an era of pedestrian journeymen, clubbable but ineffective throwbacks to a time when winning was not as important as taking part. The weaknesses Martin had previously admitted to were all ones that he was secretly proud of or did not mind having, but this new abuse had been so harsh that he had seriously considered playing as well as he could in his last innings.

At the moment of decision he had reverted to type, remained true to himself and thrown the game, but as he returned to the pavilion he wept. In other players it might have been seen as a sign of excessive emotion, but in "the mighty trunk" it was, at best, downright baffling. Mercifully no one had guessed that it was not the game Martin cried for but the absent skipper whom he worshipped like a boy, and whose disapproving silhouette he had caught sight of.

Martin's attachment to P.W. Sanders had started before he knew that it was more dangerous to punch below your weight than at it. Sanders had acted as the sixth form prefect to Martin's star struck apprentice, and for a while Martin had nearly learned to enjoy the game. Martin had pursued Sanders like an animal that seeks no solace past the company of another, imitating his style as best he could, yet somehow failing to grasp the sportsmanship which accompanied it.

Sanders, a rule-following pedant, confused his young companion's tongue-tied infatuation for dependability, and quickly bought him on to the national side. Like many sportsmen, Martin developed the knack of appearing more mature and older than he was, possessing if not an aura then some stature and, with a batting average of just thirty-two, he found himself an automatic choice for his country. The tears he shed, having deliberately run himself out, were not only for the man Sanders and countless others believed him to be, but for the Captain he knew he would never share a room with again.

Sanders' parting words offered neither help or consolation. 'Nothing will make you a bigger man than realising you get what you deserve', but Martin understood that he was not quite ready for this lesson yet. For when a certain type of man is freed from all earthly wants he does not find transcendence, he simply ceases to live. By trading his inner timetable for a pay day, Martin had swapped a future teaching schoolboys how to bat for the horrors of life as a free man. He would, he feared, have a long time to rue his mistake. Deliberately he had missed the last day of play, feigning injury and thus double-crossing the betting syndicate of their final pay out, and this obscure corner of England was the spot where he would now lie low and hopefully be forgotten.

An orange Mercedes pulled up by the ugly shelter, and Hartley Conti called out to him, 'Fucking awful place, isn't it?'

Martin's leathery eyes lit up slightly as he shouted, 'You're late!' He was never sure where he stood with this Englishman, but glad they were off to a sound start.

It was a firm conviction of Conti's that Martin was a cunt, but a different type of one from the kind he considered himself to be. He had listened to his wife hold forth on Martin's untapped potential, and believed little of it, preferring to trust appearances, which in Martin's case spoke loudly of a secretive mountebank. Moreover he suspected that he and Martin secretly thought the other to be full of shit, but they both enjoyed their exaggerated fraternity too much to call time on the pretence. Either this or they had never lost hope that the other might be in earnest, Conti's quirky intelligence impressing Martin, as much as Martin's confusion of the same quality for paranoia amused Conti.

'We're guys, we come with secrets,' said Martin, before huffing conspiratorially, 'so not too many questions, right man?' Awkwardly he pushed his bottom heavy frame into the narrow white leather seat.

'I was just going to ask you how your flight was,' Conti replied. 'I'm exhausted, you've got jet lag, we might meet in the middle with a sort of average conversation.' Winning people's confidences and entering their worlds had always been a gift of his, but in Martin's case Conti had had little opportunity to demonstrate it. At least, not since Martin told him that 'batting's like courage, man, you do it even when you don't feel like it', setting a "simple man" precedent he assiduously maintained.

'The flight?' Martin sounded disappointed, 'I guess that doesn't really count as a question. It was all right. Plenty of new things to think about.'

'You've decided to chuck cricket in, that's what I read in the papers.'

Martin's large eyes watched the last of the street lights give way to the outline of a passing tree. 'I was getting into a bit of a, you know, rut.'

Conti raised an eyebrow, 'Where does that leave you?'

'Questions!'

'Sorry, I can't help myself.'

'People always ask sportsmen so many questions about what they do. They'd never think of giving the same kind of interrogation to a milkman or bank teller,' he said, puzzled by the trace of spite he could not keep out of his voice. 'I mean, are people always asking you about your job?'

'You mean what I'd describe myself as or what I think of what I do for a living?'

'Both I suppose.'

Conti laughed quickly, 'I think I'm whatever it is a bit of a lad becomes when he settles down. And as for thinking about what I do, who does?'

'Ditto,' said Martin, 'we can keep each other company on that.'

The car veered past a burnt-out pub and off the main road, the lights of the duel carriageway switching off suddenly as they dipped into a twisty lane. 'Are you planning to stay long?' asked Conti, his voice more serious, eerily conscious of his surroundings.

'I'm in-between places at the moment so I don't know, I'm always on the way somewhere,' Martin paused. 'Yeah, maybe I'll stay for a bit. I need some time after that tour. To relax, and think.' Thinking for Martin usually meant daydreaming about money, or draining his days of purpose in the clubhouse. Unlike his sister, it wasn't the people he met in life that defined him, but those he met that made no difference at all that shaped his attitude.

'No girl left behind then?'

Martin's blood momentarily froze, as it often did when women were mentioned.

'I never had enough time for one... you know, training, nets.'

'No?' In less distracted times Conti had noticed Martin's reluctance around women. 'Well, they're not the be-all and end-all. But I think your sister told me that you had a hidden romantic streak. When you were younger anyway.'

'Yeah, I wanted to get married to my teacher when I was five. Kind of gone off the idea now.'

Martin hesitated and fiddled with his watch strap. If his dishonesty was one part of his double life, then a romantic urge

entirely inconsistent with the rest of his character was its humil-
iating flip. Put plainly, he found living, breathing women so
complicated that he wished next time he was rejected, it was
someone dead who did it, just to be on the safer side of heart-
break. To his shame he had yet to break with the habit of falling
in love with every woman he slept with. Prostitutes offered some
relief even though he found it difficult to be aroused for full
intercourse and often ended up, to their embarrassment, offering
them oral. The closest thing he had found to a solution were the
hookers he encountered on holiday, since he was too lazy to love
someone who did not speak his language, and could not be
bothered to love anyone enough to learn theirs. It was ironic that
his successes in friendship meant less than nothing to him, but
his romantic infatuation with girls had yet to be rewarded with
even the least bit of reciprocity.

'How is she, my sister?' he asked, changing the subject the
best way he knew of avoiding emotion head on. 'I was surprised
not to hear from her. She used to write all these letters. I didn't
keep up. I'm not much of a one for writing anyway.'

Conti shuffled in his seat uneasily. 'It's a long story. I wasn't
sure how to tell you over the phone,' he glanced in the rear view
mirror as if he were afraid of being overheard. 'I was going to
leave it until we met face to face, but now that you're here... I
thought it might be easier for you to see for yourself.'

In someone else, an admission of this kind may have aroused
curiosity or a question, but Martin, who in the exasperated
vanity of his ignorance had predicted his sister would tire of
English life, replied assuredly, 'Oh yeah, how's that?'

'Like I say, it'll be easier for you to see her first and then for
me to explain, if I'm able to... It's a complicated situation.' The
road had arrived at a small hill, the gap between houses growing
longer and their shape more irregular, the view from the car
obscured by thick trees, higher walls and closed gates.

'Well I guess country living here isn't the same as back home,'

Martin replied, with the swagger of a man who knew the ball he hit was a six. 'She's probably bored, that's all, man. She was brought up on a farm, our idea of a farm, not yours, maybe she finds this tame.' He pressed his finger to the window and to his surprise saw nothing but pitch black. The darkness on the Veldt had never scared him; it was natural and covered only high grass and the beasts that lived on it. Here the darkness was smaller and held in like a person concealing something that did not want to be seen. At once he regretted his remark, it was disrespectful, not to Conti or Brigit but to the land he was describing, and he was frightened that he would pay for it.

'It's a lot to take in, for her,' he said, backtracking, 'she probably feels the responsibility too, for sinking most of her inheritance in to the place, and the big allowance she still collects off Dad. But it's what she wanted, to live among the English, somewhere nice and safe so she could have time for her degree and bring up...'

'Emile.'

'Yeah, Emile, bring him up here in your countryside.'

Conti dropped down a gear as the car crossed a cattle grid. 'You're right, it is a proper boy's paradise, but...' he slowed the vehicle down and turned past a row of corrugated iron houses in to a drive, 'it's a little back-end too. You could say there's a downside to all the good you can enjoy here, a badness here that isn't as obvious as it is in the city,' he stopped himself, careful not to destroy the sane point he was trying to make. 'You'll see what I mean when you've been here a bit. Like a lot of things, country life is better recalled than met with.'

Martin looked up at the large arch they were passing under; a tall statue of a deer loomed over it, its antlers quivering in spite of being motionless. As he was about to remark on the effect, a high-pitched barking, possibly a hound waking up a pack, filled his ears. 'The Hampshire hunt kennels right?'

'No, your sister.'

A smell of burning pine wreaths filled both men's nostrils as first a nightjar, and then a tawny owl joined the din, their noise and the one coming from the house growing indistinguishable.

'She likes to lead the singing,' said Conti, 'to start as a dog and then switch to a bird. A bit of a game.'

'You must be fucking with me man?'

'Come in and see,' said Conti, and switched off the engine.

At first all he could focus on was the ivy-flecked stone. Time and neglect having reduced it to a brittle network of prowling vines over a faded grey core. Though the large door, bolted together by rusty nails, was lit by a solitary hurricane lamp, it was impossible for Martin to take in the full measure of the house. The tall windows shed no light over the walls, and the turrets and battlements created no line against the ink black sky. Even the incontestable largeness of what lay before him was trimmed by the way the house seemed to fall back, so that the bulk of it was hidden behind its relatively narrow front. Without an aerial photo, Martin could not tell where the house stopped, and night started, or even whether the building had a discernable design. If it did, he guessed, then it would resemble nothing so much as an Eastern European Asylum, for Brigit's description of it as a run down home that could pass for a girls' school fell hopelessly short of its true monstrousness.

Martin could not rid himself of the feeling that Tyger Tyger should not be there, that in a world of air travel, consumerism and pop music it ought to have disappeared or been turned in to a hotel. This was not, he sensed, because it was old, more that it did not fit into any period at all, its existence negating ordinary conceptions of time, just as its diameters could be summed up as chaos without shape.

'Be careful of the moat, it's more of a ditch but I've fallen into it a couple of times. Follow the path.'

'This is not what I expected, man.'

Looking as though he did not know or care what Martin expected, Conti tugged the scrolled iron bell pull, his face obscured by smoke from the burning pines. 'Judith, our gardener, she likes lighting bonfires at night. It mixes with the fog and the end result is that you can't see a damn thing.'

The door opened and an elderly but strong looking woman silently lifted Martin's case out of his arms and led him in to the hall. Behind him, Martin could feel Conti loitering uneasily, as though there were some magic incantation he needed to recite before steeping through his door justified.

'Martin, this is Mrs Archer, we were fortunate enough to purchase her with the house.'

Mrs Archer made no attempt to help Martin by introducing herself. Her loaf-like head and tiny refracting eyes emitted the defensiveness through which she met the world, their pointed stare supported by an aggressive self-belief. In spite of her age, Archer's shoulders were as broad as Martin's, and her legs easily as thick. Only the dimples on her chin softened her appearance, offering the promise of a speck of kindness rationed away for emergencies. As with the mauve walls she stood in front of, Archer gave the impression of appearing a different colour in daylight, the proximity of night accentuating a spiky morbidity.

'Judith will take your bags up to your room Mr Martin, she's a strong lass.'

'I can do that myself.'

'As I say she's a strong lass. Best to limit the number of trips you have to make on your own.'

'Fine, whatever,' Martin checked himself, conscious that he had replied to something he had not understood properly.

'And I apologise right off for the smell,' Archer glared at Conti who seemed to be reluctant to take his coat off, 'it's disinfectant and well needed. The carpet, this one, was covered in that stuff only an hour past, and every plant, watering can and ash tray in the conservatory smelled like a blocked river,' she added, turning her glare to Martin, 'looked like piss, thick brown urine, gallons of it. I tell you, I've never seen it this bad before, not for years now. It's unbecoming.'

'We're not sure where this silt is coming from, but Mrs Archer is right, it has become a problem,' said Conti, his tone admirably sane in front of Archer's onslaught, 'probably the plumbing. It's pretty defective.'

'Plumbing!' Archer rolled her eyes.

'How's Emile,' Conti asked gently, mindful that any inquiry could be construed as a provocation.

'Playing merry hell no doubt in his room, but safely locked in.'

'He wanders round the house at night, sleep walking,' Conti added for Martin's benefit, 'We have to shut him up in there as a sort of precaution against accidents. And Chantal?'

Archer snorted, her nostrils flaring as if she were about to charge, 'Who knows? Not lifting a finger to help about the place, that's for sure. There's a lot her daddy ought to have taught her that I don't have time to. She keeps complaining about the doors and windows locking, I say then find the bloody keys. Hopeless she is, absolutely bloody hopeless.'

Conti took a deep breath, 'Brigit?'

Archer looked from Conti to Martin and then back to Conti.

'He's her brother Mrs Archer. You can be candid,' as if you need a cue to be, he could have added.

'Well, she's up now, as you'll have heard. Quiet through the morning though, but the doctor didn't help any with his visit. I told you, no doctor would do any good, especially not that one. He's soft through and through, that man, fainted when he saw my husband's piles.'

'That as may be, I went to see him before I picked up Martin. He told me...'

'She knocked him off stride all right, had a right good giggle to herself over that, but rude I thought it was, even to a fool like

39

him.'

'What do you mean?' asked Martin, 'is Brigit pretending to be ill, because I tell you, man, that's my sister all over, a hypochondriac.'

'Oh, you'll find out soon enough,' laughed Archer bitterly, 'she was coming out with a right load of old rubbish after he left, all about opposites, how we can't have light without dark, being without non being or something like that, no good without evil…'

'I hope you put a stop to that Mrs Archer,' Conti said quietly.

'I certainly did, I said precious nonsense, if we're meant to have both good and evil, how is it you've fallen in with just one of them Mrs Conti? Just bloody evil and evil minded with no bloody good. That shut her up, that did!' Archer cackled, pleased with her erudition.

Martin opened his mouth to say something but his questions were too numerous to be intelligible. 'Jesus,' he said, 'she always said things she didn't mean when she lost her temper…but that sounds out there. Has she a fever?'

'She plays up sometimes,' said Conti, 'and kind of acts out characters if she's angry. It may be that she's suffering some kind of minor breakdown… we're not sure what's causing it. I think Martin, it'd be best if I went up to see her on my own first, then you can go up once I'm down and speak to her on your own, if that's what you want.'

Martin nodded mutely.

'Mrs Archer, show Martin the drawing room, I won't be long,' said Conti, mounting the wide oak staircase.

'Oh Mr Conti, before I forget, she wants that mattress changed again, the special one you got from that catalogue for her back pains, she says its like lying on top of a skin, whatever that means.'

'All right,' Conti called down the stairs, 'let her sleep on it for another night. And get in touch with an electrician, the sound's gone again on the TV in the kitchen, and the one in my room.'

Archer sighed loudly, once again a simple woman puzzled by life's many demands. 'So you're her brother then?'

'Yes.'

Archer frowned at him reprovingly, before shaking her head, 'Well you seem normal enough, I don't suppose it's hereditary, but whether Mr Conti fills you in or not, five minutes in a room with her, no offence meant, will tell you more than he or I can. She's a very tired woman, has been ever since oh, Easter at least.'

'Easter, that's nearly seven months ago?' said Martin, belated belligerence entering his voice as it sunk in that the woman they were referring to, was his sister.

'You must think we're all ill mannered; it'll be hard for you. When I first met Mrs Conti she was a fairly gentle thing, lovely in her way, not soft but kept herself to herself, and that's probably what you remember her as... Here,' Archer stuffed a piece of paper into Martin's palm, 'she wanted me to give you this to show you that she's still the same underneath. Those were her words she used.'

Martin opened the crumpled page and eyed his sister's lopsided handwriting, the letters bent over so the words they formed were strung like catapults waiting to be released:

'Hand in hand
On earth, in Hell,
Sick or well,
On sea, on Land
On the square, Ever

Stiff or in Breath,
Lag or Free,
You and Me,
In Life, in Death,
On the Cross, never.'

Martin read aloud, his hand unsteady under the shaking glow of the chandelier.

Archer scratched her chin, 'Does that mean anything to you?'

'Yeah. It comes from a game we played when we were little. We were like a secret society, being hunted by people who weren't really there. In an imaginary world, she liked it but I didn't. I just wanted her to leave me alone so I could play with my cars. We weren't always that close, to be honest.'

'Well that's a relief, we hardly ever tie up loose ends round here. Maybe you'd be able to understand some of the other gubbins she keeps spouting off...'

'Is she awake when she does this? She used to talk in her sleep, she had bad nightmares too. What's wrong with her do you think? I don't understand what you mean by "gubbins?"'

Mrs Archer was already ahead of him and had advanced down a passage that resembled a ship's corridor flanked by portal windows that looked out into small crannies decorated with cigarette cards and miniature golliwogs. As with the staircase, exterior, and hall, no part of Tyger Tyger resembled itself, the plans of a dozen architects thrown in to a haphazard mix bereft of order or consistency. Among the bizarre array of ornaments and etchings, Martin noticed a fresh crop of crude illustrations running below a blue chalk pentacle, 'What are those? They look like the kind of thing you find inside a pyramid.'

'Emile, your nephew leaves them there faster than we can wash them off. He draws bloody great circles on the floor too. "Scrapies", he calls them.'

Archer was ascending another staircase in to a large green room, the visibility inside was so bad that Martin could hardly see how he was expected to follow her. His bearings indoors were no better than they were when he had tried to guess the shape of Tyger Tyger House from the drive. Lacking an organic feel for things, Martin was used to working his way through attitudes until he had found one that worked, but his sense of direction had always been as good as a bushman's. He feared that if he had to leave in a hurry (and why would he even think this?) the path that led to the front door was not necessarily the one that lay behind him, 'Dark here, isn't it...' his voice faltered.

'It is, too expensive to get it all fitted with modern electrics, and we'd have to tear half the walls down to do it.'

'With all this old stuff it doesn't feel like I'm in 1986.'

Archer, ignoring the array of large black switches, paused at the door, either for Martin to catch up or, he sensed, for someone else to leave the room before they entered.

'Well, in a way, you're not.'

Slowly she reached for a box of matches and lit an oil lamp, illuminating a ghastly line of paintings depicting fawns in battle with various mythological beasts. The flickering light on these vulgarly painted oils was too much for Martin and he couldn't resist asking her, 'Doesn't it creep you to work here?' for he knew of no other way of putting it. 'I couldn't take it here on my own without no light on, the shadows are sketchy, they'd freak me out.'

Archer smiled as if she had been waiting for this question. 'There are three types of shadows in Tyger Tyger, yours, those that belong to things, and those that don't belong to anything at all, and these last... they wait for you to acknowledge them, which I never have, you see, so I've nothing to be scared of. In the end they go back to being ordinary shadows of real things, waiting to bother someone else.'

Martin tried to look as though he had been reassured. 'I know what you mean. You're saying it's all in the mind, right?'

Archer, to Martin's embarrassment, looked at him protectively, 'No, no. You see things, but they don't matter any. Harmless, for the most part.'

'That picture,' he pointed at a lecherous looking Minotaur, 'looks like a damned devil. Is that what it's supposed to be?'

'No, much too ugly, the prince of darkness is a gentleman, you'll find that in your Shakespeare.'

'You believe in him?'

'Who, Shakespeare?'

'No, Satan, you know, the devil'.

'More than believe. I know he exists.'

Martin examined Archer's face for signs of ironic intent and found none.

'My husband got him to cure his arthritis, and he did.'

'You're f...fooling me.'

'I'm not saying Mr Archer wasn't the same old misery boots as he was before but the arthritis had gone for good, the devil took it away from him for half his soul. It didn't solve our problems though. Our lives were just as hard as they had been except Mr Archer could walk without pain, pain in his joints where the arthritis was. Trouble was, he always did like to take the easy way, he was a lazy so and so. That's why he went back, I told him not to. He went back and asked for something he shouldn't have asked for.'

'A bit of inside help, eh?' Martin joked unconvincingly.

'And this time Old Nick took the whole of his soul, took it quick as a shot.' Archer's face was pale and suddenly Martin could see a much younger, almost vulnerable woman in her place.

'Did he give him what he promised?'

'Did he hell! Everyone knows the devil's a bloody liar.'

Archer stopped, a knocking from the other side of the house had grown audible. 'Be sensible and keep out of it,' she warned. 'You won't have to look far to find him. Not here.'

The knocking stopped once Conti entered the draughty room. The windows were bolted and the heating was turned up but the posts of the bed were covered in a light frost and Conti noticed a small icicle forming along the curtain rail. A cold wind seemed to be travelling in through the walls, chilly dampness was coating the furniture and floor. Brigit sat cross-legged on a pile of cushions with her sheets wrapped round her like a cloak, her gaunt face lined but playfully expressive. Beside her was a large candle, the wax of which she was playing with.

'What's all the noise for, Brigit? You know your songs aren't everyone's cup of tea,' Conti's tone verged on flippancy, a reproof of how little seriousness should be attributed to such behaviour. 'I thought we agreed it was bad for you voice. Please go back to bed, it's freezing in here. I'll get Archer to bring up another electric heater.'

'There was no singing Hartley, I was only clearing my sinuses.'

Conti eyed Brigit with distrust. He had grown wary of the schoolgirl voice she teased him in, its apparent innocence caught in the drift towards some quality that was its opposite. On the end of her nose was a small mole he had not noticed before, no larger than a Rice Krispie, its tip blood red.

'I hope you've eaten properly today.'

'Yes, and Archer changed the sheets...it's funny, isn't it, Hartley, how you've ended up with this responsibility. I was only telling our friend the doctor, a doctor who may be in need of one,' she grinned privately, 'that I felt sorry for you shouldering the burden of me...on your own.'

There was an unpleasant suggestiveness in his wife's tone that reminded Conti not to take her civility at face value.

'I don't think I have much trouble coping, if that's what you mean Brigit,' somehow he knew he had to keep addressing her by name, and noticed she visibly flinched every time he did so. 'When you love someone nothing's too much trouble.'

'But who else is there to help you other than that old Archer and her brooding daughter...or am I forgetting someone else? Am I Hartley? Someone who smells nice and who's not even a teensy bit stinky like me,' her voice was deeper but controlled, alluding to an in-joke.

'Come on Brigit, you were being sensible this morning. You don't smell, you're just too weak to take care of yourself properly.'

'The right answer!'

Irony was a characteristic Conti had adored in Brigit, its discovery an unexpected surprise in so quiet a girl. Now, however, there was something faintly poisonous in it that mocked not just seriousness, but the very idea that there could be anything that did not deserve ridicule.

'Brigit, your brother's downstairs... I picked him up from the station. You agreed that you'd make an effort with him, not to worry the guy unnecessarily.'

'Oh don't be so pious!' she rasped, 'go to the one who licks your wounds clean if I'm not enough for you. What sort of husband,' she said, 'carries on an affair under his wife's nose!'

Conti held the candle he feared Brigit would throw at him, 'Stop it! I'm here to take care of you. If I didn't want to I'd bugger off, wouldn't I?'

'You want it all ways.'

'Brigit, listen to me. Your brother is downstairs. He wants to see you. What should I tell him? That his sister is too much of a drama queen to leave her bedroom... and too babyish to talk sense?'

Brigit's face switched to a robotic stare, as it did whenever Conti threatened to lose patience with her. He had felt this was the most affected of her personas, but he now treated it as a reliable source of information when compared to her other moods. 'Gifts, gifts such as these,' she intoned in an android voice, 'are not normally thought to bring their owners to the threshold of suffering...'

'Christ Brigit! What gifts?'

'The dead and living are together in the Kingdom.'

'You aren't dead Brigit.'

'But I feel it.'

'Brigit, please, I am your husband and I love you. You may not act like you care, but if you carry on like this, one or both of us is set for the madhouse, I mean it.'

They were interrupted by a small cough. Standing at the door in his alphabet pyjamas was their son, Emile, a slight boy with Brigit's eyes, his narrow face hidden under a pudding bowl fringe. Meekly he smiled at his mother, his small teeth chattering in the cold. Just behind Emile was the shadow of a cat, searching for a physical embodiment it lacked. Conti squinted and the shadow disappeared, blending in with the door. He had reburied one of the cats only the day before, the morning his son had been sent home from school for cackling through morning prayers, stopping only once the hymns had finished. His teachers were concerned that he had fallen under the influence of an older boy. Since his suspension Conti had tried, without success, to keep Emile away from his mother who had repeatedly asked Conti to move the boy in to the room next to hers so that they could be "nearer to the light".

His sense of duty towards his son was just that and no more. An obligation landed on him by nature, the steady disengagement between the two having begun the night Emile was born. Conti had never entertained the expectations a medieval King might for his heir, but Emile had dropped below those of a eunuch. The boy was irredeemably wet, distant and twee. Although most of the disappointment had been choked up in the first few years, Conti had never completely given up hope that his son might wake from his torpor and display signs of virile life.

'How did you get out of your room?'

'My door opened itself. Like this one did.'

'Doors don't do that Emile. We've talked about making things up.'

'They open themselves. I've seen them do it lots of times. But tonight it didn't, you're right, Daddy. Felix let me out.'

'Felix is dead Emile, I buried him myself and you keep digging him up. Dead cats don't open doors.'

'He did, it was Felix the cat!'

'We both know that's another lie, don't we?'

Brigit, whose face had reverted to a pointed smirk, drew a long finger through the air and beckoned to Emile, 'What's that in your hand darling?'

'The homework Mr Stressfield told me to take home with me.'

'Bring it to Mummy and show her how hard you've tried.'

Emile smiled complicity, and limped in on one leg in the pathetic imitation of a cripple that he assumed from time to time to amuse his mother, sadder than even he realised.

Without waiting for her son to reach her, Brigit advanced and snatched the jotting book out of his hands.

'Religious *Studies*', she exclaimed, 'Well it would just have to be, wouldn't it Hartley, my God, this house must have been merry when it found raw material like us!' she laughed. Her frequent references to the house as a living thing, though not lost on Conti, always struck him as less significant than her laughter. There had always been a slightly nervous quality about it, tentative even, but now it was joyously abrupt, possessed, but not necessarily in self-possession. Still smiling to herself, Brigit flicked open a page and studied it carefully, her face showing its old intelligence.

Conti had, by now, detected a pattern emerge in Brigit's "play acting". The much-vaunted atheism of her youth, and the aversion with which she loudly disclaimed God, were beginning to enjoy a complimentary relationship. He first noticed it in the spring when she declared that she no longer wished him to call her Heavenly, her old nickname, but instead wanted to be named after something from the animal kingdom. At the time he had thought this was indicative of her tendency to take herself too seriously, or possibly a weak wind up, but she had been as good as her word, flying into an anger whenever he called her by the old name, even if he said it in a silly voice. Bit by bit he saw that it was not his use of arcane language that affected her but the actual content of the word and what it referred to. Rather than be annoyed, Conti was puzzled. It was hard for a man who had no real thoughts on heaven to fathom why a woman should wish to swap a pretty nickname, for a peculiar one, Brigit's personal preference being "rat".

Not long after this Brigit had blown up with Mrs Archer who, having complimented her on giving up her trips to London to see psychiatrists, said that an hour in church was worth four on the couch. Brigit had wished Archer gone and teased her for not knowing about her daughter's abortion, knowledge that Brigit had never alluded to before. It was the first time Conti had witnessed Brigit act hatefully, seriously weakening his view that her behaviour was little more than a tasteless game brought on by boredom. When asked what was wrong with her, she contrived not to understand the question, insisting that her behaviour was perfectly normal and that Conti was overreacting. All of which made her interest in her son's religious studies homework somewhat unlikely, if not worrying. The knocking beginning again as Conti tried to lift the book out of Brigit's hands.

Before he was able to do so, Brigit threw out an arm and tossed it across the room, muttering in pain, 'It's burning me Hartley, the words are burning!'

'Get back to your room, Emile, and stay in there. Mummy's not well tonight.'

Normally Emile would linger and spy on his mother's upsets, but this time the boy quickly did as he was told, not through obedience, but from instinctual symbiosis, which Conti felt, came through Brigit.

'Help me Hartley, I'm so hot!' Brigit fell back on to the bed clutching her hands. Grasping her by the wrist, Conti emptied a glass of squash over her clenched fists, rubbing the liquid between her fingers and knuckles. Instantaneously Brigit stopped wriggling, closed her eyes and allowed her body to become dead weight. Conti bound her in the bedding, as though rolling up a carpet and watched her for a moment. Though seemingly asleep, froth was collecting at the sides of her mouth and she had begun to breathe in slow phlegm-inflected grunts. The room, meanwhile, had grown even colder. Conti picked the book up off the floor, still open on the page Brigit had been reading from, and saw underlined in red pen, 'Earth, *if chosen instead of heaven, will turn out to have been, all along, only a region in hell, and earth, if put second to heaven, will prove from the very beginning to have been part of heaven itself.'*

Conti put the book down and looked around the room. Fear was wrapped round his neck as tight as rope. It seemed to him that there was a shadow common to all these moments, not unlike the one of the cat, only vaster and more indistinct. In some elementary way it had been there all along, before he had met Brigit or moved to Tyger Tyger, responsible for every anomalous thing that had ever happened to him, but something he had never sought an explanation for. Normality had been the rule and nights spent sweating under his covers as a child were the exception. His years were defined by a superficial interest in politics and the arts, not by examining why he always turned a light on before switching one off. Ignoring the unknown, which was how he treated everything he did not know yet, had replaced curiosity and become his working method; revelation and surprise were properties of a long abandoned self. Was this why, ignored and passed over for so long, the shadow had finally come to find him, angry that he had worshipped banal everyday truths over those it could provide? Leaving the room backwards so his eyes did not leave the bed where his wife lay, Conti hoped that he had got it wrong and that normalcy would return as inexplicably as it had left, his bearing too British to give up on so reassuring an outcome.

Chapter Three

The bulk of Martin's brain was aching under the weight of recent use. He had never suffered the sensation of a room listening to his thoughts before, and did not like it. When Conti entered by way of a lot of noisy coughing, Martin raised his head hopefully like a donkey over a gate, frankly grateful for the escape his presence offered. 'Martin, would you mind leaving her until morning, she's nearly asleep now.'

'Morning is fine with me.'

'Mrs Archer, one minute,' Conti approached the house keeper who had lingered on the dark staircase, 'this message you left me, the phone call, from Tom Elmhurst?'

'Why yes, he called this afternoon inviting you to a party in London...'

'He was killed in my car twelve years ago, and the place where the party is apparently to be held,' Conti folded the note, trying to control his voice, 'closed at about the same time.'

'Don't blame me! Am I supposed to know...'

'I'm not, but it isn't the first time it's happened, there have been other phone calls too, haven't there? So be prepared if whoever it is rings again.'

'It was a she. She sounded foreign.'

'She then, and keep her on the line if I'm in, I want to speak to her. Check on Emile too please, he wasn't properly locked in and came in on his mother, which is the last place he ought to be. They were in the garden again a few days ago.'

'Doesn't sound like there's anything strange in that,' interjected Martin.

Conti scowled impatiently, before checking himself. 'They woke up in the garden together at eight in the morning. England's a cold place to sleep outside, in winter.'

'What were they doing, camping?'

'According to Emile they flew there during the night, though Brigit claims they both sleep walked. Either way I don't want them to catch colds.'

'A boy's place is with his mother, I used to say,' muttered Archer.

'Not this mother or boy, which reminds me, I agree with your suggestion, about the vicar.'

Archer did not need to say anything, so complete was her air of vindication. 'I'll call first thing, goodnight sir, and you too Mr Martin, sleep well. This place will look far less interesting in the morning!' she added, curtsying slyly.

Martin crossed his heavy legs.

'Are you tired?' Conti asked as he pulled out a tray and poured them both a large brandy. Martin could see that Conti was no longer tired, his pointed cheekbones twitching with suppressed agitation and, if Martin read him correctly, fear. It was Martin's first indication that painful surprises, far from being the bane of Conti's life, were perhaps preferable monotony. 'Or would you prefer to drink?'

'A drink, yeah, why not... That woman, Archer, she seems, a bit, a bit tricky. I find her attitude strange to be honest, man.'

'Strange?' Conti chuckled, 'She's bloody mad. Were this place not so out of hand, I'd have sacked her, but she has made herself indispensable. I need her, the crafty witch.'

'I'm going to have to ask you, I didn't want to pry, but no one's told me anything. What's going on here?' Martin sank his drink in one.

'You'd be mad if you didn't pry.'

'How bad is my sister?'

'Ugly at times, but a price worth paying for living with someone who made my life.' Conti, who was shifting his weight from leg to leg without going anywhere, emptied the rest of the bottle into Martin's glass and opened another bottle to furnish his own. The measures, Martin could not help but notice, were liberal even by the standards of a professional sportsman.

'Brigit told me that you wouldn't want to come here,' said Conti measuring his words carefully, 'even if you were in England. Because you hated the countryside.' She had also said that he did not care about her enough to come but Conti passed over that. 'Which meant I didn't have to make any provisions for letting you in on our predicament. When you rang to say you were definitely on your way I thought I might usher you through without you cottoning on to what's going on here…then you said you wanted to stay and… well no one can bullshit that well. Brigit can give you her own account in the morning.'

'I haven't cottoned on to that much yet, though Archer was giving me some advice when you came in. Sounded like old wives' stuff, about the devil.'

Conti frowned, 'I said that I agreed that she was mad, but in a mad house it might be the mad ones you should listen to.'

'Maybe you've got some crazy advice for me as well?' Martin grinned archly, impressed at how easily he had slipped in to this way of conversing.

'You're probably best off following your own advice, Martin. Perhaps it's me who should be asking you about your sister. You've known her for longer than I have, after all.'

'No way, I'm a stranger in a strange land, remember, tired after a long journey. I'm asking you the questions.'

'Advice can go two ways, it can protect you if you listen to it,' Conti raised his glass, 'or make you doubt my sanity and endanger your own if you discard it.'

'Put me in danger if I don't listen to you! Sounds like you've got a bloody high opinion of your own advice, man! I'd like to hear some of what you're offering, if you think it's all that great.'

'Not great, useful.'

'Go on, for God's sake.'

'To start with,' said Conti, examining his drink, 'I think you should close your bedroom door every time you leave your room. I do.'

'You think I should what?'

'Close the door every time you leave your bedroom.'

'I heard you the first time, I just didn't believe it. To avoid draughts?'

'No, to avoid seeing faces at your window, when walking back up the drive or coming back in to the room.'

'Come again?'

'If you don't close doors, shapes appear in your room, the wind blows them in. I've seen them looking at me, it's not a pleasant sight. But I've found that if I close the doors it doesn't happen.'

'What faces are you talking about? People who work here you mean?' Martin guessed this was precisely what Conti did not mean, but what he might mean, belonged too far from sanity to credit. 'You mean staff who'll go through my belongings? I don't find you funny, if that's what you're trying to be… you haven't been on the bottle all day?'

'No, I'm serious. These aren't the faces of people, not real people, there's something missing from them that stops them from being… natural. I don't know what they are, but if you close your door you won't see them, and that way you won't have to ask yourself what they are. Of course, you might then wonder whether they exist at all, but never so much as to actually risk not closing your door, believe me.'

'So you're telling me, *you* act as if they exist, even though you don't really believe they do, eh?'

'That's quite a clever way of putting it. Realistic but not real, sure, why not.'

'You're fucking kidding me… this is a wind-up right? Like the singing?'

Martin wiped his mouth and waited for Conti's expression to change. Instead it grew sadder. For a second he contemplated the deliciously brusque idea that he had the English cocksucker where he wanted, admitting he was as good as mad and terrified of imaginary faces. The trouble was that Conti did not strike him as insane, only scared. 'So I'd better close my door just to be on the safe side!' Martin laughed weakly, 'Anything else I can do to stave off the little green men in your head?'

Conti, who was resting on the arm of a settee, nodded like a good sport prepared to take a joke against himself. 'It's a lot to take my word for, I know. And as I say, you don't have to. Think of it like crossing your fingers under a ladder or avoiding the number thirteen.'

Martin took a sip from his glass, not losing eye contact with Conti. 'Faces' he sniffed, 'now I really have heard it all.'

'I'm not trying to scare you. You may have an uneventful stay here and decide I'm full of shit.'

'So we're talking about ghosts, right? Why not cut the crap, you think this place is haunted.'

'I don't know... I've wondered, but haunted houses are meant to stay the same aren't they? Ghosts repeating the same old re-enactments throughout eternity...but this house feels like it's always moving.'

'Jesus, it's all happening here. No, this is too good, man, go on, where else should I cross my fingers and touch wood?'

'Personally, I wouldn't make yourself comfortable anywhere apart from your bedroom. In a big house I know it's tempting to make use of the space, but if you want a catnap do it in your own room with the door closed. Start to relax somewhere else and the next thing you know you'll have heard some gorgeous singing and fallen asleep...'

'And?'

'And before you know it you'll have woken up wanting to kill yourself...'

'If you're still kidding me you're getting sick, you know that?'

'You'll think I really am if I tell you that I drifted off in the drawing room right above this one,' Conti pointed to the ceiling, 'which unlike this one actually looks habitable, and woke up pleading with some *thing* to fuck me...'

This time Martin laughed involuntarily, 'Now that might say something about you English!'

'As a forfeit to stop my family from burning in hell.'

'You are a sick bastard.'

Conti poured himself another brandy, ignoring Martin's empty glass. 'Usually when I'm leaving in the morning, and I'm closing the door after I've helped Brigit up the stairs...'

'Can't she walk up them herself?'

'She claims to have a bone disease amongst other things, but we can go back to that. It's when I close the door I'll see something that chills me...her body will be normal, except for her eyes. They'll be yellow. Or else her hand will beckon, like a claw...'. There was a frustration in Conti's voice directed not at Martin but towards a more general presence in the room, 'Even when I've left her, I never feel like I'm on my own in this place, never alone with silence anyway, that's why I think it's something to be avoided.'

'I thought a bit of peace and quiet would be good.'

'Good? No shit. Talk to yourself, hum, sing, but don't catch yourself being quiet for any length of time. Or it'll be like falling asleep in one of those rooms except it'll happen to you when you're awake...some voice suggesting that'd it'd be quicker if you used the window instead of the stairs, even though you're on the fifth floor, you know, that kind of thing. Forgive me for going on like this, but you've arrived here at a ...'

'No, you just keep going, but you know what I think, no disrespect Hartley, but it sounds like you have a real problem, and it's not just to do with living in this place. It's with your head.' Quickly he topped up his brandy. 'I always find that if I'm scared of something I try and become part of it, do you know what I mean? Kind of like "if you can't beat them join them", so if a guy is scared of the dark or of silence he imagines he's part of it,'

Martin paused, this was easily one of the profoundest discoveries of his life and he wanted Conti to relish it. 'That way you feel like you're on the inside of it looking out at all the other scared guys. That you've become part of what they're scared of, so you don't have to be frightened any more. You've got to start thinking like that.'

'I would not want to become part of anything here.'

'Listen to me, man, I grew up in the wild, I'm not frightened of the dark like you, you know, it shows that you're still a city kid at heart,' the alcohol made Martin brave, but careless also, if he had not been he might have noticed a shadow flicker across the room. 'I mean, what with you and that old woman winding each other up all the time, it's no wonder Brigit's gone nuts. No, I'm just fine in nooks and crannies, the dark, you name it, bring it on...' he paused, mindful that this was not what he had said to Archer earlier, but that seemed a long time ago. Conti's reticence was emboldening Martin, a tonic for his own shortcomings, 'This place is only bricks and mortar; nothing changes just because the lights aren't on. The chairs are in the same place, and the walls don't move. Trust me.'

'That's easy to say when there isn't anything normally threatening about those things, but here the dark isn't some neutral substance. It promises to reveal things to you when what it really wants to do is draw you in. Fear of it is good, it's a sign that you can still remember yourself.'

Martin shook his head. His certainty was interrupted by a loud knocking. The sound was disconcerting; a few gentle raps, and then a sudden outburst of louder ones. Though he could not explain why, he knew that what he heard was directed at *him*, and like a clean bowled batsman, his swagger evaporated. The brandy was still there, but dragging him to uncertain conclusions, the kind he had woken up to the morning after the last Test. 'What is that, I thought I heard it earlier, old pipes?'

Conti emptied his brandy and glanced at the corner of the

room where the shadow had become one with a Persian rug. 'Maybe. I had them checked at Easter,' his voice dropped, 'they were okay for a while and then they got worse, not just them, the electrics, the plumbing, everything.'

'You can date that?'

'I try to, but I keep going back, and the further I go the more I recognise it was always wrong here, right back to when we lost our friends, the real ones, when we first moved out.'

'I don't see a link man.'

'Our *great* mates, we began to feel uncomfortable round them. We swapped them for less challenging ones, though at the time we convinced ourselves that the ones we loved and who really loved us and had known us for years, were misfits and alcoholic delinquents. We'd become yuppies and we did what yuppies do which is upgrade to people who want coffee after dinner and not stay up all night on acid.'

'What does that have to do with the house and Brigit?'

'None of them liked it when they came here, Brigit joked it was because they had invisible protectors, or guardian angels that repelled the influence of Tyger Tyger, making them safe from its effects. Even then we knew this place wasn't for everyone, but we guessed it was because of its old atmosphere, and that these art school anarchists were probably jealous of us for turning into country squires. They were the first to get out of our lives, the ones we would have needed the most. We drove them off.'

'What about the yuppies? Can't you talk to them?'

'Talk to them about what I've been saying to you? And end up sounding like a new age dickhead with fairies at the bottom of my garden and UFOs flying over the drive? I'd have to be mad, mad and out of a job, this is still England remember? Anyway, Brigit made a good job of scaring off the nosy ones without me having to bare my heart. I don't talk to everyone this frankly, Martin.'

For the first time that night Martin suspected that Conti was lying to him. He did not believe Conti's thoughts, dark as they were, had cost him as much to air as they would a normal man, or that living within abnormality was out of character for him. After all, Conti had made no secret of his support for the ANC, he freely admitted he took drugs and had slept with many of Brigit's friends before marrying her, which for Martin was far weirder than a case of the spooks. If it had not been for the very real fear he had experienced minutes earlier, Martin would have guessed that some kind of premeditated manipulation was taking place. 'Look here Hartley, lots of people believe in ghosts. I've even met guys who claim to have seen them. Don't you want to get to the bottom of it? There must be some kind of expert who deals in this stuff?'

Conti stared into his glass. 'It isn't about ghosts; they're a red herring. Brigit knows what it is, the way she grins to herself as if she's on the inside of it. It's not ghosts.'

'But the inside of what, man? I don't want to wait until she tells me, what's wrong with her?' Martin flinched at his own question. What if Conti was poisoning his sister for her inheritance and all this haunted house stuff was a decoy... it was too absurd, but then how normal was it to be asked to shut your bedroom door to avoid coming face to face with the un-dead?

'According to her doctors, nothing's wrong with her. She'll complain of agonising stomach pains, this bogus bone problem, and furniture falling in to her all the time but they, and I mean private specialists as well as our local beardy, they all say there's nothing to it. Not a disease, not allergies, not arthritis, nothing.'

'It's all in her head?'

'That is about the worst thing you can say to her,' said Conti clutching his glass. 'Mention psychological problems and she goes nuts, I mean literally, the whole thing's stood on its head and I'm accused of inventing problems.'

'But didn't she dine on these quacks for years, at university and after, paying a fortune for their ear? She was into that crap from way back.'

'I know, all that was difficult enough to stomach when she was well. That's why when she started ranting and raving about how blind they all were, I agreed. The idea of her working in the garden and getting some fresh air in her lungs instead of burying herself in libraries and giving those old fossils a subject for their bullshit theories seemed a good trade off. I didn't see it then, but it wasn't only going to be them she was turning her back on...'

'Why don't you just leave then? If this house is what's making her sick. Get in a jumbo jet and go.'

'I had thought of that,' said Conti, 'in fact I raised the subject a week ago. Your sister said she'd kill herself if we did. That she belongs here, that this house is "her place".

'You believe her?'

'It's not something I want to exactly call her bluff on.' Conti glanced at the clock.

Martin saw him do so and said, trying to muster some friendly sarcasm, 'Eleven thirty, we're damned near the witching hour, yeah?'

'No, that's actually three.'

'What?'

'Three in the morning, it's worse than midnight because there's longer to wait if you can't sleep, and the fear that you'll wake up in time for it if you do. Are you all right?'

Martin cleared his throat and put down his glass. 'It's nothing. I woke up feeling sick at three this morning, actually every morning since I left Africa,' he pressed his forehead. 'You were right, I should ask Archer the questions. It's jet lag, I'm tired, I'm sorry, I think I need to go to bed,' Martin hesitated, 'if you're comfortable leaving it like this.'

'I'll show you to your room,' said Conti courteously, 'and then I'll lock the doors.'

If Martin thought he had left his host at a loose end, or worse, feeling foolish for confiding in him, he was wrong. Conti was not concerned in the slightest with what kind of impression his confession had made on Martin, so confident was he that Tyger Tyger would speak for itself. Since his first affair, barely three months in to his marriage, Conti had bracketed off his responsibilities from his enthusiasms and tonight was no exception.

The doors, which had already been locked by Archer and her daughter when they left for their cottage, were of no interest to him, but Chantal was. Conti knew by now that he possessed a temperament calm enough to propose on a volcano and take bets in a crashing plane, switching from the contemplation of horror to sex in a finger flick. Atmosphere and context, though intimidating, were never so pressing as to get in the way of pleasure, which in this case meant making love to his au pair of three months standing.

It had begun well. As an agnostic, Conti's wishes were imperfectly realised prayers, and privately he had longed for something more diverting than an above average housewife to flirt with. An advert for an au pair in the Hampshire Chronicle had, to his immense surprise, met the need, and within a week Chantal had been installed in the old butler's quarters. Put uncomplicatedly, Conti found her so sexy that he could not believe anyone could think otherwise, and though many people concurred with his judgement, those who did not would have described her as a slim, muscular girl in her mid-twenties, with a boy's backside. Her overall appearance was fundamentally androgynous, with little feminine hints flecked here and there, her fiery eyes more likely to be noticed at a second meeting, than on the first. Conti did not view this relationship as either a compliment to, or contradicting his love for Brigit. In fact, he did not bother to think of the attachment morally at all. Desiring more than one partner was a practical matter that had nothing whatsoever to do with ethics.

It was Conti's guess that Chantal had inherited her benign

fiendishness from her father, as her mother was a shy and disappointed woman who had remarried a local farmer. It was her failure to settle at her mother's farm that instigated Chantal's move to Tyger Tyger, her years in France with her father an evasive blank she rarely alluded to. At twenty four, and perfectly fluent in English, she had little business advertising herself as an au pair but as there were few takers for the job, Archer had grudgingly agreed to accommodate her. Attracted to her, as he was, Conti had been wary of what he thought was Chantal's essential distrust-worthiness. Privately he had prepared himself for months of second guessing her, building up to what she could screw him for, the inevitable result of an affair, or so he feared. In this he was wrong, Chantal, though morally flexible was not interested in anything as practical as a future or the possessions that would help furnish it. The quality of her sex life was how she measured her self-esteem with neither money nor status making much of an impression. For her the fact that Brigit was difficult justified their transgression, and if sleeping with Conti caused offence, the fact that they were "pretty cool people" put them clear of any real wrongdoing.

Of all the inhabitants of Tyger Tyger, Conti noticed that Chantal was the least touched by the building and its effects. Not because she did not believe in them – Chantal was as superstitious as she was cautious, checking her star signs and barely venturing out after dark, but if Conti tried to draw her on particulars she would blow her cheeks out and sigh 'boring, boring, boring.' Rather than fear it, Conti sensed the house did not appear to interest her any more than Brigit's psychobabble or Emile's imaginary pets did.

This Gallic blankness, instinctive or cultivated, had affected her relationship with Emile, best characterised in her pitying incomprehension of him. 'He's just like his mother,' she complained, 'he likes making up secrets and dramas, and can't see how much of a drag they are for anyone normal.'

Predictably a falling out had occurred between Chantal and Brigit, forcing Archer and her daughter to take exclusive care of her. Brigit, who had taken to calling Chantal "the whore" on the rare occasions their paths had crossed, now referred to her simply as "the guest", a moniker Archer readily concurred with as it had become increasingly difficult to tell what Chantal's job actually entailed. Though he promised he would, Conti rarely spoke to her of her duties or her increasingly ambiguous role in the life of his family, the very subject feeling like an ex-partner they could not be bothered to mention, their consumption in one another insularly final.

Gently, so as to not surprise her, Conti opened her door and entered the old play room she occupied. Chantal was standing on her desk pinning a red flag to the wall, dressed in a tight sailor top that he could see her nipples through and plimsolls. In the corner of the room stood a large iron bed with rails, the floor around it strewn with luminous socks and leggings, her walls hidden under posters of dancers and tennis players.

She grinned and he frowned back. This was his own way of smiling at her since his natural reaction on seeing her was always to laugh. Not because everything else in his life was bad, he reasoned, just that she was very good.

'Hello,' he said, and slipped his fingers under the seat of her trousers, her hole at the back and the one at the front closer together and moister than those on any woman he had fallen in love with before.

Martin did not know what had woken him up. His hands were stretched above his head as though they had been holding someone else's and he could hear loud breathing at the end of his bed.

'Brigit?'

There was no answer and in a single movement he was a huddled ball sweating under the heavy duvet. It was a position he had been familiar with as a child, a masochistic thrill taken in knowing that ultimately, the fear was imaginary and therefore could be ended whenever he wished to cease scaring himself. But this was different, the hot breath on his toes was as independent of his imagination as his feet.

Underneath him the house felt unsteady, as though it were moving on stilts and if he drew away too quickly he would fall off. He did not know how many hours passed before he fell asleep and woke, or whether he even had, the shadow in his room not lifting until dawn.

*

It was not her insensitive behaviour, but theirs, that had bought Brigit to this place. She could hear them; listen to every word they thought, downstairs in the kitchen. "The guest" stirring her blackberries into her yogurt to protect the size of her little arse, Archer and her wobbling daughter marinating in the swill of reactive pleasantries, and worst of all, her doltish brother feeding his greed, the ingestion of food so much easier than the comprehension of life. Brigit appealed to the baby intercom, wired to the kitchen. 'Eve ate the apple for knowledge; she did not eat for hunger!' adding, lest her listeners be in any doubt that it was their breakfast that displeased her, 'Pull your snouts out of the trough and bathe in light!'

'She's been like that since Mr Conti left this morning, I'd pay her no mind,' said Judith, Archer's daughter. Her mother smiled proudly. Brigit's attacks and many implied ironies had no more impact on them than fallen bat droppings, regrettably dirty but easily cleared away. Or at least, that was the impression they had decided to convey.

Martin chewed his sausage and tried to look unruffled. The attractive girl washing up her plate had been an unexpected sight and she put him off his stride, for he found it difficult to eat unselfconsciously around beauty. Nor had Archer patting him on the head every time she passed, or her daughter, crashing round the kitchen like a speeding dumpling helped his normally robust passion for fried food. In fact, the sight of Judith bent over the table was exactly the kind of view memory was created to paper over, and he resolved to eat the rest of his meal with his eyes closed.

'Feeding time is not clean!'

Judith allowed herself a nervous chuckle, 'When we eat, it sometimes winds her up. I don't know why.'

The thought of getting out of there, there and then, hurried across Martin's mind, but with enormous effort, he smiled weakly. The thin girl in sparkly leggings at the sink was apparently unaffected by either the tension coming from upstairs, or the variant found round the table. With deliberation he turned his attention to the small television set depicting a far off famine, soundless images of children waiting for aid calming and assisting his digestion.

'The chaste rarely urinate!'

This time Judith laughed openly, 'Get her! To listen to Mrs C you'd think she'd be the sort who'd like nothing more than spending the day thinking of how miserable all her friends would be at her funeral!'

'Now, now, Judith,' said Archer reinstalling discipline, 'she may seem funny to us but that's Mr Martin's sister you're talking about. Different people from different places have different ways of doing things.'

Martin nearly choked on his egg, and Chantal, quiet until now, laughed quickly, made a vague sweeping motion with her eyes at all those present, and left, the smell of fresh lemons wafting behind her.

'Good,' said Archer, 'we don't need madam here with all her airs looking down her little nose at the rest of us. Listening all the time and never saying a word, making out she doesn't understand. He's a fair man, but he's made a mistake with her, letting her loaf about the place.'

Judith, who Archer considered her intellectual superior on account of her O level in Geography, licked her lips knowingly. 'It's a well known fact that foreigners and children are prime candidates for making things up,' she announced, ignoring her mother's earlier warning, 'and we've got a fine mix of them here, Mr Martin. There's the little boy Emile, who says that there's a man in the house, that we've never seen, who comes up behind him and says things in a creepy voice like "hello"!' she paused to laugh, 'and the cat of course, that's only dead, which follows him everywhere too, so he says, and then old vinegar tits upstairs, Chantal, she says this lad keeps coming to the house to sell her things like washing up cloths who again, none of us have seen...'

'Fair's fair, Judith,' interrupted her mother, 'there are a lot of local folk who believe in that lad too, goes by the name of the Stig, released from the Borstal, lives out on a dump and likes coming to the door to sell you things.'

'Get away with you! I say she's just answering the door and talking to herself...and what about that black man in a cowboy hat Mrs Conti was talking about! A black bloke, round here!'

'That's enough Judith!'

Martin put down his fork. 'When can I see my sister?' he said.

'Why! Whenever you want to of course. She's your sister,' replied Archer.

'Can one of you take me up there now?'

'Certainly.'

Martin pushed his plate away and stood up. He did not want to say anything but he knew that if he did not he may forfeit his right to grumble later. 'I woke up in the middle of the night and I thought I heard someone breathing or sleeping in my room, and there was a kind of animal smell too. To be honest it put me on edge. I wasn't dreaming.'

Judith bent her head, as if to say, bloody foreigners, and her mother nodded to show she had taken his point in, but did not think it worth further consideration.

Without knowing how to finish something he wished he had not started, Martin followed her mutely into the hall, his lingering embarrassment dwarfed by the apprehension that in a few minutes he would at least be face to face with his sister.

'Don't take anything she says personally, Mr Martin, you must remember she's very, very tired... she doesn't sleep well at nights.'

Rapidly Martin tried to wrack his memory for an image of his sister to compare this changed version with, but all he could find were visions of himself, alone with his distrust and fear. 'Are you coming in with me? It might be better if she sees me with someone she knows.'

'Me? But she can't know me better than she knows you, her own flesh and blood? Oh I don't think that would be right, do you Mr Martin, not after all this time. Best the two of you catch up on your own, I say...'

Conti made his way through the group of boys, acknowledging their attempts at adult familiarity with the ease of a slightly more experienced sibling. In spite of there being centrally heated class-rooms for them to spend their breaks in, most of them preferred to brave the cold, swapping robot miniatures that turned into cars for science fiction figurines bound with rubber bands.

'You all get too much pocket money. Your parents have more money than sense,' he called cheerfully.

'You just don't get paid enough yourself, Sir.'

'Of course he does, he lives in a castle.'

'But it's a very old one that no one else wanted to live in.'

Although their questions were never innocent, Conti preferred the frenetic chatter of the yard, to the dry one-upmanship of the masters' common room, his presence there slightly akin to an impostor's. In his three years at the school he had learnt that he was most effective around teachers in small doses, a spectacular fringe player yet to make his peace with the adult world.

'Do you own any shares, Sir?'

'I'm too poor Pardoe-Williams, and life is very short.'

'Everyone's buying shares sir, my dad has bought shares for me in Telecom and Cable and Wireless I think.'

'I'm sure you'll have cause to thank him one day. But I don't really understand them.'

'Mr Conti, do you think the school fees are too much. Dad says they're going up all the time, but that's because everyone is earning more money nowadays.'

'I don't know about everyone...'

'Do you think roller-balls are common compared to cartridge pens Mr Conti?'

'You can't go wrong with a sharp pencil Stretton-Hill.'

'Who do you prefer Sir, Linda Lussardi or Sarah Brightman?'

'I tend to not go in for slags Bateson, but if I had to, I'd opt for both.'

'You're by far our favourite grown up.'

'God bless you.'

'Sir?'

Blocking his path was a first year with a Chinese surname he could never remember the pronunciation of, but for whom he felt sympathy, the boy having been marked out for both his ethnicity and for having a grandmother instead of parents.

'Sir?'

'Yes...Lui?'

'That's not my name Sir. I've told everyone that my name means Angel of the Light in Chinese, but a senior says that he checked a dictionary and found out it means "man that pounds on your door in the middle of the night."'

Conti held the boy's eye and said, 'They just want you to switch to your English first name, to make you one of them, if I were you...'

'But you aren't sir.'

'No, but I know the others try and make your life hell. It's important to stand up to them,' his words were not registering, individually correct but unhelpful. 'You can talk to me anytime you want to.'

'A black man is coming to your house sir.'

'What? What are you talking about?'

'I had a dream. That your house was a door that someone was walking through.'

'A door?' asked Conti, a déjà vu with a bad ending already upon him.

Looking frightened, the boy stepped back and disappeared into the throng. Compassion had been too much for him to take, thought Conti, standing motionless, the cold sun in his face, as more and more boys swarmed past him like dying planets round a dead star.

The first thing Martin noticed was the draught. The entire house felt as though it existed over a fault line, but on Brigit's floor the temperature dropped to below that of a cave. The sub-divided stained glass windows were not doing their job, thought Martin. It was little wonder that his sister was ill, the real surprise being that Conti should still humour her by allowing them to stay. In an ideal world Martin would have shipped out of Tyger Tyger that afternoon, but the small matter of not daring to be seen on the African continent, and having no self-organising ability, made an English country house, replete with servants and free meals, bearable for the time being.

There was an abrupt knocking and then silence, reminding Martin of a primitive Morse code, its inexplicable source marginally less unsettling in daylight, of which there was not much in the dark corridor. The stretch of floor in front of Brigit's room was bare, the carpets pulled up to reveal a linoleum floor, the walls stripped of prints and, Martin assumed, anything else breakable. Unlike the other parts of the house he had seen, which, like the modern kitchen attached to the tatty parlour, were incongruous and unkempt, Brigit's "patch" was scrupulously clean, exuding a hospital air. As he approached the door, a gamey smell reminded him of his sleepless night, but it was too late to do anything about it, he was already inside facing the welcoming gaze of his sister.

'Martin. I've too much to tell you,' Brigit's expression was soft, her smile as thin as the flesh that supported it.

'Jesus, you look so skinny!'

'When you lose your appetite the fat follows, brother.'

'But you were never fat!'

Brigit pinched her arm self-deprecatingly. An odd spot at the end of her nose marred her pure white features, the skin was completely drained of contrast or tone. With obvious discomfort, she hauled herself up and sighed, 'I just don't seem to be in the mood for food anymore. It makes me feel disgusting knowing it's going in me, turning to shit and flab. Silly, I know.'

In spite of himself, Martin felt sympathy swell in his chest, his guard and natural caution were down. Brigit, still pretty, bore little physical resemblance to the sprightly and athletic figure she had cut before. Instead her Spartan features reminded him of a torch lit chanteuse addicted to slimming pills. Though on a wavelength he had never cared to understand or enter, her continual interest and affection for him, undeserved and unreciprocated, provided him with a continuity he had taken for granted. Seeing her in this condition was upsetting.

'What's happened to you Brigit?'

'I wish I knew, I started to get sick...'

'What sick? No one will tell me. Then I hear all this shouting. What are you playing at, are you pretending to be mad, or are they driving you that way? What's been happening here?'

'Dizzy spells, colds, my joints, moving round became hard,

my balance, and terrible nightmares, brother...'

Martin flinched, she had never referred to him as "brother" before and there was something odd about the way she now did.

'Do you need help going to the toilet,' he asked sniffing the air.

'At times, it's one of the more embarrassing side affects of my...condition. And then later terrible migraines, it just been impossible for me to get around. And even voices... I hear them'

'Voices? I don't understand.'

'You never did,' Brigit smiled again, this time Martin recoiled slightly; there was an unnatural aspect to it.

'What are you talking about, Brigit?'

'I thought it was the house at first but the house was waiting, for me to come to it.'

She laughed to herself and Martin felt a cold hand move through him. He had slipped, Brigit had seen into his secrets, and read his heart; all in the moment it took for him to drop his guard and... *sympathise with her.*

'Come and sit by the bed, brother. Keep me company...'

Like a small boy, Martin did as he was told, his sister's eyes boring through his mind, their actual conversation a left over she would save for later.

*

'Admit it, Mr Martin, it wasn't so bad, was it?' said Archer handing Martin his tea, not from the handle but from the scalding mug end.

Martin, who could not work out whether it was mere loathing or active hatred he felt for Archer, nodded in a way that could be taken for assent. 'Maybe a bit of, what do you call it, post-natal depression that got out of hand. She's weird, but not as bad as you're all making out,' which was a lie, or at least only half a truth.

Experiencing Brigit had been frightening, just not in the way he was prepared for. Carefully Martin tried to impose a sensible shape on what happened. Her languid look, like a stroke victim bored with enforced inactivity, had wrong footed him from the moment he entered her room. Even with a good will he lacked, he could not have equated the tired looking woman with the healthy teenage girl whose underwear he put peanut butter in to, and forced to eat worms. Of the first half hour sat on her bed, he remembered nothing, like entering a trance that he woke from on her bidding. The next half hour was clearer, but his recollection was still hazy.

Brigit's lack of surprise at finding him in the middle of her world, and her tolerant smile as he answered the expected questions that were not asked, about family and home, unnerved him. The shrieking that he heard over breakfast had not come. There had been some nonsense about not everyone wanting redemption, and at one point he helped her move on to her back, "to stop the stars falling into my mouth", but these asides were an aberration.

It had fallen to him to turn interrogator, for her silences were provocative, as if it were now his turn to know what it felt like to be around an unresponsive "trunk". Though Brigit agreed the energy in the house was not as benign as she thought, when asked if it had been a mistake moving there, her manner was offhand and assured, compared to his, which was faltering and timid. Even the odd Mrs Thatcher inflection in her voice, which Martin presumed was an affectation she had adopted to fit in to English society, felt more normal than his aversion to it. And all the while he had sensed another presence spying on him, telling Brigit things he wanted to keep from her, the occasional questions about "the girls in his life" frightening him more than they should. Finally he had been forced to play his trump card, and ask outright about her "fits", which she explained away airily as a side effect of missing her medication, adding that anyone would become irritable if they were in the pain she was. Not once had she raised her voice, finished his sentences for him, or acted discourteously, traits that he had all too readily inflicted on her in the past.

The point was that the woman he had conversed with was not his sister. Her care and control belonged to someone, or something, else.

'How did it go?' whispered Judith, pretending to dust a stuffed parrot that Emile had wiped toothpaste over the beak of.

Archer winked slyly, gesturing towards Martin. 'You know how Mrs C can turn on and off, saving herself for the priest this afternoon, no doubt.'

'A priest?' asked Martin, 'What does she need one of those for? She was never religious.'

Archer shrugged her shoulders nonchalantly. 'After the doctors it's always the priests, isn't it?'

Martin blinked, the usual sign that an idea was occurring to him. If he could see Brigit again, this time with a priest, perhaps he would be able to obtain a better location on her. After all, they were supposed to be hard men to lie to.

'I'm going to lie down; I'm still tired after the flight. Can you wake me when the priest arrives?'

'Of course Mr Martin,' answered Judith, 'we'll all be interested to see what happens then...'

It was only when Martin reached his room, reassured by the daylight streaming through the one large window, that he recognised the change. The very feeling of considering a person to the extent of being antagonised by them was novel. If this, he thought, was what living through a period of transition felt like, then his father really was right when he told them more change meant less good.

Although he had never really got to know his sister, her willingness to accept him as he was, had been an anchor to plot his own development by. That had now gone. Cautiously, Martin took out the card he had stolen from Brigit's notebook, under the auspices of clearing her bedside table of clutter. On it was written "bereft of praises, betrayed by despicable fate, most handsome angel and most knowledgeable, take pity on my wretchedness.'

'Jesus,' he groaned, 'what are you on Brigit, what are you on...'

An image of a naked man, his genitals on fire, followed by a woman mounting him, filled his inner eye. Neither view was arousing. Instead there was a frightful sense that his virility, slight as it was, would never work again. Martin clenched his temples and screwed up his eyes.

In seconds he was fast asleep, the pillow lodged protectively behind his neck.

The knocking stopped once Judith closed the door behind her. Usually she was indifferent to it, but this time it had come on too loudly for her to remain blasé. On the bed Emile was sat colouring in a comic, cuddly Smurfs unsuitable for a boy his age his companions.

'Was that you?' asked Judith. She had never held a successful conversation with Emile, one-word altercations were more their style, though much as she chose to mock him, his seriousness scared her a little. Conti, who had always gone out of his way to be relaxed, but above all kind to her, seemed an unlikely father for this sombre child, leading Judith to speculate on the matter of his parenthood.

'Was what me?'

'You know,' Judith pointed to a small cricket bat, 'making all that banging.'

The boy smiled and went back to his colouring, more feverishly than at first.

'I'm going to tell your dad,' said Judith angrily, 'and he won't be pleased, he doesn't like stuck up little sneaks.'

Emile purred soundlessly, a gentle scratching coming from under the pile of toys.

*

Vicar Augustus Crook sat in silence with his thoughts, his bottom lip quivering like the recipient of a disappointing orgasm, his Barbour jacket spread over his legs like a shawl. Next to him, lying pole-axed on the sofa was Martin, his left hand shaking due to the effort of steadying the trembling in his right. Crook, a large-bottomed man of feminine countenance, had taken to the cloth in midlife, having enjoyed a successful but ultimately unfulfilling career as the owner of a Beauchamp Place boutique.

In spite of his interest in the sciences, and progressive attitude towards the social issues of the day, Crook had always accepted that Tyger Tyger house was haunted, for in his parish it seemed impolite not to. He was quick to recognise that although he was prepared to believe in ghosts in theory, he was not so ready to accept their existence in practice, there being something childish and self-centred about such beliefs.

Over the years Crook had made a handful of pastoral visits to Tyger Tyger in order to welcome its owners to village life and had usually been relieved when the time had come to take his leave. On this occasion however there had been no mistaking the change in atmosphere and his first thought had been that the haunting had stopped and whatever had once dwelt there had left. Unfortunately the thought that followed was decidedly less optimistic, alerting him to a different force in the house. It felt as if something truly *evil* had driven out the old presence, much as a larger beast would chase a smaller one.

On his arrival, Archer, a stubborn crank whom Crook had never been able to stomach, led him and Martin up the main staircase to Brigit's room, with each step feeling like a falling away from faith. It was once he got in there that it all made dreadful sense, the initial impression of beauty vanishing as he remembered the horror he had purposefully forgotten about the village he had moved to.

The dazzling light in her chamber had been too beautiful, like a premonition of heaven sent by one who wishes to deceive. Crook had lasted barely fifteen minutes in her company, and Martin only ten.

'So vicar, how did it go?' asked Conti, turning on a lamp. The sight of the two men sitting in defeated silence struck him as a bad sign, as did the empty bottle of sherry lodged between Martin's legs. Calling the vicar in, for no specific purpose, had struck Conti as something of an embarrassment, but no more absurd than paying another head doctor fifty pounds for an hour of cerebral masturbation. The fact that Brigit appeared more agitated about seeing a priest than a psychiatrist, a professional with the authority to actually section her, interested Conti. After all, if he were in her position, a visit from a cunning quack would hold greater terror than one from a well-meaning fool who, at worst, was capable of inflicting only minor boredom.

Crook raised his head from its angle of contemplation, his piggy eyes squinting in the light, 'Sorry, so sorry,' he said, 'I must have forgotten where I was.'

'Don't be,' said Conti, 'I often forget where I am. I blame it on advanced powers of concentration. Mrs Archer seemed to think your trip here may help Brigit come out of her... dip... which she's been in for a while now.'

It was the first time Conti had described his wife's condition in this way, the presence of a priest awakening his secular tendencies. 'The doctor was here earlier in the week, what he had to say wasn't very encouraging, to be honest...'

'It was like hearing a rack of barbecued ribs speak,' said Martin, aroused from his trance. 'She was disgusting. Totally foul, I mean, what the hell is going on in her head, man? Can someone be normal and still behave like this. I don't mean normal, I mean normally mad, she isn't even that, man.'

'Yes,' muttered Crook, his reedy lisp barely decipherable, 'the good Mrs Archer has, I'm afraid, unwittingly misled you. My visit seemed to light a fuse.'

'How?'

'It pretty much started from the moment I entered her room, calling me names, most strange it was. She implied that I was homosexual.'

'I...I apologise on her behalf. She sometimes comes out with things like that.'

'I am, as it happens, or at least I was when I was able to. I just wonder how she knew.'

Conti nodded tactfully, omitting to mention that even his son referred to the priest as 'a giant Gaylord'.

'After that rebuff she wouldn't open up, she said she would only address her equal, which was rather hurtful, not that I'd pretend I'm very high up in the hierarchy of men.'

'What do you think she meant by her "equal"?'

'I think her exact words were something like, "I am far higher, and below you" and then, "I am everything you are not from now until the end of the world, I speak to another, my equal."'

'She has quite an animus against religion. The difficulty for us is knowing when she's sincere, and when she's acting up,' he husband summarised.

'I don't think she knows herself,' grunted Archer.

Crook stared at his hands awkwardly. 'There was a knowing sort of awareness about her that I couldn't in all honesty call mad, she boasted to me that she's very good at reverting back to being the "normal her" when she wants to, and fooling the psychiatrists she has seen. The poor woman...'

'She propositioned me,' said Martin, who had picked up and was sniffing the empty bottle, 'sexually. Her own brother! Damn it, man.'

'And then the noise started,' said Archer from the doorway, 'all over the house.'

'I know about that,' Conti said addressing the vicar, 'She's learnt to throw her voice like a ventriloquist but without the dummy, she can even simulate the chatter of several people.'

'But it wasn't like that,' replied Crook, 'this sounded more like a crowd of animals stamping their feet, from far away to start with and then getting progressively louder. It didn't appear to be coming from your wife at all.'

'Like the sufferers in hell,' said Archer rather too enthusiastically, 'isn't that what you said, Vicar, amplified like the sounds of the sufferers in hell.'

Crook coughed, 'Well, yes, I must admit it shocked me at the time, which isn't to rule out a more mundane explanation...'

'No, let me have your un-mundane explanation. I've already had the mundane ones,' Conti leaned forward keenly. 'If my wife is a witch, or even a straightforward common-garden psycho, please, say so. My mind's open enough with what I have had to endure here.'

'Very well,' said Crook, 'Her problems may have been medical in origin, but they aren't now. I accept that this may very well be a religious matter, though I hope you'll forgive me, not the sort of religious matter I'm very well equipped to deal with.'

'He's right,' blurted Martin, 'he was like a frightened hare up there.'

'I didn't realise that you belonged to that sub-sect of the Christianity that isn't religious,' said Conti impatiently, 'What do you mean, "not equipped to deal with", you're a priest, aren't you? Even the most obdurate atheist would accept that putting theology to one side, you've an opening here!'

'It's not that, Mr Conti. I know my religion from books, teaching, and the example of the men who made me feel humble. My lack of what you might call "spirituality" makes me a fine foot soldier for the Church of England, and I mean that most respectfully to that great institution. If you had asked me to advise you on your son's choice of degree, or to raise money for a new spire, I should be able to help, but this problem with your wife is not my bag at all, and the failing is with me, or in me, to be more precise. Unfortunately I'm not a hero and I certainly don't want to be alone with my God or the Devil. I just wish to continue with my job; one I think I'm rather good at.'

'Jesus,' growled Martin disbelievingly, 'you can always rely on the God squad when in a fix, eh?'

Ignoring him, and straightening his crucifix on its chain, Crook continued, 'I'm aware that this is not what you wanted to hear, or what you would have necessarily expected from a man of the cloth. You must think me a moral coward... and that I suspect I may be, actually. But I stand by what I say...'

'*Actually*, I'm not all that concerned about what manner of man you consider yourself to be, Vicar. I *am* shit scared over my wife's health and sanity, and that you haven't so much as told me what you think is wrong with her yet. Should I just give her up and send her to a clinic...'

The vicar cleared his throat.

'I believe that she may be demonically possessed.'

'What?'

'But that she may be the safest of you all, because at present she enjoys the protection of whatever wishes to preserve her.'

'Stop. Hang on a minute. You said she's *demonically* possessed?'

'Yes, that is what I said.'

'Possessed? But how do you know she's not just insane, in the bog standard medical way? Asylums must be full of stir fry crazy souls who are "possessed", claiming to be so, precisely because they're mad...'

'Or because their possession has driven them insane? The properly insane are usually unconscious of their tragedy, your wife is not, I don't hear reasonless laughter coming from her. Rather controlled bursts from... somewhere else. A force coming to her aid against us that can travel to and fro as it pleases.'

'I had thought the supernatural weirdness in this place was

the fault of the *house*, not my wife. I knew that she was more sensitive to whatever was watching us here, haunting us I mean, but I didn't think she was the one responsible for it.'

'Forgive me Mr Conti, I accept I might be quite wrong...'

'And you might not be. No one has been able to give me an explanation that's equal to Brigit's behaviour yet,' Conti pulled out a cigarette, a jittery agitation about his movements.

'In the last instance, one can never be one hundred percent certain about such things. We're not Catholics you know.'

'But you've said you think she is... Whatever you want to call it, she is under some kind of evil influence... There are some tell tale signs, aren't there, possessions must have their version of garlic and upside down crosses... not being able to be seen in mirrors, that stuff.'

'The victims of possession usually tend to be poor, simple or very religious whereas your wife is highly intelligent, wealthy and, well, I've never seen her in Church... Yet now there's all this talk of light, and biblical illusions and blasphemous Latin she's scrawled over the walls and floor. It points to something.'

'I expect it does, but mightn't a sceptic say she read a book or saw a film on the subject? Do you see what I mean, that depressed people are susceptible to a bit of "let's pretend".'

'I admit my explanation isn't perfect but...'

'Damn it, man, if you have something to say hurry up,' encouraged Martin, 'I saw what she was like, remember?'

'Years ago, when I first came to this village, I saw something similar. There was a girl from a very poor family, with a history of making up stories and an abusive father in jail. Personally I agreed that she was rather too keen on Hammer horror films, and Dennis Wheatley paperbacks, but the long and short of it was that her mother demanded that I attempt a sort of exorcism. They were all the rage at the time after that film... Anyway, in truth I was surprised at what I found.'

'What did you find,' asked Martin, 'what happened?'

'I failed her badly. It affected me.'

'How?'

'I became like a normal person, or as much like one as somebody like me can be. I sort of lost my faith because I couldn't take the ceremony seriously, or take myself performing it seriously. I heard a voice, laughing at me all the way through. I didn't know who it belonged to. Before that I was more confident of my relationship with God.'

Conti shook his head witheringly, 'And what happened to the girl?'

'She ended up in Southcrawl working as a tart for a darkie,' piped in Archer with gloomy relish. 'Last I heard, she had a whole fleet of little black bastards and weighed seventeen stone.'

Crook stood up, knocking over a cup of cold tea as he did so. 'If I tried to exorcise your wife, quite apart from being completely unfit for such a task, but if I did, then whatever it is in her would win. It, or your wife if you prefer to still see her in those terms, would make mincemeat of me. Today she had me in her complete control as I was listening to her, even as she abused me, I found myself, shameful as it is to admit, yearning to slavishly debase myself at her feet and ask her to teach me more about myself.'

'Christ, are you crackers man?' screamed Martin, 'she said you sucked dicks and fucked arses, for God's sake!'

'No, let me finish, this isn't easy for me at all. She was my superior. Do you understand? I made the mistake of responding to her on a personal level, as an individual and not as a representative of the Church, and she pounced on my egotism. We all have our doubts and I feel that she could see through all of mine. I was worse than naïve in front of her, I was nothing so far as she was concerned.'

'I think you're right,' Conti said, 'you'd be useless.'

'And the validity of my doubts would assist her. It was much the same with that little girl. There was a cold unloving inhumanity in her I couldn't match. The force of telepathy in the possessed is astounding, astounding. Your wife was communicating different thoughts to me without so much as moving her lips...'

'She called me a cheat,' deadpanned Martin, 'she knew I was a cheat without me opening my mouth, or her opening hers. I heard her voice in here,' he tapped his head.

Conti squeezed the back of a chair, 'but if we asked her, accused her, even, of being possessed, she'd deny it. And who wouldn't believe her? Faced with a pack of devil hunting morons, or a vulnerable and sick woman, only a crank would take our side.'

'Yes, that is a difficulty. We can't get past the pretence. I had always assumed a possession was in part a human cry for help, but your wife eschews that. It's too powerful.'

Conti shook his head. 'I'm beginning to think your God views religion with the same indifference as he views everything else.'

'What if it isn't Brigit but the damned house that's the problem,' said Martin excitedly, 'it's freaking us all out. Even the kid knows this shit-hole's haunted to the gills, anyone can see it. Brigit was fine before she came here, get my sister away from here and she'll be all right again. We're wasting time talking. Let's just get out of here!'

'You're wrong,' said Crook quietly. 'Running away would make no difference now. This house is rotten, I've known that all along, it affects the whole village, but it's only an enabler,' his words were helping him to regain his composure. 'The house is not the cause, some force in it was looking for someone to unleash it, and it found that person in your sister.'

Conti crushed his cigarette on the stump of a dead pot plant. 'I've thought it before about Tyger Tyger, but... something a boy said to me the other day set me wondering. It's like we're in the cupboard those children find in that kid's book, the one they can walk through to another world where it snows all the time,

Narnia. Tyger Tyger is like that, a threshold. Everything wrong here is right on the other side, all the anomalies we see are just the excesses of the other reality bubbling over... I mean, am I making any sense to you?'

Crook hesitated. 'There is a man, a man who can help you, an Exorcist. He's, how can I put it, slightly unconventional and his methods have been criticised as unsound, he may even have a little of the devil in him too, but he is known to the Church and accepted as someone who gets results.'

'He sounds like the cavalry. Who is he?'

'He goes by the name of Todger Wade, also known as "The Rector". The curious thing is he sometimes pretends he's Welsh, but he isn't, he's half black actually, from Surinam, I think, or maybe Haiti, no one's really sure.'

'You must think we're a pair of cunts' said Martin.

The Vicar blushed and stared at his nails.

'Todger? My wife's soul is to be entrusted to a man called Todger?' laughed Conti.

'I wouldn't go as far as trusting him with souls, in fact I'd say that the part of you that occupies the eternal world ought to be slightly cautious of him, but the animal part of you that exists only in time, well, it would be wise to accept whatever help it can get.'

'Cup of tea, Vicar?' Archer asked, 'and maybe some *fruitcake* on the side?'

'Todger,' repeated Conti walking over to the narrow bay window, the dusk clouds reddening before him like bleeding lizard skins, 'an Exorcist. It's a nuclear option that doesn't leave us any room to double back if we're wrong...'

'Yes please,' said Crook lifting up his plate greedily, 'some cake would be nice.'

'What are *you* doing in here?' hissed Brigit, 'I told you to never come in here again.'

'I'm here to change your piss pot you grande vache!' replied Chantal, and spat in Brigit's face. Drawing her shoulders back, Chantal pushed her breasts against the tight nylon squares of her T-shirt. With a lone finger she pointed to her buttocks, hanging below the demarcation line of the string panties she barely had on. 'Kiss my fiery ass.'

'Ha! Lazy and narcissistic when left alone, and rebellious when monitored, you are my pet Chantal, my pet!'

Chantal bowed coyly, and mounted the bed. Obediently she ran her hand through Brigit's matted hair, straightening the knots and lumps, her mistress's wan face smiling with the ruined grandeur of cities set ablaze.

'All my life I have waited,' whispered Brigit, thrilled by the one eye that watched her every move, 'and at last you have found me.'

Outside the wind picked up and battered against the windows, 'Let me in, it says,' sighed Brigit, 'but I already have. You are the falling morning star, and I am your echo, the echo that comes before the noise.'

Book Two

SHE'S LOST CONTROL

Tell me *how* you are searching
And I will tell you *what* you are searching for

Wittgenstein

Chapter Four

Did Brigit want him to know for sure? In the two days since the Vicar's visit, Brigit had become someone else, not an amalgamation of cryptic personas but, for several hours a day, a specific human being known to Conti from his past. Disturbingly this identity belonged to a girl whom Brigit had never met, and who Conti had not seen in fifteen years, it belonged to his first childhood sweetheart, Tanya Raffle.

At first Conti had not been able to place the expressions Brigit used, or why she talked in a London accent, the sheer outlandishness of her impersonation too disparate to arouse suspicion. But the accuracy and consistency of her banter, along with her knowledge of Raffle's A-level subjects, had eventually forced him to make a connection. This could only point to perverse powers or an intimate acquaintance with Raffle that Conti knew Brigit could never have had. If he could establish what the link was, or find some clue that offered a rational explanation, no matter how bizarre, then saving his wife from madness was still achievable and could be in his hands, not an Exorcist's.

Which was why Conti now found himself in the West London of his youth, turning his car in to the concrete quadrangle that stood behind The Ship in Distress, the pub that Raffle had thrown her life away in. Surveying the unpromising scene, Conti wondered why he had left Raffle, his first great love.

Was the answer hopelessly prosaic; that she would not take it up the arse and Lilly Sparks would, (though in the end she had not). On such small things lives hang, thought Conti, as he turned off the engine, his garishly coloured Mercedes already attracting the attention of the natives. Raffle had probably been the last person, since Chantal, he had practised truly monogamous sex with, that is, without the help of virtual pictures and voices to help him finish the act. At the time he reasoned that rather than point to any deficiency in him this simply meant that he must want sex with hundreds of girls, or at least with more girls than the one he was actually making love to. But after Chantal he could not be so sure. The correctness of how he felt with his au pair showed that no supposed fact from his past could be guaranteed to mean what it had, his lovemaking included.

Stepping out of the car, Conti examined the pub, built and owned by Raffle's brother, its brutal modernist finishing complimenting the surrounding high rise it was constructed to serve. The newly completed gravel grey pillbox entrance, jammed between two Union Jacks, was a telling portent of what was to come. Pushing open the heavy iron door, the proper location for which would have been a police station, Conti stepped on to a spongy carpet that reeked of oats and spilled drinks, his shoes slowly absorbed the synthetic brown mush. He knew the smell rising off it well; it had been on Brigit's breath when she talked like Raffle.

The yellow walls that had been decorated by those who lost their way to the toilets were now a regal purple, and Conti noticed that the light shades had been changed to pink, otherwise everything was the same as before. Not for the first time he had the sensation of travelling between countries. It was all so much worse than he remembered, yet closer to him than the years of success he had lied his way through. Carefully suppressing the urge to shout 'hello', Conti strode unselfconsciously to the bar and leant against it, the passing years vanishing in an eternal pub moment.

'A pint of lager,' he said with precise annunciation, the chorus to "Make me smile (come up and see me)" playing away in the background.

A man in his forties moved away to a tap and stood by it, waiting for further clues.

'Hofmeister,' said Conti helpfully.

87

The Ship in Distress had always alluded to a bleak version of the preceding decade, the asinine locals incapable of thought or laughter, comforted that to be kept was no profit and to be destroyed was no loss.

They had tolerated Conti's intellect because he was a good laugh, and from them he had learned that not everyones subjectivity was of primary importance, not even to themselves. This was his justification for not looking back or keeping in touch; the past acknowledged only as a lingering form of homesickness.

'Look who's changed with the times,' said a voice he thought was Brigit's, before realising that this was what Raffle sounded like now. He turned to face her, their meeting was planned as he had called the night before to check that she still worked there.

'You look great.'

'And you, you've changed too, give me a turn,' he said less convincingly. The girl before him was still Raffle, less her sparkle, confidence and breasts, which had, judging by the sagging indentations in her jumper, begun the long journey south. Though her hair, styled in a poodle perm, was the same colour as it was in her youth, its texture was as uneven as her stone washed jeans, their ends held together by clunky laminated zips.

'Very up to date.'

'I probably look awful, I've been really ill. You always said people get old quickly here. Shall we sit down, John can bring over the pints, I know it's a bit early but I'm nervous seeing you again!' she laughed falsely, 'and I still drink as much as we used to! Remember? Pissed all the time we were! Must be years since I last got a Christmas card from you. You were good like that.'

'I know. I've stopped sending them because I don't like getting them.'

'Charming!' said Raffle in a "posh" voice she used for Conti's benefit.

She smelled of heavily perfumed soaps, and Conti briefly

contemplated asking her whether she alternated these with the seasons, before realising that even ten years ago, this would have made him sound somewhat worse than a dick. Instead he said, 'You smell nice.'

'Full of compliments! And you look great, very nice threads.'

'Well you know what they say, you can't be judged a complete failure until you've lost your vanity...' which was a little kind on delusion, thought Conti, as he fiddled for a lighter.

Opposite them an old man, sipping his pint like a fellating dog, had got up and moved to the side of the table facing the wall so as to not look over. Conti remembered strange customs like this, never sure whether they lay in respect for privacy or distaste at intimacy.

'So you at least remember who I am!' said Conti in a way he intended to be self-deprecating, but was afraid sounded arrogant.

'The funny thing is, I'm not sure I do!' replied Raffle, her tone completely in earnest, 'is that what you came here to ask me?'

'In a way, yes...' Conti could tell this was not a rebuke or the beginning of a polite enquiry, but a question they both sought an answer to.

'Of course I know who you are, but I don't really...remember you. That sounds funny doesn't it?' Raffle adjusted the baggy woollen jumper she was wearing, the brown leather collar too tight for her neck. 'You must think I'm topping up!'

'No, no it doesn't sound funny. But how do you mean it, Tanya?'

'Not really remembering you?'

'Yes' Conti said, 'do you literally mean that you don't remember me?'

Raffle paused for a moment and stared at her fingers. 'Up until recently,' she said raising her head to meet his eyes, 'I mean, days ago, until then, I missed you, Hartley. I feel so stupid for saying it, especially since it's been years since we meant anything to each other, but I really missed you and thought about you a lot, a hell of a lot. That's why its so weird hearing from you now...'

'You said days ago, you mean just *days* ago?'

'Just days, and then it was like the past had really gone. Gone and vanished out of me. Funny way for us to begin a conversation, isn't it?'

'Tanya, this is more important than you might think, are you sure you didn't try to deliberately forget about me? Remember that was what you said you'd do once we left school, you said that you'd forget all about me?'

'This isn't the same as that. It's like it had nothing to do with me. It happened when I was ill, like I first told you, I've had a funny sickness, it's gone now, but it was like a bit of a turn.'

'That left you with memory loss?'

'Not exactly that, I still remember everything else, it's only stuff about you that I've forgotten. And the way I was around you, who I was, I've forgotten most of that too. The weird thing is it felt good to start with.'

'How did it happen? Did you get a knock on the head or was it more like flu? I'm serious Tanya, this has nothing to do with my ego, it's important that I know...'

Raffle looked at the bar expectantly, 'Where are those drinks?'

'Here', Conti offered her a Silk Cut, 'I know it's crazy me turning up out of nowhere asking you these questions, but I have to. Something dangerous is happening around me Tanya, and I think you can help me understand it if I can understand what's happened to you.'

Raffle lit the cigarette and ran her finger along the serrated metal edge of the ashtray. 'It was so weird; I haven't told anyone about it, I just said that I was tired and stressed out. I don't know; I was sat here after closing time about a week ago, knackered and a bit pissed up, relaxing with a fag. I'd turned the lights out and was alone and feeling really, really chilled. And then I started to spin out a bit, like I was falling and I thought, well you're just drunk aren't you? But it was happening in a nice way, like I was being taken care of, know what I mean?'

Conti nodded, his feet twitching anxiously under the table.

'Then it wasn't good, I mean, it became really fucking dark and bad. I felt like someone's hand was inside me, really powerfully, controlling my feelings about the past at first, so they didn't hurt or confuse me anymore, which was in a way what I wanted. That was nearly okay but I knew I didn't have any control over it, which scared me. But then it sort of changed direction, and it wasn't just the bit of the past that had hurt me, that the hand was getting rid of.'

'What else did it want?'

'It was pulling out who I was, you know what I mean? Like all of me was being rubbed out, erased or whatever you call it, like it was taking something, who I used to *be*, and it was being taken from me forever. Even the stuff that I couldn't remember about myself and I had forgotten, but that had shaped me and made me who I am, it was going for that too.'

'And this had something to do with your memory of me?'

'Totally. It was who I was when we were together that it was after, like when we thought we'd get married and grow old, all of what you formed in me, what I reasoned with, or tried to.'

'How long did this… experience go on for?'

'I've no idea but when it stopped I felt like a fucking zombie. Have done for a few days now, though it isn't so bad now as it was, but I was scared it would happen again, though somehow now, I don't think it will.'

There were tears in Raffle's eyes. 'Smoke' she said lamely, and made her hand to wave it away. 'The weirdest part is, that though I don't remember stuff, I still know I loved you and that you loved me.'

Conti cleared his throat, thought twice about what he was going to say, and then said it anyway, 'Time moves on, but love doesn't, it stays still, fixed at whatever point it came into our lives. Nothing about our current attitudes can change that Tanya, though whatever it was that happened to you wanted to destroy that awareness.'

He reached his hand over the table and Raffle took it.

The old man had turned round almost as soon as they had started talking, and was staring at them with the patience of an astronomer waiting for an eclipse, his rummy eyes trickling water. Above him was a framed sign Conti had written out and hung there years earlier which read, "*AND YOU'RE PLEASED TO CALL THIS REALITY?*' the relic of a forgotten art project that the management must have taken a warped pride in. Smiling, the old man raised his glass to his lips and let the alcohol dribble down his chin onto his soiled tie.

'Tanya, there's something else I need to ask you. You said apart from your memory and feeling out of it for a few days, there were no side effects…'

'I don't think so… well you know how I never really had a temper?' Now I feel more pissed off, especially when I think of nice things. They really wind me up, things that are supposed to make you happy. Like puppies and having a laugh.'

'Like something inside you is making you mad, something you don't have any control over?'

'Yeah, yeah, that's it.'

'And you say you haven't told anyone else about this?'

Raffle's face dropped like a fallen Christmas decoration, 'My brother, I told him. I know he's the last person I should have said anything too, but I did. He said this was what happened to people who had abortions, that they had to live the life of two people, their own and the person they've killed. He said what happened was a punishment.'

'That's bollocks. Your life is for you and what matters is that you are who you are and not anyone else. He's a mad, bitter tosser.'

Raffle smiled, more out of politeness than conviction, 'Enough about me, eh? What do you do with yourself now, Hartley?'

'I advise people on what school to send their kids to. My heart's not in it, but it's probably better that way. It's not the kind of thing you want to take too seriously.'

'I always knew you'd do something special.'

Conti raised an eyebrow, 'I don't know whether it's special but at least it's an easy job to take a day off from, not that I usually do. I wouldn't want them to realise that they can do without me...'

'And what else have you done, Hartley, are you still being naughty?'

'The only "naughty" thing I've done is fall in love with two very pretty girls, one of whom is possessed by the devil and the other of whom is a prick tease.'

He waited for her to laugh. Raffle lifted her lip sourly, and said in a voice too like Brigit's impersonation of her for comfort, 'poor old you, Mister.'

'Your drinks,' said her brother putting down two flat pints of Hofmeister in front of Conti, 'both for you are they, Flash?'

Conti did not bother to even acknowledge a person whom he considered so stupid, that in spite of his stupidity he still insisted on playing dumb. Years earlier the two had nearly ended up killing each other in a game of slaps changing Conti's view that underneath it all, people were all the same.

'So what are you doing back here, checking out your exes, eh?' said Les Raffle, stroking his moustache and beard, neither of which looked like they had anything to do with each other, 'That'll be two pounds for the drinks, and ten grand for wasting my sister's time by coming back here and trying to get your leg over.'

Conti winked at him. 'It's a thin line between justified rage and jealously, eh, Lesley?'

'You what?'

'I'll pass on both thanks. No offence Tanya.'

'Someone like you would, wouldn't they,' said Les warming up, 'coming here and giving the bloody large in your ponce suit and slacks, who do you think you are, a showroom yuppie? An old iron like you should know his limitations.'

Conti eyed him with distaste. 'Then I'd rather have mine than yours,' he said getting up to leave, 'you drink them Les, there's a good lad.'

As Conti approached the car and looked into Raffle's frankly mottled face, he felt a physical gratitude for the sensations of the past they had imparted to one another. He touched her arm and said, slightly melodramatically, 'If you don't love you're dead and if you do they'll kill you,' before kissing her. It may, he reflected, be corny to carry on in this way, but it was his personal aesthetic and she may as well live with it as he had to.

A swift inrush of serenity later and he was in the car and changing up from first gear to second. As he looked in to the rear view mirror and waved from the window, Raffle smiled in a soft twisted way, and he noticed a shadow emerge behind her.

Suddenly he realised there was someone in the back of the car with him, breathing heavily.

'What are you doing in here?'

Brigit smiled swinishly from ear to ear with glittering malice.

'What are you doing here?' he repeated, before realising that he was addressing an empty seat, the blue and grey of a London winter tickling his freezing spine.

*

'Do you know where he's gone?'

Archer and her daughter smirked knowingly, waiting for Chantal to repeat her question, as they knew she would.

'Did he say where he was going today?'

Judith removed the orange headphones of the walkman that

had been switched off the second Chantal entered. 'You what'?

'Who do you mean, dear?'

Chantal put her mug down loudly.

'I think,' said Judith, 'he mentioned something about London, a woman he had to meet, quite an important one I believe.'

'A woman?'

'Yes, you know dear,' said Archer savouring the French girl's petulance, 'a woman. Probably a dainty little thing like you, or maybe a little taller…is there anything the matter with that?'

'Perhaps if she knew he was going to London she could have asked him to bring back some of that funny chocolate spread she likes,' chuckled Judith to her mother, 'she's very particular about that, aren't you, Chantal, though heaven knows what's wrong with marmalade and Bovril.'

Saying something in French that neither of them understood, Chantal poured the rest of her coffee down the sink and left the kitchen. 'Well someone cares more than she lets on,' said Judith watching her go, her morning well and truly made.

It was the last letter she had sent him, some months earlier, and it had, like the others, remained unopened, the wonder being that he had kept this one at all. Why he should choose to read it now, when she was only one floor away from him, was clear. His sister may have been too learned, hot tempered, and deep for his tastes, but she had never been unapproachable, loving conversation in a way that had bored him, when it had not left him uncomfortable.

The idea of asking the woman downstairs a question that might result in an honest answer was laughable, as indeed was the notion that Martin was putting Brigit's welfare first. It was not concern, or even a variant of family pride that pricked his curiosity now, rather an animal fear that he might be next.

Taking a nip from a can of cider, lifted from the stash under his bed, Martin tore open the envelope and took out the card. On its front was an old photo of the local Cathedral, a member of the Royal family stood outside it, and emblazoned on the back of the card was a message, 'When you go you'll wish you had been doing something else with your hand.'

Martin read it again, attempted, for a second or two to understand what it might mean and then tried to laugh.

Below him the discordant and tuneless sound of a badly played recorder stopped, replaced by the discordant and tuneless sound of his sister's singing. He had watched the boy, who cut a vulnerable figure, be chased from the garden by Judith so that he could practise his instrument with his mother. The observance of this sort of nicety was the equivalent of opening an umbrella at the bottom of a lake. Didn't any of them realise that the house was on *fire* and Brigit with it?

He knew he was in danger, and had done since waking at 3am on the plane back to England. On that flight he remembered the flame in the Malaysian bookmaker's eye, the twinge in his trousers as Sanders changed out of his Jock strap, and his sister's advice to him on his last visit, 'Of all the masks you can choose, normality is the flimsiest.'

She had always been full of "deep" riddles that he had never taken any notice of, not thinking that they could all have been warnings until now.

'You had it coming, 'but what have you done to me...?' He touched his crotch. Concentrating with all his might he tried to remember the bodies of various bar girls he had idolised, but instead of lust there was only the pathetic reminder that he had not had an erection since entering the house.

Prudishly, he sat up straight on the bed, terribly alert to someone else having come in to the room with him. 'Drink up mate, you and I need to talk...'

'Sanders? Is that you?'

'Trunk!'

*

'We can stop our music lesson for today.' Brigit put down the tiny electronic keyboard, which she used like a conductors baton.

'Thank you mummy.'

Emile did the same with his recorder. When she was well his mother often asked him whether he loved her. Sadly he knew even then that he did not, the feeling he got when he thought about love was sick and claustrophobically binding. Yet he sensed the strangeness that bound mother to son was strong, the fear of what lay outside their bond performing the role that love would have in a normal relationship. More than that, he had felt sorry for his mother, always trying so hard to be like other parents, to do the things they did, hardly aware that she could never be what she was not. But as that desire, to fit in and collect him from the school gates died, so did the woman he trusted, a new and alien one taking her place.

'Aren't you proud of me, Emile, you should be. How many other mummies are like me?'

'I don't know,' he shrugged, 'not many.'

'None, there are none like me who would do for you what I would! And the other boys at school, do they talk about me?'

'No mummy,' replied Emile, trying not to look at her face. It had not escaped his notice that in the last week an unpleasant rash had spread from her nose to her cheeks, forehead and chin. The mother he had always found so pretty now looked like a woman in a girl's body with measles, her skin cut in the places she had scratched it.

'Are they boring Emile,' Brigit rasped, 'do they bore you by doing what they're told all the time, by behaving like good "ickle" boys?'

Until his mother had told him that there were other things to do than follow the rules, Emile had never even considered being disobedient. Having seen, however, that it was the only way to gain her confidence, he had succumbed to being bad, increasingly with the conviction of a natural.

'They *are* boring mummy. I don't like them, I wish daddy would take me away from that school.'

'I'm afraid daddy is scared of looking bad in front of the other grown ups by letting you do what you want. Do what though wilt shall be the whole of the law. He doesn't love you like I do, no one can.'

'Thank you mummy.'

'But our new friend, he isn't like that at all. He tells us a man will come here to hurt mummy and to hurt you too Emile. Beware of that.'

Emile, sat cross-legged under the shadow that loomed over him, nodding his head and trying to ignore the purring he could hear. Dementedly his mother began to laugh, choking hoarsely with mirth, until Emile covered his ears and prayed in the way he had been taught to at school.

'Let him in Emile, let him in!' exhorted Brigit, 'you can't be hurt child, nothing has harmed or done you wrong, what you feel is the pain of one still outside the Kingdom, your mother is so lonely without you, come down and see me, make me smile...'

Conti could barely disguise his exhaustion as he tumbled into his office and began to shake the large black answering machine he had yet to master the usage of. His attention to detail, even in the midst of storms, impressed him, and picking up a biro, he stabbed the plastic grille with concentrated determination.

'Here, allow me,' said Stack twisting its dial in the correct direction, 'it's not a depth charge.'

'God bless you,' said Conti, unfurling on the sofa, 'is there anything on it I need to be aware of?'

'All run of the mill stuff I dealt with, there'll be no new parents for a week now as it's half term coming up.'

'They like to see the school in action, eh?'

'But there was a funny message from a chap with a strange accent, Bodger or Hector or something like that he said his name was, does that mean anything to you?'

Conti looked to smirk but his face turned serious, 'Yes, I'll follow it up.'

Stack turned her not inconsiderable rump round and stepped into her annexe, causing Conti to wonder whether jumping her from behind might cheer him up a little, before dismissing the urge in marginally less time than it took to feel it. With Stack it was difficult to get past the abortive beauty of what had been, a fleshy willingness that exacted his compassion, but did not do much for his crotch. He prided himself on his loyalty, at least his loyalty excluding the London lot and his leftist bohemian friends from university, which really only left Stack. Gazing absently at her arse, it was still possible to think back to what it was like not knowing what he thought, listening to Stack's fledgling life philosophies and the accidents they were based on, the summer of 1977 steaming off her naked back.

'I hear that the Hatter's child is settling in well at Claysmug...Hartley?' Stack shook her head, the ends of her blonde bob sticking to her make up, 'anyway, they say he's coming on.' Clumsily she stuck her thumb under the thick wraparound belt that separated the two parts of her grey smock, 'which ought to give you some job satisfaction.'

Conti sighed: he had never even impregnated Stack, the flickering urge to still do so no more than lust's unfinished business. Fate was moral, and the time spent fantasising over her after they had broken up made up for the times he had thought of someone else when they had petted as a couple. Stack's fading image long since topped up, and ultimately rescued by other fantasy composites.

'You know what I love about you, Melissa' called Conti, addressing the ceiling from his place on the sofa, 'that there's something of the familiar novelty about you, like spring coming round every year after an awful winter...'

There was no reply from Stack's office. Conti hauled himself up and peered into the annexe. The faculty of care, though strong, was usually deferred, he knew he was capable of it, but like death, would confront it only when it was necessary for him to do so. From what he saw, it did not look as though he had long to go. Stack was lying with her arms wrapped round her typewriter sobbing, her posture indicative of someone who wanted answers and not insincere flirtation. Conti cleared his throat, 'Is there something the matter, Melissa?'

Stack lifted her head off the table, the swollen tracts round her eyes puffed up like a boxer's. 'As you get older, you need to hear things you've never heard before, Hartley. New things that give you hope and the energy to live.'

'You're not making many allowances for me today,' said Conti bluffly.

Stack wiped a bundle of snot from under her nose, 'You, Hartley, of all people should know that the more different we are from someone, the more likely we are to make allowances for them. You and I are too similar for me to make allowances for you, the only difference is that you've got to where you want to in life, and I haven't,' her voice faltered and she raised her hands, 'Why someone else and not me? It all seems so arbitrary...'

'There, there,' said Conti, his tone kinder than the implicit condescension carried in it, 'There's nothing wrong in loving a great man unconditionally, all you had to do was ask if I felt the same way...'

Stack spluttered a little, laughing clumsily, 'You're giving back something to me that you had no right to take in the first place, you bastard. Self respect.'

'Yes,' said Conti, soothed by the belief that even a little goodness could make the most shallow of lives worth living, 'Better than not giving it back at all though, isn't it?'

Stack gazed up at him affectionately, 'Why do you always

have to be so bloody charming, I...' she stopped, her face paralysed between two movements. For a second she did nothing, to make sure she saw what she saw, and then screamed.

'What!'

'Behind you...'

'What?'

'Your wife, standing there behind you, looking at me horribly. She was saying... couldn't you hear?'

Conti clutched Stack by the wrist, 'Calm down, Melissa, there was no one in here with us, you must have...'

'I saw her, Hartley! You know I did, I can see you're scared too, what's happening?'

'Melissa, relax, nothing's happening!'

'*Your use of me is only a hint of the pretensions and vanity that you permit yourself!*' screeched Stack, her green eyes whitening under the light.

Conti struck her with his open hand, a weird lapse between the slap and noise separating the two events.

Stack raised a trembling finger to the red mark, 'Why did you do that?'

She seemed surprised, and gazed over at the window, 'What's happening to me?'

'Nothing, I was afraid you'd....'

'I don't...' Stack paused and burst in to tears, harder and noisier sobs than those she had just shed.

'Melissa,' said Conti, glancing round the room warily, 'oh Melissa I'm sorry.'

'No, I'm the one who should be sorry, I don't know what happened...'

'Take the rest of the week and next off Melissa, we're both in a bad place.'

'I must be cracking up,' cried Stack, 'don't leave...'

'I'm not...'

'Please don't leave me.'

'I'm not leaving you Melissa, I'm always with you, time will prove it, but believe me now. There's something I'm going to try and do, and if I can't do it then I don't know how I'll be able to carry on as me.'

'But what about me?' said Stack wiping a teary lump of make up from her eye, 'I don't want to be on my own any more.'

'*You're not!*' hissed Brigit, seemingly everywhere at once.

Minutes passed before Conti and Stack let go of each other, the smell of rotting mice that filled the room was so putrid that fear was forgotten in their haste to leave.

Conti left Stack by the Old Priory with a kiss that cost him nothing, and walked briskly over the quad, conspicuously ignoring the crowd of boys that had gathered for their evening banter, a light drizzle thinning their number. Using a footpath that led straight to the Cathedral Close, Conti made his way along the paving stones of College Street, past its split Georgian maisonettes and in to the car park of the The Green Man pub. There he noticed something he wished he had not.

Maurice Squeers was crouched in a back doorway with a chorister. Conti could not tell whether the boy's trousers were actually undone, but he was certain that Squeers had not bought the youth there to lecture him on the subtler points of Platonic love. As he approached them, he realised that neither had noticed his presence, and he heard Squeers whisper loudly, 'would you prefer a Prozzie to a pretty girl? I bet you would, but I bet you don't know why yet, do you?'

Conti stepped forward triggering off an automatic light. A cruel line flickered across the boy's face. Conti realised at once that it revealed his true character and wondered how many years would pass before the boy realised this too.

'No substitute for one to one tuition Maurice?'

The boy dashed out of the murky yellow light into an adjoining passage. Squeers resuming a standing position, his wobbling legs suggesting drink, cramp or both.

'Just telling Oliver here,' he slurred, his bandy face struggling to adjust to the new situation, 'that the world was his lobster. The sort of advice I could have used when I was a boy. But adults never bloody talked to us like that, did they? All so bloody closed and stiff upper thingy.'

'I suppose the lonely have to take love as they find it. You could be ruined for this you know, sacked I reckon.'

'Sacked? You overestimate the English, oh you do! They'd be more put off by the scandal than the offence, and think it awfully poor form of you for bringing it to their attention and breaking ranks. Telling tales is not our style, leave that sort of thing to the East German chappies in grey. Humph! Not as if I'm in the IRA or one of those striking miners! Worst I'd get is a slap round the wrist, be demoted to school photographer or historian, still welcome at lunch and still able to supervise the boys' games, ha ha! Only in a place like this! Oliver where art thou? Has the pigeon fled?'

Conti was standing so close that he could see the stained filth on the rims of Squeers glasses and smell the deep intestinal odour of what he dearly hoped was not what he thought, on his breath, 'You need help.'

'I don't want it!'

'You're evil, aren't you? Truly evil,' Conti heard himself say, the moral judgment implied in this remark rare for him.

Squeers clucked, clearly untroubled by the accusation, 'Ahh, the heart's goodwill thwarted by the mind's defect, we aren't all as lucky as you Conti, but even a hypocrite like yourself must wonder from time to time why Christ has deserted him.'

'What are you talking about Christ for?' asked Conti foolishly, realising too late that he had bitten a hook.

Squeers grinned lopsidedly and jabbed Conti in the ribs, 'You ought to be seeing God's love on your wife's breasts, not the devil's private parts!'

Conti pushed Squeers firmly away, hesitating to take the insult, if that was what it was, seriously, 'They might not sack you for playing with little boys, but they certainly will for being a washed out drunk. It's not hard to fathom why you've lost your touch with the fair sex.'

Squeers face crumpled like an old tissue. 'The fair sex? Bitches you mean. They're all the same, after a while you end up meeting the same woman, in one modified way or other, some of them souped up, others scaled down. Don't believe any of this crap about the uniqueness of the human soul. Not that you do anyway, not really, we're the same like that, not like 99% of the swinish multitude...'

Conti pushed Squeers against the wall, '*Maurice*, the move from thinking 90% of people are below par, to believing that 99% of them are scum is the shift from a properly critical attitude to a misanthropic one. I don't hate people, I can't be bothered to, and in cases like yours, I don't even feel sorry for them.'

'Oh Satan, where art thou when I needed thee most,' lisped Squeers theatrically, lifting his fingers into a cross. His manner, supposedly playful, was far too desperate for Conti to believe that he was witnessing anything other than the prelude to a collapse.

'So far as I know, it isn't common practice to make emotional appeals to the devil. You can expect a more than polite shunning in the staffroom if that one gets out.'

'Bless you Conti, you forget that your God does not like contented worldliness, of which you seem to have too much of,' sneered Squeers, his eyes twinkling manically, 'What is Christianity if not a dose of Greek navel gazing and tiresome Roman legalism? I...' he clutched his head as if he had just remembered something and stumbled onto Conti's shoulder, 'Your wife, tell me quickly, how is she?'

'Change the record, I thought you'd found a new subject tonight,' said Conti stepping back from Squeers who was advancing towards him like a prostitute howling for hire.

'Tell me, I need to know,' implored Squeers, the edge in his tone at odds with his wordy soliloquies, 'has she…changed?'

'Changed?'

'What does she now speak of?'

'Actually she's started to refer to you a lot,' Conti lied.

Squeers froze and clasped Conti's arm, 'How? How does she mention me?'

'Pretty much all the time in just about every context.'

'So she is… aware of me then… she needs my help, and I hers?'

Conti laughed, hoping to sound dismissive, 'Don't worry, you're beyond help Squeers, even Satan isn't interested in you now, you're just another identikit damned soul, free to continue as you are into perpetuity.'

'Then you both belong to the kingdom too?'

'No, I'm an adult. Allowing piss poor demons to enter your second rate life is your line, just like the pointy horns from Oxfam and the broomstick you bring out every Halloween.'

Despite his bravado, Conti felt the emergence of a connection he did not want to make. Squeers behaviour wasn't perplexing; it was *entirely of a piece* with everything else. His son, wife, secretary and old girlfriend, all under the same spell.

'So, she has escaped from the life that exhibits itself? Listen to me Conti, I know full well what goes on within that contraption you call a *home*.'

Conti wrapped his fist round his keys. 'Save it, save the stupid voice, freaked out looks and the rest of the camp drunken special effects. Forget whatever you think you know about Brigit, because you could end up some place worse than where you are.'

'Your wife is a teacher, I wish to be taught.'

'Ask someone else.'

'He has ancient fires for eyes,' cried Squeers collapsing to his knees, 'We people of the fire, we…you burn the house to roast the pig!'

Avoiding his waving arms, Conti brushed off the unfortunate schoolmaster and walked out of the light to his car, the starless night's silence barely spoiled by the climatic ham of Squeers' breakdown.

'Do you have any aspirin or any of that kind of stuff?' asked Martin, his two day old growth taking on a greyish hue. 'I'm bunged up badly. This headache, it won't go away.'

'We might have, but you're not to mix it with that,' Archer pointed at the bottle in Martin's hand, 'I know you sports men like letting off steam after matches and all that, but you're in danger of waking up in a very lonely place, Mr Martin.'

'What do you mean, "lonely place"?'

'Well I know you care about your sister, but drinking yourself sick isn't going to make her any better,' she said ignoring the crazed look in Martin's eyes.

Martin laughed, 'Yeah, that's right, I care about my sister. Now where are the aspirin?'

'Over there in that cupboard, second shelf down in a plastic bottle.'

'Hallelujah.'

Conti surveyed the body that had once been so familiar, and often precious. A thin white mist was spilling through the curtains heightening the scarlet in Brigit's lips, her red tongue curling from her mouth like a baby dragon's phallus. The parts of her that did not resemble food on the turn appeared to be crafted from silvery wax, uncanny inhumanity pervading every inch of her sleeping body. Nasty splashes of red, like scurvy, had spread from her face, to her arms and hands, daring Conti not to call for a doctor.

He had already rescued Emile from one of the rooms he had not ventured into for months, the boy having locked himself in after being chased there by Chantal, "whose breath had smelled funny", and who "talked in a voice like a rough old man like mummy does". Mummy had also explained that he would have to marry her when he grew up, an assertion that had nearly made Conti laugh had it not been made in earnest by his wife to their son. Watching her sleep reminded Conti of a house where, though the owner has left, guests still feel frightened to mention her by name lest she hear.

Even unconscious, Brigit seemed aware and all seeing, her breath retracting like sensors taking in new information, her closed eyes a ploy to put Conti off his guard.

'How were your women?'

Conti grimaced and Brigit, licking her lips, let out a peal of hideous laughter, 'Your women Hartley, your *girls* lined up you know which way in the harem of your mind!'

'I think I know what you're doing Brigit...' Conti paused. It was happening again, the immobilising passivity he was inflicted with whenever Brigit turned on him.

It had all been so different when Brigit's eyes had waited for his to do something first. Coming second best to her would continue unless he accepted what she was. So why did he still refrain? His uncertainty, a sense of the ridiculous and an attachment to an agnostic world view, were the weapons Brigit beat him with. The only reason he held to those things was because they seemed undoubtedly true, not for any ideological purpose or commitment to reason. Now that they were clearly inadequate in the face of a different reality, what was to stop him from abandoning them? Why couldn't a pragmatist believe in the devil?

'Ha! I'm tired of her, that non-entity Raffle, how could you have ever loved a zero like that? Perhaps it's time for the frigid slob Stack! I wonder whether there isn't too much gristle growing over her soul, too much fat on those thighs...'

'Melissa is innocent...' protested Conti, his shock lagging

behind the audacity of Brigit's second sight.

'Still carrying a candle for roly-poly! Couldn't you have tried to be a better husband to me instead?'

'I was never bad to you Brigit... I tried. I'm still trying! What the hell do you think I'm doing now?'

'You were always off with other women, I know all about them now, a certain someone... has told me. You won't get over me until you've got over her, Hartley! You always need to be two women ahead to mend a broken heart, and I know there's someone new now. Cupid, messenger of the old gods has come with his bow and arrow, but beware, the old gods never existed, they were demons in disguise.'

'You know this can't carry on. Any of it. I can't let you.'

'Why ever not? You don't think I'm another average self-fulfilling tragic woman, do you? Oh Hartley, thou comest when I had thee least in mind!'

'I'm going to bring in someone to help you, somebody who really can. Trying to cope on my own hasn't done you any good. You need to be cured of whatever's ruining you.'

'But I have Chantal.'

'Chantal?'

'Yes Chantal!' Brigit gasped feverishly, 'Fuck her, fuck her small spiteful tits! Oh new experiences, they upset and they excite, they show what is over, but they also show that which replaces will end too... the process is everything. The process hates, Hartley, it hates...' Brigit let out an agonised groan, seemingly out of breath, and began to cough dark brown tar into her hand. 'See,' she said wiping the muck into her night gown, 'we want the good without the bad, to believe hell is simply the absence of heaven, that evil is nothing in-itself...'

'Please Brigit, you are going to kill yourself if you don't stop!'

'Mine hour is not yet come,' she said archly. 'You're lucky you have such a slender spiritual life or else I'd say you would be in jeopardy too... I can't stand in *their way* forever.'

'In *their* way? Don't tell me, you're actually offering me conditional protection from something worse? Like a supernatural protection racket? What are you talking about, Brigit? Why don't you tell me plain and simple what you mean and what you want me to do? Do you really think I don't care, standing around watching your life go to shit and not even knowing why? Why do you think I've stayed? We loved each other, when there still was a "you"...that could love.'

Brigit rocked her head back, braying loudly, the noise of her teeth grinding louder than her words, 'Please help me Hartley, if I die like this I die unclean.'

Conti rushed to the side of the bed, 'Of course I'll help you Brigit, a priest is coming here who can cure you of this...hex you're under, I promise. But we need you too, to help us get rid of your disease...'

The corners of Brigit's mouth upped in to a patronising smirk.

She had the news she wanted, 'You say you care for *me*? The man that you bring here will try and put *God* where he doesn't belong, but I shall put him out of where he should be! Pray through your arse and shit through your mouth Hartley, the one you seek help from can do nothing for us, me because I believe in his foe, and you because you believe in nothing...'

'Brigit...'

'From who do you, Hartley the modern man, issue a counter-challenge from? Some force "larger" than your self? Humanity? The Campaign for Nuclear Disarmament or The National Theatre? What use are they Hartley, what use? Don't you long for a master, haven't you tired of killing the fascist inside yourself? My Master has no use for free will or choice, he rules by coercion and temptation, the carrot and stick!'

'Your master isn't God, is it Brigit?' said Conti, 'Who is he?'

'Thinking again, are we? You know it doesn't suit you, poor boy!'

'You were lovely once, why are you doing this?' He felt

emasculated by the question, naked in his pathetic helplessness.

'Because you asked me about God, ha! God seeks to woo you, by using precisely nothing at all. I need my temptation, I need my Master.'

'Why do you gloat? As Faustian pacts go, yours is a disaster. Look at you Brigit, you smell as if you've been dead a week and talk cack like a Speakers' Corner bag lady.'

Brigit twisted a sticky plait of hair around her finger and sneered, 'ahh, Hoth suth, hoth suth! A black one in these corridors.'

'What the hell?'

The door opened and Archer strode in purposefully, looking Brigit up and down with barely concealed revulsion, 'A man on the phone for you Mr Conti, says it's most urgent...'

'Shut up white crap!' squeaked Brigit, in an accurate imitation of Archer's daughter, Judith.

'White crap that has your measure my dear!' bellowed Archer. Turning to Conti, she said firmly, her voice rising above Brigit's jabbering, 'A man who says his name is Todger Wade, but who is known, professionally he says, as *the Rector*.'

No sooner had Archer uttered these words, than the window pain shattered as if punctured by a howitzer, Brigit screaming at the top of her voice, 'Sludge hai choi, sludge hai choi, he will kill me! Whoever forces himself to love begets a murderer in his own body! Keep the black away!'

'Looks like we're going to get some results at last,' said Archer grimly.

'I know,' agreed Conti, averting his gaze from Brigit's demented face, 'but will they be the right ones?'

Having said goodbye, Conti put the phone down on The Rector. Avoiding Martin, who was staggering down the main staircase looking for friends, a bottle of Thunderbird in hand, Conti passed through the annexe doors, connecting the newer part of the house to the old. Without bothering to turn on the lights, a precaution he would normally have superstitiously observed, Conti felt his way down the steps to Chantal's quarters, daring whatever hidden power he feared to do its worst. There he found Chantal, her head bowed in apparent concentration over a book. To his disappointment she did not look up, but carried on reading as though he were not there. Conti accepted that he had no formal claim over the girl and that, having sought her out for excitement and not support, had no right to play the injured lover. But her aloof way of rising above the humdrum, often so liberating, also dismayed him, just as it was useless to deny that her indifference to his family's predicament stung him more than he cared to admit.

'What's that you're reading?'

Chantal raised her eyes coyly and slowly pushed the book away, 'Jacques Derrida.'

'Oh, a self help book for clever French girls?' It was characteristic of Conti to be at his most offensive, and least aware, precisely at that point where he believed himself to be being gratuitously sinned against. Chantal's radical disassociation and lack of responsibility from the feelings she caused in others, chilled him. It simply had nothing to do with her if someone should fall in love with her.

'Subtle, is he? One of those, "everything means something else" merchants?'

Chantal rolled her eyes impatiently, as if to remind Conti that he may have given his heart to someone who was not exactly blown away by the privilege. Sensing this Conti sucked his cheeks in and gazed meaningfully at the door, hiding the one thought love could not help him with; that he did not know the one he loved.

'He writes about the things we can't say.'

'Very profound.'

'For example, I can't say that I've never fucked Emile.'

Controlling both his anger and the urge to tear her clothes off and ravish her, Conti replied, 'The fact that you haven't obviously isn't a strong enough reason…according to Derrida?'

'I can't say it's *true* that I've never fucked him because truth is to do with finality and one day we might fuck each other… according to me.'

There was, Conti felt, an unpleasant symmetry between Chantal's game playing, and that of Brigit's. Beneath the guise of a challenge hid an intention to wound. In both cases the coldness of the attack played on and made fun of his natural warmth, rendering him weak for possessing it, or so he felt as he said coldly,

'Chantal, why are you doing this? Deliberately trying to make me hate you, don't you think I've enough crap to be getting on with? Do you even know what's happening upstairs, do you care?'

'Behaving like what, Hartley?'

'This!' he gestured round the room, 'locking yourself in here when I… when I need you to be natural with me. Like you would be if you gave a shit about anything.'

'I'm sorry Hartley, I thought you were a big man…'

'I'm not asking for your help, Chantal, it's just that I could live without its opposite. What the hell did you think you were doing chasing Emile into that airing cupboard, in one of those rooms I asked you not to go in? Don't you realise what we're living in?'

'I didn't! He ran in there himself! He's trying to wrap you round his little finger like his mother has. You're so blind to them both.'

'Bollocks, you're the one wrapping me round their little finger, and since this seems lost on you, he's my son, and she *is* my wife.'

'And me, who am I to you?'

'You?' Conti gazed at Chantal, who had slung a leg provocatively over the desk, her hand resting where he wanted his. 'I don't know who you are.'

Chantal waited to see what Conti would follow this on with, and hearing nothing she snorted haughtily, the effect of which was drowned by a violent hiccupping from upstairs.

Conti sat down on the side of the bed and glared rather foolishly at Chantal who was giving nothing away. He had been able to excuse himself for failing Brigit, who though mad, had at least been sinned against. But he had given his best to Chantal, who if anything, was failing him, having chosen to abandon the cheerful role he had elected her for. The perfect situation Conti had greedily conspired towards, a wife upstairs, a mistress downstairs and a career somewhere in-between, had come unstuck. Perhaps it was the baseness of this desire that created the space in which sickness and evil enjoyed a free hand. Who could be surprised at the appearance of "the Devil" in circumstances such as these?

'Do you believe in the Devil, Chantal?' he asked, the desire not to make a fool of himself dropped along with common sense, 'because Brigit does. And I'm beginning to. Not the guy in the bible but some kind of force of primordial evil in the world. That kind of Devil.'

'The Devil,' Chantal laughed uneasily, 'is that who she's pretending to be today?' Her manner was jumpy, and Conti observed that her Gallic cool was ruffled, though whether this was because she found his line of questioning embarrassing or too close to the bone, he could not tell.

'Yes, the Devil. I think he has his hands a long way up Brigit, and perhaps in me and maybe in you as well. He likes it here. It looks as though we've created, or inherited, a comforting environment for the bastard.'

'What are you talking about? Your wife is ill in the head, Hartley. She should go to hospital, that's all. And the longer she stays here the crazier we all get. If she said she was Napoleon, I suppose you'd believe her, yes?'

'I think you're lying Chantal, and you're doing it because

you're scared. I can understand why, and it doesn't make me think less of you. I was scared too, and then I pretended I wasn't because I didn't know what to do about it. I only stopped when I realised that that's exactly what Brigit or whatever's in control of her wants us to do, to go on denying its reality until it's too late.'

Chantal snorted again, weakly. 'There are a lot of weird people in the world...and heavy things. Only donkeys like Archer believe the Devil is behind them all.'

'But you *know* this is different, don't you? What does she say to you, when you go in to her room? Does she still taunt you or say anything about us? Come on Chantal, don't pretend you haven't got an opinion and this is all so tiresome for you. I know she gets to you, gets under your skin like she has with me.'

Chantal's expression had changed, a film of water coating her eyes, 'I hardly see her, Hartley...what could she have said to me?'

'Archer's told me she's watched you going in and out of her room... there's something going on between you two, admit it, I won't be angry.'

'I... I don't know, when I go in I'm scared, and then I'm not, but I don't remember what happens, it's like I fall asleep and by the time I'm awake I've left, and I know that I'm not scared but it doesn't make me feel good. It's like knowing something dirty has happened to me that I can't remember. Sometimes I think she might have hypnotised me. I keep finding myself in rooms and don't know why.'

Conti was ashamed at the relief he felt, especially since this latest discovery could hardly be considered good news. But Chantal's admission was significant, ensuring that even if his view of reality had been bent into strange and ghastly shapes, his sanity was not in doubt, for even if it was, it was partaking in an illusion that was affecting them all.

'It's like a complete mental black out. I hate it but I feel like she's in me. I feel like I have to go to her... I should have gone away from here the first time it happened but I was afraid she would have stayed with me, following.'

'Why, what stopped you from leaving? It couldn't just have been fear?' asked Conti, hoping very much that the answer involved him.

'I couldn't go. She wouldn't let me. She said that you needed me.'

'And didn't you need me?'

'No, I only wanted you. I do want you.'

Chantal's change in tone had made them both uneasy, their usual means of ignoring the rest of the house stripped away. The hiccupping had stopped and a smoky mist was congealing in the centre of the room, a development Conti knew to be another sign of Brigit. Again, to his elation and shame, he saw terror in Chantal's eyes, and with it the chance to not fail another woman. Steadily the smoke thickened the air with noxious fume trails and little gaseous clouds of soot. Conti opened his mouth to try and calm Chantal, who had joined him on the bed, but no sooner had he, than the heat entered his throat reducing him to coughing intelligibility. A strong draught was pulling them towards the mist. Roughly he held Chantal's head tightly to his, evaporating clumps of phlegm sizzling on his tongue like burning straw in a boiler, the entire room throbbing in a devilish warmth.

'She's using me,' he heard Chantal say and then she screamed; a pair of flaming eyes leered at them through the smoke and vanished, the air clearing to reveal an envelope on the floor.

'Don't, please don't,' gasped Chantal.

'Don't what?' said Conti, his shaking hand on her lap, the fright so sudden that he found he was laughing.

In a way it reminded him of how he had been able to overcome his fear of spiders, killing them in the presence of those more scared than himself. His fright had been too extreme to credit, leaving disbelief where terror ought to have been. The same was not true for Chantal, who was literally tucked under his shoulder, her small fingers digging into his ribs.

Leaning over the bed, his mind curiously lucid, Conti picked the envelope up and read the scrawl on it aloud, *"The living have one thing over the dead, they know when the dead are going to die."*

Though he had grown accustomed to Brigit's habit of leaving cryptic notes around the house, when she was still mobile, these messages had not materialised out of burning fogs or dry ice before. Conti removed the card from the envelope, *"You and yours are invited to Tom Elmhurst's 21st birthday Party at The Kosmokrator Club on the 1st November, All Souls Day..."*

The print and feel of the card was old and sepia tinged. 'Elmhurst again, the 21st, two weeks from now...do you know about this?' he turned to Chantal, 'has Brigit been in here?'

'No,' she shook her head, 'No, and I've never seen that envelope. Never. What does it mean?'

'I don't know, an invitation from death perhaps. Tom Elmhurst was Brigit's first boyfriend and my best friend. He warned me she was no good, but I always thought he was jealous. Perhaps he still is warning me.'

'Warning what?'

'Maybe that we don't have long,' said Conti, the perverse impulse that enjoyed it when things went wrong nearly greater than salvation he neither expected nor sought.

Martin finished relieving himself over the drive and, forgetting to return his member from whence it came, stumbled on towards the tiny cottage Archer shared with her daughter, his mind not fixed on any particular plan. For the past few hours the disembodied presence of his old team Captain, P.W. Saunders had been yelling all kinds of homosexual smut at him. No matter how much he drank, and he had been overdoing it since the first night in Tyger Tyger, it persisted in its unwholesome instruction. Martin had first heard it enter his room as a lewd whisper but it had since grown in to a menace that he had been left to struggle with on his own. It had watched his every humiliation. In spite of what he viewed as his good start to life in the house, the other inhabitants' attitude towards him had changed markedly, from what he assumed to have been acceptance to disinterested rejection. Led by Conti they had made their minds up, brushing him off as a harmless insignificance. Hearing Judith describe him as a dull lad was the last straw, but what could he do to show he was interesting? Admit that he was soft and in need? Or confess that the only kind of woman he felt safe with is one he knew he did not have to satisfy?

'Who told you?' he cried, 'how did you know?'

If only he were still the mighty trunk that swung at every ball, not a detestable fool playing cricket at night with a "voice" for company. 'He that is filthy,' he cried out, bitter tears of reproach welling in his grey eyes, 'let him be filthy still!'

Martin thrashed at the gravel underfoot, kicking at wet pebbles, more out of self-pity than rage. Given the choice, he would have ideally chosen the role of abuser over victim, but Tyger Tyger appeared to have no use for him in either capacity, preferring instead to make an ass of the fallen cricketer. Like a child watching a horror movie from behind the settee, the others were privately amused at Martin's spooked face, quizzical expressions and oafish bad humour. Had he not started to feel everything so *emotionally* he would probably not have noticed, let alone minded their antipathy, for the only emotion he had known before was romantic love towards the unsuspecting. Ordinary sensitivity had been a stranger to him, but as well as feeling unusually low, he was jealous of the attention Brigit attracted through her ghoulish antics, especially since she was no longer the only Botha-Hall chased by a demon.

'I don't like not being part of the team,' he grumbled drunkenly, 'I'm a team man, a god damned team man, damn it.'

'A gay man, a gay man,' laughed the voice Martin had identified as Saunders, despite sounding strangely like his own, 'a great big gay *black* bear!'

'Shut your mouth!' Martin yelled, 'I love women, I've always loved women.'

'Sure you love them but you can't fuck them! You think of men!'

'I don't!'

'You do! You mooned after women but you lust after men, you fat fake!'

'You don't add up, show me your face!'

He heard no reply. Looking back, he half expected to see the voice hovering genie-like over his shoulder, a physical manifestation preferable to the vacuum occupied by his invisible tormentor. There was nothing however, only blue darkness, strong and cold, and the wretched outline of Tyger Tyger, its turrets looming over him like giant wickets. Martin squinted, the eyes of the house following, or so he feared, his every move. It could certainly hear his thoughts, for he could make out irregular and jagged shapes darting across the battlements and lights flicking on and off in the uninhabited rooms, their activity an outright provocation. 'Damn you, you bastard,' Martin shouted at the building, a fist raised pitifully in the air, 'come out and fight me…'

'Shhhh Mr Martin,' scolded Archer, the light of her torch falling squarely on his contorted face. 'You've already woken Judith, and Lord alone knows what else you'll wake if you carry on like this. Noise carries a long way in the country.'

'Woken *Judith*! You mean she can sleep in this…hell! I thought you women were meant to be more sensitive!' Martin could barely hide the joy an encounter with a human had bought him, even one as unappealing as Archer.

Archer tutted good naturedly, the cords of her dressing gown swinging loosely beside her large hips, 'Just because we can sleep doesn't mean we don't notice things. But we enjoy a certain protection, it's why it doesn't affect us like it does you.'

'Us? What affects you? Who's us?'

'Always questions with you Mr Martin, no wonder you look so tired. "Us" is those of us who believe in God, have seen the good he can do and know he spares those who believe in him. Why else aren't most of us murdered, starved or drowned at sea? Who sees to it that we aren't, eh? If God gave me the due reward for my deeds he would see to it that I was sent to hell alright.'

Oblivious to the unlikelihood of the first theological conversation of his life occurring with his member hanging from his cricket whites in full view of a pensioner, Martin replied quickly, 'You must be joking, I've always believed in him, always! It was Brigit that never did.'

'But you don't believe he loves you, do you?'

There was an edge to Archer's voice that Martin had not noticed before, a lurking femininity that he felt both sickened and drawn to, 'Why should he love me?'

'Well maybe he doesn't, but he hasn't hung you out to dry, has he?'

'Things have been happening to me like Brigit, but none of you British want to know.'

'British are we now? What rubbish! You're just a scared silly billy Mr Martin! I haven't seen you sending clocks crashing through the air, or your face blistering up like a tomato, not like Mrs Conti's. There's nothing wrong with you that a few days off the sauce won't cure. Mulling about the house like a yak with scurvy, you've been.'

'A voice follows me round, I hear it everywhere I go!'

'It's your own voice you hear! You're imagining the whole thing. No, you aren't like your sister, the French girl or the little boy; they're in it up to their necks, they are. Your sister the worst of all, God help her. Whatever's in that house, grown men is one thing it isn't interested in.'

Martin bridled at the hierarchy of pain he appeared to have been omitted from, 'You knew what was happening to her, didn't you? Why did you let Conti arse fart around, chasing his tail if you knew all along…'

'He had to find out for himself, just like we all do. Fact is, I didn't think Mrs Conti would last this long without switching and giving in to it, and the funny thing is, if she did that, we'd have all thought she was all right again and everything would have gone back to normal. It's a special person who can handle the fright of being taken over by a Devil without the horror of it killing them, which is probably why it went for her, especially since she invited it in…'

'She what?'

'Yes, she invited it in. I was there that day, I found her in the garden. See here, unlike most simple folk who are possessed, but are too daft to see they are, your sister has plenty of grey matter. That's why she's fighting it and why she's ill. She can't help the goodness in her resisting, tearing her apart, killing her. If it weren't there, and she was bad, she'd be well.'

Martin stood there mutely, lost and dumbfounded, Archer gazing patiently at him, a warmth of sorts surrounding her, 'What if you forget to say your prayers,' he said, his wine red lips parting to reveal stained teeth 'and God goes missing one night. What happens to your protection then?'

'Nothing to worry about, God's useful if you want to be on the safe side, but if worst came to worst, well, me and Judith would scare out any spirit ourselves. We're a pair of toughies.'

'I've always prayed but, but nothing happened,' Martin croaked, the alcohol, the cold and fear descending on him like slates, 'I prayed but… he didn't listen, I… he doesn't love me, why the hell should he, a shit like me… I've so much love to give, you know, to girls…''

'Shhhh now,' said Archer, one hand around the base of Martin's frozen penis, the other taking him firmly by the arm to her bosom, 'tonight me and Judith are going to look after you for him.'

'Husband?'

Conti stopped outside Brigit's room but did not reply, a soft yellow moonlight illuminating the linoleum floor. The voice was soft; reminding him of the voice she used when she took her vows at the Registry office, years before.

'Has Tom's invite arrived yet?'

'If you mean the note you somehow smuggled in to Chantal's room, yes.'

'And aren't you going to go?'

'I haven't made up my mind; there's so much to do here. What's the point of moving to the country if I spend all my weekends up in London?'

Brigit chuckled to herself, 'Very good, very good Hartley, so glad that you're still game. But if you don't go to London for his party he'll have to have it here…we both miss him don't we?'

'You married me, Brigit. Live with your choice as I do.'

'Oh I have! Don't go, let's talk a while…'

Conti moved towards her door and stopped outside it.

'Sorry,' she cried, 'just leave me, go away and live your life, leave me…'

Trying the handle he found it stuck.

'Of course I want to help…let me in. The door's jammed.'

'It's too late Hartley. We should have taken our chance when we had it. Please go.'

For a moment he stayed as he was, then resumed his journey to the floor below, heavy steps following a pace or two behind him, until he reached his bedroom door. Swiftly he shot a glance in their direction and saw a dark shape, distinguishable only by a ponytail and donkey jacket, turn its back to him and disappear into a wall. He held his breath for a moment; absolutely sure of what he had seen.

'Tom, is that you?'

He could hear Brigit's tears through the floorboards and a low whistling coming from the garden.

'Tom, if there's something you want to say to me, then tell me...' Brigit's crying grew sharper, sounding more like laughter, and for a moment Conti thought he could hear another voice, calling him to the window, telling him to trust it.

He came to the following morning in the garden by the compost heap. In his hand was another envelope, on it written *"Trust the Rector, beware of Dr Mikes"*. Hastily he pocketed it and made for the house, his mind a complete blank.

Chapter Five

The Rector thanked the fat man for the lift and pulled his case from the boot of the dilapidated Land Rover, taking care to remark, 'Strange looking place, isn't it?'

'Why's that?' asked his driver. The air had combined in such a way as to feel both humid and cold, the overcast sky stubbornly refusing to declare its hand.

'Not quite how I imagined this part of the world to be, high hedges and walls, narrow lanes and a couple of main roads leading out. It doesn't inspire.'

'It's flat and ugly all right, but not dull,' said the driver pointing to the stag standing over the entrance to Tyger Tyger, 'Alert looking bugger that one.'

'He looks life-like, doesn't he? You know its owners?'

'Village people and them don't have any in common, we get on with our lives and they get on with theirs. Never fancied that place, mind, can't think of ever enjoying what you might call a good experience there.'

'I have positive associations with few places, and most places I go are bad,' the Rector smiled, 'I'll manage.'

The fat man nodded warily and reversed out on to the road, 'I do believe you will,' he called, the first rays of sunshine piercing through the early morning cloud.

'Am I as you expected me, boyo?' asked the Rector.

'I didn't know what to expect,' Conti answered honestly, 'Thank you for getting here so quickly. I didn't think you'd make it overnight. How far did you have to come?'

'From the hills,' laughed the Rector removing his narrow brimmed Stetson and leather trench coat to reveal a small Afro and mauve corduroy suit. Even without his Chelsea boots, he would have stood a foot taller than Conti, his pencil thin moustache and knotted black tie more Haitian Gestapo than Church of England.

Carefully he licked a long black finger and held it up in the air. Martin, who had returned dishevelled from the Archers in time to bump into the Rector on the drive, growled at him warily.

'I'm just taking the temperature,' said the Rector brushing past Martin and entering the great hall, the original dining room that had remained unused since the Conti's arrival. 'Normally I'd say these kind of presences, you know, the *thing* you have here, are as known to us as we are to them,' his voice was smooth and sonorous, reminding Conti of a DJ toasting over a sound system, its Welsh inflection oddly natural. 'I normally feel both, good and evil, but not here,' he said running his hand over a dusty mahogany armchair. 'You don't mind me getting straight to business, do you Mr Conti?'

'You're making me feel less mad already,' ventured Conti cautiously, 'and I also like the opportunity to be nice to black people. I don't think I've met one to talk to in five years.'

The Rector laughed sharply, its piercing echo producing the first of a series of low groans from the room Brigit had been moved to. 'I saw it on your face when I came in, you're giving up, you shouldn't, we've a good chance of turning it around.'

'I beg your pardon?'

'Your wife's problem.'

'You may be up against more than you think. It's worse than my wife, it's the whole house, our histories... you're probably thinking I'm overdoing it but believe me, I'm not.'

'Not at all. It's here all the time,' the Rector said inspecting the walls, 'Real, external, like the plumbing, not like how you might expect a haunting to be.' He flashed a salesman's smile, his gold plated teeth catching the sunlight.

'If you mean what I think, then yes... Mr Wade or Todger?'

'Rector please, this is business, Todger's all right for the pub and Wade for the TV licence people, but it's Rector for when we're at work.'

Martin made a disbelieving noise and slumped into the armchair so his back was turned to the Rector. A stale odour, like bread soaked in iodine rose off him.

'If you're too polite to ask who this belligerent ox is, it's my brother-in-law,' Conti explained, 'he's over from South Africa.'

Martin leant his head back, as one whose body is too consti- pated to move might, and grinning clownishly said, 'Martin Botha-Hall, currently of Fartmouth Swineshire, at your service my good man.'

Acknowledging the interruption with a tolerant nod, the man from the hills continued, 'It's subtle, like a serpent, it can even reassure, allowing you to believe that someone kind is watching over you, a dead ancestor perhaps, until you realise there's no warmth in this presence, or tenderness either, that the substance of this thing is not sturdy or dependable.'

He looked at the others like a consultant fishing for a second opinion, and smiled confidently into the giant looking glass that hung over the dining table. 'But it isn't the house itself I'm talking about, you know that too, don't you...this place is one giant doorway.'

Martin snorted again and followed it with a raspberry, 'You don't mind starting in the deep end, do you, man, must make the God you're asking so much of enjoy your act even more.'

This time the Rector grasped Martin's shoulder and said, 'It's not a question of *asking* God for anything, just try not to hide anything from him, a lack of openness can only help the enemy.'

Martin moved to get up, but the Rector, leaning down on his shoulder kept him where he was, 'You've a face that inspires pity; you've been through it, haven't you? I don't blame you for wondering who the hell I am or what gives me the right to come in here and talk to you like this. It's not often us humans are able to reproduce God's trust in us with each other, but it's important that we try.'

'Jesus, man,' spluttered Martin, 'you haven't based your look on that guy in that movie, Dr Kananga or whatever his name was? You don't sound like any Christian I know.'

The Rector let go and laughed again, his eyes twinkling with ruthless sensuality.

'I didn't know how hard it was to find a good Christian until I started to look for one,' Conti cut in, 'I guess it's why I wasn't scared to venture off menu with you...Rector.'

'Rector!' Martin gasped, 'I've never met a Rector like this, what kind of Rector is he?'

The Rector nodded good-naturedly, 'Voodoo man, charlatan, the Devil too, I've been called them all. It helps to have some of Old Nick's darkness in you for this line of work. After all, he's never been scared to borrow God's ideas when it suits his purposes.'

'So you believe "the Devil" has something to do with our problems,' asked Conti.

'This one's name is Iblis,' snarled the Rector, all jollity having left his face, 'and it lives between two layers, those of truth and deception.'

'And how would you know, Kaffir?' asked Martin, determined to keep the inquiry at a brute level that as far as he was concerned befitted the one he was addressing, 'What makes you such an expert?'

'I apologise for him,' said Conti frowning at Martin, 'he seems to have gone downhill rapidly these past few days. You say this Iblis, is that who we normally mean when we talk about the Devil? A real thing, not just some *idea* or mental representation that someone with nervous illness like my wife could imagine...but the biblical one.'

The Rector picked up a candleholder and swung it playfully over his shoulder, 'No, not that. The Devil is the human form for a force far worse than the being you're thinking of or, to put it another way, it is the form something else takes when it enters a human soul… for our purposes we can call this energy the Devil, or as our Muslim brethren have it, Iblis. He, the Devil, is actually an "IT" a "THING", but I find that we all know where we are if we refer to "it" as a he, especially as that's the way he seems to humans when he appears, and to your wife, of course. But don't misunderstand me; the idea of a man of wealth and taste with a pointy tail and horns growing out of his head who inhabits a gentleman's club called Hell will be of no use. Far better to think of him as a slobbering eviscerated corpse with a needle sticking out of his arm. But then you already know far more about him than most people do.' He turned to Martin, 'Why are you laughing?'

'Because,' Martin exclaimed, 'you come in here like some kind of children's entertainer talking about the devil and expect me to take you seriously, man, I can't believe you're for real.'

'I'm sorry, he's still drunk.'

The Rector, walked around the armchair, his gaze running through Brigit's brother as if searching for clues in the crumpled leather. '*He* is real. Yes, it first hits you when you relax, doesn't it? Perhaps in a chair like this one, of which there are many in this house, I don't doubt. Or in your case, when you drink.'

The Rector clicked his tongue and pointed the candleholder at Martin, 'So you begin to think this place isn't so bad, normal like other homes, where even the silence reassures you at last, and you feel like dozing, and then bang,' he slapped the candleholder in to the palm of his hand, 'it hits you, you realise it's in you and there are no covers to hide under, not even your skin can keep it out because it's already in everything, yes?'

Conti nodded in assent and Martin allowed his head to fall into his palms, 'That, I suspect, is the sickest part, that this energy has already been working in you for an age, from the beginning, strongest when you were most relaxed, its filth oozing in, silently telling you things you didn't want to hear, but not in its own voice but in that of a friend, but it's no friend, it's a superior ruthless bastard that's further in you than even you are...' the Rector let his voice trail off, '...like the switch from mono to stereo, and just when you feel the noise fade out, isn't that stillness...possession? After that the noise starts.'

Conti, whose feelings concerning the Rector had moved quickly through bemusement, distrust, fear, and now cautious respect, said, 'It's shocking that you should see it so clearly. If I knew what I do now, I'd have taken us away on our first night. But the point is nothing happened for a year, this was just a frightening old building that gave me the creeps. The things that went wrong, stuff moving about, doors opening themselves, were so small and explainable that...'

'Of course they were. Who do you think Old Nick uses to announce himself and herald his arrival if not his demons? The insignificant little tics that lay the way for him so to speak, the ones that mess you up slightly with the trivial stuff you mention. He likes them to pronounce his each syllable before he talks, it helps cover the hiss and makes him sound more human, more like what you think of as the Devil...the evil slowly growing out of what you've already got used to.'

'The Devil, Iblis or the Grim Reaper? Make your mind up man!' Martin interrupted, 'I can't make head or tail of your riddles. And you,' he turned to Conti, 'don't just lap it up, this guy could be anyone!'

'Joke? Riddles? You wish it were so. I'll tell you who you're up against,' the Rector spat, the acceleration of his wrath alarming Conti, who raised an elbow defensively. 'It's a force that won't cut you any slack just because you're weaker than it. Iblis is the opposite of God in every respect, he knows he's better than you and hasn't got any of God's modesty or love to soften the blow, you can't meet him as an equal and that's why the *terror* of an encounter with him *paralyses*...'

Martin stood up and said in a raised voice, 'All right, all right man. There is terror here, you are right about that.'

'Damn right I am and don't be scared of admitting it. Jesus wasn't scared of crawling, humiliation, even disbelief. Your only hope of equalising the odds is God and the Lord Jesus Christ our Saviour. He's the only one that the beast is scared of...'

'Now you're sounding like a proper priest,' Martin said with no trace of irony, 'There is an enemy of mankind in this building. I believe that.'

'And I believe in independent and sovereign evil speaking to me through the darkness of eternity. Amen,' said the Rector, winking at Conti playfully. Conti acknowledged the communication with a nervous smile.

There was another loud groan and a noise that sounded like a post falling over. In a single and graceful swoop, The Rector placed the candleholder back on the old oak dining table, and picked a heavily bound document from the snakeskin briefcase he had carried in with him. Conti noticed that his manner was changing again, his temper had vanished and a legal formality entered his voice, 'Thank you for telling me about her PhD thesis Mr Conti, very interesting, but I was already acquainted with it. Before you ask how, my radar's tweaked for things like this, it's my job. I've bought my copy with me, The "BODY WITHOUT ORGANS", have you read it?'

'I tried to once, years ago, but gave up after a few pages.'

'Why was that?'

'I had no idea what it was about and found it boring.'

'Anything else?'

Conti paused, 'I suppose there was something a bit out of character about the writing up of that PhD, in the part I read. I remember it being rather hysterical and over the top for Brigit. She was always drier when talking about these things. It was like she slipped into a different personality when it came to writing it, which is normal for intellectuals, maybe.'

'Indeed,' said the Rector, 'but if we cut through the jargon, that I suppose was fashionable at her place of study at the time, what I find in her words is a kind of materialist black magic, all forces and energies and no spirits or souls. If you want my opinion Mr Conti, in this thesis we find if not the *genesis* of your wife's problem, then an early manifestation.'

'Are you implying that what's happening to her now is somehow connected to what she was writing then, all those years ago?'

'Yes, though you would have to know what you were looking for to see it. Take one paragraph here, your wife is saying all of life is only "matter", you follow me, very scientific and proper of her. But then she shifts gear...'

'Shifts gear?'

'She becomes insidiously *satanic*. Her materialism evolves, and ends up unlike any I've encountered. This post-modern world of so-called "animal becoming" that she treats the reader to stinks of paganism, and the parts where she pretends to be "rational" are the least honest.'

'Let me get this straight, you say she openly admits to worshipping the Devil in her PhD, am I right?' asked Martin.

'Not so crude, but in a certain way, she's trying to tell us she's discovering someone. I became suspicious at her inconsistency, because nowhere does she renounce transcendence, only a moral and supernatural deity, the place of which is taken by a "Dark Precursor"... so you could say that she's been in training for her present predicament for some years now. All she needed was a sympathetic incubator, which turned out to be this house. Think about it. Everyone who came to live here wanted something, and heard the voices in this place tell them they could have it, but at a price: their soul. Man is greedy, but most of us, when the choice is put like that, aren't going to give up our sanity for a few water-colours, a new Porsche or an agricultural business. We're not Faust. But your wife, she wanted knowledge, the ultimate Faustian Pact and the easiest to be cheated on. And this was the place where the deal was always going to go down. Here in Tyger

Tyger.'

'Read some of it out,' demanded Martin, 'one of the easy bits.'

'All right,' the Rector said, flicking through the pages, 'here's a section I underlined near the middle, when she starts to really warm to her theme, "Is it really so sad and dangerous to be fed up with seeing with your eyes, breathing with your lungs, swallowing with your mouth, talking with your tongue, thinking with your brain, having an anus and larynx, head and legs? Why not walk on your head, sing with your sinuses, see through your skin, breathe with your belly: to become a body without organs; to be done with the judgement of God." And then this, "It is when she flees, launches down a line of flight, that she becomes animal, that she might touch the unutterable existence of the thing higher than a deity." The Rector looked at the other two as though nothing more needed to be said and closed the binder.

'It is obvious that this thing made an intellectual approach to your wife, several years ago, even before you had met her, and lay there, not unlike a sleeper cell, waiting for its moment... I'm sorry, but it's not as uncommon as you might think. Sometimes the invitation is issued as early as childhood. Watching a human for that long is nothing for one of those that has come out of eternity.'

'It sounds absolutely fucking ghastly. If what you're saying is right...'

'It is right Mr Conti.'

'Then it was here all the time. In her from the moment I first knew her, watching everything we did together, listening to our conversations, knowing her thoughts.'

'Right in the heart of her "creative process",' said the Rector slapping the binder, 'the part of her that she thought was most free.'

'It's too much... even the worst things I thought, lag behind this,' Conti ground his knuckles together, 'if I'm not tearing my hair out and screaming black hell at the top of my voice, thank my upbringing, because even after what I've witnessed, what you're telling me, so calmly, shocks me to my core. If I hadn't seen it myself in the last few days, I wouldn't have believed you.'

The Rector pulled out a chair, Conti sat on it automatically, a horrible look of recognition dawning on him, 'When she's making sense, she claims to have never been so *inspired*, ideas keep coming to her like she's already thought of them before, a channel for creative energy – except that it's destructive…'

'Exactly, Mr Conti, this isn't poetry she's engaged in, and when she yells the house down it isn't unconscious lines of scattergun "creativity" you hear. What is pulling the strings in her is a cohesive alien body communicating a very specific, and consistent message. Its deception and success lies in making her believe that she has discovered the real *her*. The special powers she has developed, the ability to move objects, her visions and insights are all sops planted by a diabolical spirit to gain control. But the one thing it couldn't do, especially in a woman of your wife's sort, was arrive as itself. The danger now is that these "effects" have formed the very core of your wife's inner life, they are what, in her own mind, makes her unique… Why should she let go of them and join the rest of us poor unenlightened beings? Her possession is one of the most subtle I've encountered.'

'I tell you there is nothing subtle about it,' said Martin, correctively but without aggression, for he was being taken in to the Rector's world, the outrageous phenomena under discussion excusing the peculiar excesses of the speaker.

'Subtle compared to my last case, a religious girl who had been chained and hooded in the garage and raped over a four day period by a paedophile gang who wanted her to accept the seed of "Satan". It was taped, video nasty stuff, nothing left to the imagination, very sick.'

'Jesus, man. There are Satanists that do that kind of shit?'

'Not Satanists, degenerates. The gang were easily traced and arrested. I sat in on their interviews, nothing but a bunch of amateurs playing out fantasies born of inadequacy. The Exorcism her parents wanted me to perform would have been a shambles. That girl needed care and some medical attention. But your wife Mr Conti, she's different, she feels like the real deal.'

'She *is* in bad physical shape...I don't want anything you do to make that worse, medically speaking. If we push her any further to the edge, I'm scared that the person I loved will never come back. I can only see her in glimpses as it is.'

'What will be worse for her is if we leave her as she is, be sure of that.'

'A doctor came here, he believed further psychiatric tests would be useful.'

The Rector twitched impatiently. 'Sure, I can give you all that technical medical hokum if you want; I've kept abreast with latest papers and can hit you with the up to date quack speak. For example she's almost certainly suffering from DIM, Disassociative Identity Disorder, bought on by traumatic memories, that it's turned her in to a group of actors, all of whom experience dissociation with each other, and that's why she's confused her own role in the process for the Devil's... Maybe we could give her what they nowadays call spiritual release therapy, but we know better than that don't we? We know what she needs is love, an exorcism and the grace of God.'

Conti looked at the Rector, his spidery eloquence supporting the plausibility of his hypothesis, and wondered whether this man really was capable of administering divine grace, or whether he was the latest turn in Tyger Tyger's attempts to strip him of his reason.

The Rector appeared to perceive his latest and, most severe, doubt. 'Free yourself of your scepticism Mr Conti, let it go. I know it's natural to wonder who or what I am, appearing at your door like this, but where will it get you? We both know by now that all the options have been exhausted. It's why you sent for me. If you go to the psychiatrists again, all you'll get is a lot of guff about thought forms that represent anger, personality integration, cognitive restructuring, re-patterning brain techniques, regression hypnotherapy and maybe a spot of counselling once your wife is dead...'

'It's all bullshit then, is it? No one's going to help us except us, and you.'

'Correct. Though you never know, somewhere along the line God may intervene with the odd miracle. He has some past form. Now if you would, ask your domestic help to bring down your son. It's best to start with the Achilles Heel.'

Chantal did not know whether she slept or dreamt, only that her trainers were on her feet.

She and Brigit were carrying bouquets of lilies from Foyles bookshop on the Charing Cross Road to Trafalgar Square, their chosen path, a vast tunnel that she had no memory of and which ought not to have been there. She could see through it to the other side faintly, the view yielding a vision of the city unlike any she had encountered on her previous visits. Rather than red buses, The National Gallery and Nelson's Column, what lay in front of her was the crumbling brown stone tenements of the Bronx, or perhaps a mythical Gotham she half remembered from comic books. Nor were they alone. Rotting figures armed with axes hobbled towards them, like zombie extras from a budget horror, their proximity and foul breath disconcertingly real. Chantal knew that they were in danger, even if this were only a dream, and as the first figure lunged at her, she punched it and tried to turn round and run. Grasping her wrist, Brigit ordered her to stop and follow her; they were too close to where they needed to be to give up...and then Chantal understood that the tunnel was not a tunnel, but an arm, and that the city not a city but *his face.*

'Kiss his mystery,' said Brigit.

Chantal closed her eyes in front of absolute horror and opened them lying on her bed in Tyger Tyger. 'Protect me', said Brigit, 'protect me from the one who has come here to harm me.' Brigit's eyes, which seemed to have been carried in to the room from the nightmare, vanished, but her voice reverberated clearly, repeating the request, before fading.

Chantal sat up and waited for reality to come to her. A moment passed, she got to her feet, looked about her and shouted, 'No!'

A storm of revolt stirred, but the burning hand in her throat, squeezing her insides so that she could hardly breathe, was proof that she really did not have any choice. She was Brigit's prisoner.

Unwillingly, but carried by a will stronger than her own, Chantal stumbled to the door of her bedroom and tried the handle. It was locked from the outside. She tried it again and began to rattle the frame, panicking she screamed, 'Let me live! Let me out! Hartley help me! Please Hartley, it's me, Chantal, can you hear me?'

'I'm sorry,' Archer called from the other side, 'it'll just be for a little while dear. For your own good.'

Throwing herself onto the bed, Chantal covered her mouth to stifle the onset of hysteria, the looming prospect of being forgotten taking its place next to newer fears. Terror of the unknown was nothing to being passed over by a man she had tried not to fall in love with, or so she once thought. Now she was not so sure. From the far end of her room she heard her cupboard door slowly open, and a coarse voice say, 'Just close your eyes darling and we'll go for another of our walks. Just shut your eyes!'

She recognised it at once, it had been speaking to her all along, telling her what to remember and what to forget. She closed her eyes as instructed. Soon she would be back in the tunnel again, standing at the gates of the Kingdom, the tip of a ghost white lily in her hair.

'Think of Ahab and the Great White Whale. I've been after him all my life. Wherever I go I seek the bastard's face in whatever shape or form its taken,' the Rector lit a thin cigar and tossed the match on to the floor, a loose deliberation to his movements, 'Evil is never banished from the world, once it is driven out of a place, it moves on in a search of a new spot to occupy.'

'Like the common cold?'

'No, like a swarm of locusts,' replied the Rector, crossing his legs. 'I've hunted "Iblis" for years, through estate agents, film extras even a Scottish Laird. I've encountered him as the arch demon every time, though I am no closer to being able to tell you what that demon *is*, than I could account for why I'm me and not you.'

'I thought as a priest you'd know,' said Martin, 'Isn't the answer somewhere in the Bible?'

'First causes are God's line, not mine. For practical purposes, Iblis is whatever the holy books of any religion tell us he is.'

Conti, Martin and the Rector were sat in a semi circle, smoking and awaiting the arrival of Emile. The scene was deceptively relaxed and convivial, for both Conti and Martin were in a state of heightened excitement. Each had become, to varying degrees, men of reaction, waiting for the next disaster to happen in a defensive posture neither felt temperamentally suited to.

'Her thesis,' said Conti, 'she was finishing it when we met. She interested me like no one I'd met but I was never drawn to all the theoretical stuff, I just liked to hear her talk, sort of humouring her over her work. Most of her friends did too, but this diabolical dimension, how come her supervisor, the examiners, the people who actually read it never noticed?'

The corner of the Rectors mouth twitched sarcastically, 'You think the Professors in a Philosophy Department would know the devil if it goosed them in broad daylight on the high street? To my knowledge Iblis doesn't feature greatly in the lexicon of linguistic analytic philosophy, and don't even get me started on the Continentals. There could be no safer home for him to dwell in.'

The Rector tightened the knot on his tie, hard. 'The reason no one saw it coming, Mr Conti, is because good and evil have become *too much* to be true, haven't they? Quaint, embarrassing, pre-scientific concepts, replaced by "the banality of evil", "Foucauldian" power relations or some other quasi-sociological flim-flam.'

'Only egg heads think like that, man,' said Martin, 'Most people are still superstitious buggers.'

'Maybe so, but the rest of us are content to do without moral absolutes, you only have to turn on the news to watch the fall out. Truth no longer moves through knowledge because truth no longer exists,' the Rector tapped his chest, 'Your wife, Mr Conti, thought that she could think her way beyond good and evil, both of which dwell in what she called ontology and I call God. In the academic atmosphere she moved in, what was the use of a close reading of Aquinas next to the blasphemous freedom advocated by Nietzsche? The Christians lost the intellectual arguments long ago. Meanwhile out there in the real world, Iblis is having a ball.'

'Lost, maybe, but I sense you don't think you are wrong.'

The Rector inhaled deeply on his cigar, releasing the smoke in a slow trickle. 'Ideas that are of eternity are never wrong; though occasionally they slip out of fashion. There is no moral neutrality in this world and no ethically disinterested processes in life. Your wife simply chose to ignore the moral dimensions, invoking evolutionary psychology, post-structuralism, whatever. But neutrality and agnosticism have never been options, all both are saying is, "I have no faith, I choose cynicism, I choose to wait and see." They think they're with the smart money but they've succumbed to the greatest delusion of all, that it doesn't matter whether you make your mind up, that there is always tomorrow.'

Martin smiled, 'I like it man, keep talking.'

There was a knock on the door and Archer walked in, blushing slightly as she avoided eye contact with Martin, 'Mr Conti, Judith is giving Emile his medicine and will bring him in once she's done. Is there anything else?'

'Have you seen Chantal?'

'She's gone out.'

'Then could you go up and sit with Brigit and prepare yourself for whatever she does next, I appreciate your help with this more than ever, Mrs Archer.'

'I'm always prepared for her,' said Archer briskly.

'Let's get down to it gentlemen,' the Rector said putting out his cigar on an antique plate, 'The reason I've asked for the boy and not his mother, is that he's the front line we have to smash through to reach the woman.'

Conti flinched at the analogy. The Rector, noticing this, added, 'It'll be hard for you but trust me, just as I have to trust God.'

'My son isn't the most robust of children. Do you have to involve him?'

The Rector nodded patiently, 'We can't ignore him. The cat business you mentioned to me isn't the sign of an ordinary disturbance. It's part of a different pattern.'

'The kid keeps digging the kitty up, doesn't he,' said Martin, pleased to add context to the discussion, 'and I've noticed that shadow, like a big tiger or something, that follows him round, you reckon, you know, is ah, the boy possessed too?' he looked apologetically at Conti and, unintentionally imitating the Rector's diction, added, 'Best to check all the options, man.'

'I know Emile is disturbed but he hasn't dug the cat up for over a week now,' said Conti defensively, 'and when I buried it last, the cat's name was Felix for what it's worth, I didn't bother moving it from where I stuck it in the ground before, so perhaps... it's a stage he's passed through.'

'Hmmm, it would be comforting but wrong to think so. The truth is that your son doesn't need the corpse of the cat around because its physical presence is no longer important.'

'Don't tell me he's being pursued by the vengeful spirit of a dead cat,' said Conti.

'Nothing so simple,' grinned the Rector, 'Emile has no privacy of mind any more. Like your wife, he's being fed his lines. The boy is suffering from classic familiarization, that is, the dead cat has "come to live with him". But not entered or possessed him, there was no need since his mind is so pliable and young. There is nothing Emile thinks or feels that "Felix" doesn't know too.'

Martin looked at them both querulously, 'I met that kid when he was four, no disrespect man, but he was always damned weird.'

Conti groaned, 'He was worse once that cat snuffed it. He began to sleep with his back to the wall because if he didn't it looked at him... he didn't exactly say what *it* was, but he said a frightening face would emerge from the wall and scare him, and, what really got me was he insisted that *it* knew him... I hoped stupidly that compared to Brigit, Emile's problems could have had a rational source. I noticed his behaviour got worse and more disturbed when I lied to him, or when I'd been naughty, but it wasn't like a kid's intuition on his part, more an allergic reaction. There's no way he could have known what I was up to, so perhaps that's another one we can chalk up to Iblis, eh, Rector?'

The Rector tutted correctively, 'Mr Conti, you place your son in *something else's* company every time you lie or deceive. His awareness of evil is variable on the morality or immorality of your behaviour. I would view your son as one of your wife's satellite states, his new friend wants him to denounce you, and you're making it easier by leaving a vacuum for this friend through your incomprehension of the boy, and if you'll forgive me, by what I imagine is the immorality of your personal life.'

Although wanting to refute the attack, Conti could not resist the temptation to be provided with answers, 'It may even make sense. If I were to accept that I was the most evil man on the planet, deserving of this most special of punishments, then yes, why shouldn't I admit that the reason my son has gone mad is because I've exposed him to the evil of an adulterous relationship carried on under his nose? It's preposterous, but it's true, I've let them both down. I thought I deserved my holidays from life, shagging around, for putting up with their weirdness.'

'Very likely you did. None of us are perfect Mr Conti, though few have had your bad luck; that I grant you. Think of it as their revenge. Your wife no longer thinks of you, she only wants to be closer to the power that runs her, and the boy too. You've become irrelevant to them, left out of their diabolism and uninitiated.'

Conti laughed coldly, 'I can't believe it and yet I do. Iblis, possession, "immorality"…if it hadn't happened to me I'd have told you where to go, but you're right. Brigit was always jealous, and Emile was always clingy. She still pretends to be but as a red herring I think, to make me think she still cares about anything that happens in this life.'

'She's about to again,' said the Rector, taking a cross from his case and hanging it over his neck.

There was a knock on the door and Judith entered with Emile. The boy, despite his bright tracksuit, looked paler than normal. Instinctively Conti moved to hold Emile's hand but the Rector shook his head and frowned. The lack of physical contact between father and son had never struck Conti as unusual, he and Emile having so little in common and even less to share, but the boy's loneliness fell like lashes, urging Conti to clumsily state, 'Don't be nervous Emile, this man is our friend. You haven't done anything wrong and no one's going to tell you off. He's a doctor who helps people who see dead animals get better.' Conti checked himself, he had nearly said 'dead cats', which even in the circumstances would have been an absurdity too far.

Emile stared at his ill-fitting basketball boots. 'Mummy says you and your friends should leave us alone.'

'Of course she did,' said the Rector calmly, gently pushing Conti to one side, 'because mummy is not mummy and Emile,' he looked down at the boy, 'is not really Emile.' It was the last remark he addressed to the child, for he followed it with, 'Felix, I want to speak to Felix.'

Emile smirked slyly, and stuck his hands down the elastic of his tracksuit bottoms.

'Felix, I have no quarrel with Emile, I want to speak to Felix.'

'What are you going to do?' asked Conti.

The Rector brushed a finger over his lips, and continued, 'Felix are you with Emile now? If you are come out and declare yourself.'

Emile giggled and said, 'Meow Priest. Would you like me to be a cat?'

'Show yourself, don't be shy; let us see you.'

'Meow! We want to stay inside!' Emile's voice had become multiple, a chorus of smaller voices, childish but not childlike, 'It's not polite to disturb us! Hasn't anyone ever told you that's all you are, a rude and strange man?'

'Your evil stupidity is a sham that won't protect you...' the Rector paused to wipe the phlegm that Emile had spat at his face, and continued, 'are you frightened Felix? Is that why you are wasting our time? Remember, Iblis will abandon you, for he fears God, even if you do not.'

The moaning upstairs had picked up again, rising to a crescendo, and Emile clutched his ears protectively, 'You're not grown ups' he cried in a voice that was a perfect approximation of his mother's, 'you're hurting me,' and then shrilly, 'What kind of father would let their son be tortured by a stranger, what kind of brother would let his nephew be murdered by a kaffir?'

The Rector glanced at Conti coolly, and mouthed, 'Get ready.' Turning to face Emile, the Rector made a sign of the cross and said 'Release this child. You have fallen from heaven, Lucifer, Son Of Dawn, cut down to the ground. Once you dominated peoples. But you shall be bought down to the bottom of the pit. And all who see you, will despise you....'

Emile whined cattily, sprang on to all fours and darted under the table, no longer a small boy but a feline line-of-flight. Martin threw a horrified look at Conti who returned it with an expression of disbelief that even Judith mirrored, 'Come out from under there,' she cried in an attempt to introduce common sense to the proceedings, 'Don't be being such a silly boy Emile, come out here and stop all this pretending.'

The Rector held a finger to his lips, picked up a chair and brandishing it like a lion tamer shook it at Emile, who scuttled down the far end of the table where he mewled and scratched at the floor, 'This manifestation is of no great intelligence, but behind it is Iblis, remember for the moment that it's not the boy but his "friend" that we are dealing with.'

A banging had started upstairs, sounding like a body throwing itself up and down on the floor, and Emile responded to it by yelling in anguish, hissing and spitting at the adults as he did so. The difference from the boy who had walked in was as great as what separated the living from the dead. Swallowing his disbelief, Conti tried to recognise his son but could not see past the imitation of a cat, Emile's tiny fingers contorting into claws, his voice breaking into Brigit's again, 'Perverts! Bullies! Sadists! Leave the boy alone to play with his pet!'

'Go up and help restrain Mrs Conti as best you can,' the Rector told Judith as he bent down and looked at Emile, 'she is about to lose an ally and she won't like it.' Carefully, he manipulated his tall body, so he was level with the boy under the table.

'Please take care with him,' said Conti.

Crawling towards one another, the two eyed each other, the Rector pouncing first, grabbing Emile's arm whilst fending off his bites and flying nails. Swiftly he dragged the boy out from under the table and, pinning him as firmly as he could to a tangled Persian rug, said in his ordinary speaking voice, 'Supreme intelligence that leads all others in revolt against the truth of God. Your minions are legion. Watch them crushed as you were, grand claimant of nothing.'

Martin's jaw was shaking with adrenalin, confident that he was a team player again. Conti's feelings were more complicated. Paternal love was trumped by the anger of seeing it manipulated, his son no more than a glove puppet for the diabolic hand inside.

Emile's face tightened between lines of scorn and circles of agony, his open mouth spraying a jet of concentrated urine over the Rector's Aquascutum tailoring. 'Gentlemen, if you could help me with his arms and legs, I don't want to hurt him but you'll have to be heavy with the boy, he's not quite himself at the moment.'

'No shit,' said Martin and landed clumsily on Emile's legs, twisting one badly. He looked at the boy apologetically and transferred his weight as best he could to the leg that was still kicking. Conti steadied the boy's flailing hands by drawing them in, shouting, 'It'll be all right Emile, just take it easy.'

It was apparent, had an impartial deity been there to watch them (and what watched them then was not impartial), that neither Emile, Martin nor Conti knew whom they were acting for or what they were fighting against, their assigned parts having imploded in the fog of war.

'Lurking coward, father of all lies, defeated rebel, traitor be shamed, be thrust into the pit, promiser of vain victories, be thrust into the pit and everlasting death,' the Rector incanted, his voice barely audible over Emile's screams, 'Iblis, Lucifer, brightest of all of God's creations and intelligences, where shall you go, where shall you hide from an avenging Lord?'

A licking sound came from deep within Emile, leisurely but deliberate, like a chewed up tape rewound in slow motion. The boy had stopped struggling. Above them was the shadow of a large cat climbing onto its hind legs; it's paws hacking at the air in an effort to keep its balance and re-enter the body it had left.

The Rector let go of Emile, faced the shadow and said, with slow deliberation, 'Now get out.'

For a moment it hung there, clawing desperately at the walls, its shrill whining echoing round the room.

'Go,' shouted the Rector, 'through the boy and out of our minds!'

There was an instant of atomic stillness before the shadow disintegrated into a plethora of hissing molecules, its parts falling away like a routed army, the whole floor reverberating with the sound of a hundred little footprints fleeing in panic.

The Rector waited until the air was still and the banging on the ceiling had ceased before checking Emile's pulse.

'Music to my ears,' he said, handing Conti his gently stirring son, 'There are certain things I wouldn't have the nerve to ask God's help for, but that was not one.'

'Oh man,' said Martin, his cricket whites never to be worn for their intended purpose again, 'oh man, man. Is it always? This stink when you've finished? Jesus, no, no I don't.'

'Evil never smells nice.'

'I'm sorry,' said Conti to his son, two large tears rolling off Emile's chin like broken spires from a falling steeple, 'for not feeling more than I have for you.'

The boy clung silently to his father's midriff, their connection enhanced if only for a moment.

'Never mind that,' said the Rector squeezing them both firmly, 'the lady of the house is probably wondering where we've got to.'

Brigit was speaking too quickly for her reluctant listeners, the words tumbling over one another in a race to escape their infernal source, 'I am a great red wound with heads and horns, ready to be devoured,' she babbled, *'devoured, you hear, devoured.'*

'You be quiet or else we'll make life difficult for you, whoever you say you are,' sniffed Judith, her wavering voice falling short of the commanding bark she was aiming for, 'Enough from you.'

'Women who set their minds on main matters, and sufficiently urge them, in these most difficult times, I find not many!' continued Brigit, her words clicking away like a hammer on a typewriter. 'Me? I dance upon nothing, take the earth bath, shake a cloth in the wind, go off at a fall of leaf, piss when I can't whistle and loll my tongue out at the company...' Looking pleased with herself, she lifted her eiderdown in the air, watching it fall away from her hands with exaggerated naivety, 'See? Like the cloud in the Persil advert!'

'It's like being stuck with a maniac,' said Judith in a stage whisper, rubbing the spit off her T-shirt, 'She needs a mental hospital, that's what she needs, muck and filth all over her. Who does she think she is, talking to us like this? We must be just as mad to stand for it.'

Her mother, who had dragged Brigit back to bed from the floor which she had earlier rolled onto, answered, 'No, she needs that man downstairs. He'll fix her. And hospital after that. Let her go before he sorts her out and she'll be back even worse, and not just for her but for us too.'

Judith eyed Brigit coldly, 'She's like a witch, ain't she? A ducking chair, that's what she needs. Look how she broke those windows. Normal people don't work like that.'

At this Brigit chuckled, and said in a mocking falsetto, 'A witch? Double penetration sisters! One in each hole! Or two sloppy snatches on one fat sausage! You filthy you-know-whats, taking advantage of my poor little brother! What did he look like, the little plum, sticking it into one slippery mess after the next, one after another, everyone taking turns. The rot's too foul, I can't bear the smell!' Brigit stuck two fingers in her nostril and broke wind loudly, bouncing herself up and down on the bed like an epileptic gymnast. 'Crabs, trouser tics!' she screamed, 'swill troughing, cock chaffing sluts!'

'I don't believe it; I've never been talked to like that before! We never did anything with your brother, you witch! Mum bought him in frozen drunk with his trousers round his ankles and we put him straight to bed, that's all.'

Archer put her hand on her daughter's shoulder, 'I don't like this at all. Try and ignore her. I'm serious girl.'

Brigit folded up on the bed laughing, her eyes watery with mirth. 'What a pair!'

'Can't you see she's making us for fools, speaking in that damn voice, it's her and her tricks underneath it, laughing at us,' exclaimed Judith as she made her way to the bed, 'I'll show her.'

'Judith, careful!' shouted her mother, 'She wants you to see red, she'll trap you!'

Brigit stopped suddenly and kicked at her bedpost, the wood snapping in half as though an axe had been taken to it, knocking Judith over with the force of a cudgel. Before her mother could come to her aide, the second post gave way, the heavy canopy it supported pushing the elderly servant on to the floor, where Conti and the Rector found her moments later.

Chapter Six

'I can't wake her,' said Conti, 'should we call an ambulance?'

'I think not,' the Rector replied.

Brigit was lying in the collapsed wreck of the bed, the mattress and bedclothes having slid onto the broken posts and her with them, an unrepentant sneer painted over the lips of her shrunken face.

In spite of the storm of sunlight piercing through the shattered windows, the room was cold and stank of the pub carpet at The Ship in Distress, a grubby odour of footprints, yeast and immaterial disillusion rising off the floor.

'Brigit, what have you done,' said Conti, holding the broken back of a mirror in his hand, 'you'll kill yourself.'

The ache in-between his ribs, where traditionally he felt heart ache but now only guilt, pounded steadily as he tried to lift her out of the mess to no avail. 'I can't understand it, she's as heavy as a dead body, but there's nothing to her to look at. And what's on her face? Jesus, God!'

Brigit's complexion, though having deteriorated since becoming bed bound, was now showing signs of open cracking, her skin breaking apart in dark fault lines that spread over her like spiders' webs.

'I don't recognise this... this person as my wife. It's something else.'

The Rector waved him to the door. 'She's in a self-induced trance. Leave her there for the moment. It's not for nothing that Sunday school tells you cleanliness is next to Godliness. The filth in here helps evil concentrate its energy.'

Conti let Brigit down, a wintry sense of failure animating his steps back to the door. For months each parting with Brigit had been like saying goodbye to someone who had already left, the occasional glimpse of aspects of her old self teasers to lead him on, in the hope that the real her was only hiding. 'I should have done something earlier instead of waiting for...something like this to happen.'

The scene in the corridor resembled a conjuring trick gone wrong. Judith lay stretched out with a large pack of peas pressed to her shoulder, her ankles wobbling in shock, as Archer nursed a small cut on her hand, her arm jangling with barely repressed rage.

'You've got to do something now.'

'Patience, please.'

Above them, Martin, bepissed and beshitted, stood somewhat ludicrously with a jug of water and towel wrapped round his waist. Emile held awkwardly in his free hand. 'She bought this on herself, man, she asked for it, asked for it. Too many bloody books.'

Wriggling free of his uncle's grip, Emile briefly acknowledged his mother with an apologetic look that spoke of betrayal, before turning and running down the stairs. 'I don't want to live here any more,' he called back, 'I want us to go to town where it's light and there are other boys.'

'Shit,' said Martin, 'I know what he means. Downstairs was enough for me. I'd rather not have to go in there and see her now.'

'You seem to be in control of the situation for the moment Martin, but don't worry; we shan't need you for what's to follow. Hartley, a few words please.'

The Rector led Conti down along the corridor, stopping by a porthole window that he pushed open. A gust of wind blew over their faces, happier times and other places carried in its promise of elsewhere.

'That's God's breath' said the Rector, his eyes closed.

Conti said nothing, the freshness lifting him as he had always hoped country life eventually would. Dimly he remembered standing in the same spot with Brigit a year earlier, some remark of hers having made them stop. Stood there, Brigit had wondered what all their friends were doing at that precise moment. Having run through several possibilities, the one thing they had been able to agree on is that wherever they may be, their friends would all be happier than they were. Recollecting how sad Brigit was that day, Conti felt like crying, a spasm of self-revulsion preventing him from adding to his embarrassment. Squeezing his fingers into a fist he said, 'We're minnows, small fry, why us?'

'Why not you?'

'Because what are we compared to the real evil players in the world, how did he even notice us? The CIA fry the genitals of liberation theologians, the Russians bomb the bugger out of Afghanistan, this very village is probably full of kiddie fiddlers and rapists, but the Devil, according to you, chooses my family and me. I mean, I know *fairness* isn't a quality we associate with him, but perverse as he is, we're slender pickings.'

'It's not as simple as that.'

'I know, and don't misunderstand me, what you did for Emile was a miracle, unbelievable, I saw it with my own eyes and I believe you. But what I can't accept is why all this *madness* should have happened to us in the first place. That's why you may find me ungrateful. I can't help it. We haven't really deserved it, and if I accept this Iblis as evil I have to accept God as just, and that I can't do. None of it makes any sense.'

The Rector cut in quietly, 'You're asking why lightning misses me and hits you, why you should rise and I should not, why there are dangerous snakes in these woods but harmless ones in yours? All this stuff you never thought of asking, now strikes you as relevant, because you didn't expect life to mean anything before. You never did anything to deserve these calamities, sure enough, but then what had you ever done to deserve a *good* life?'

'You're right. I got on with life, unexamined. My apologies if all this is a bit old hat to a seasoned veteran like you.'

'Only a martyr wouldn't want answers.'

Conti tried to force a smile. 'I'm not one of those. I don't know what Brigit's suffering is supposed to mean, and I want to. Like knowing why the Ethiopians starve, or the Jews were gassed.'

'Should it mean anything? It's truth and truth is the production of reality, it doesn't have to *mean* anything.'

'The truth shouldn't be meaningless, why…'

The Rector slammed the window shut. 'Listen, "why?" sounds profound but it's what children ask, "why, why, why?" Infants not yet reconciled to our condition. What did God stand to gain from making us? His power rests *precisely* on our not knowing. Life is to be withstood, not understood. The only thing that has changed is your attitude to it. We know what we need to know to survive, there's an existential spuriousness in aiming any higher than that. Take this news on the chin, because you have all you need to worry about at the end of that corridor.'

Conti reached into his pocket for a Silk Cut, pulled one out and lit it, the familiar smell of tobacco having the grounding effect he had counted on. 'If you think you can do to Brigit what you did to Emile, exorcise her too, then I'd be pleased to never entertain an intellectually curious thought again. And then in maybe 40 years time I can look back from my time share apartment in Majorca and laugh about the winter when I believed in the Devil.'

'I'm sorry to disappoint you, but what you witnessed downstairs was no exorcism, only the chasing out of a very bad smell. Proper evil needs stimulation, a smart host body to dwell in. Where stimulation is lacking what you end up with is brute animal spirits like those in the boy. They're simple to dispatch. Iblis will not be quite so easy.'

'I didn't think so.' Conti was crestfallen.

'This is what I needed to say. Augustus Crook, the purple priest who told you about me, warned me that your wife's possession is "perfect", which means the demon would not surface or declare itself. If your wife doesn't wish to acknowledge the possession, or pretends it's just her being herself and accepts its hold, then she's incapable of freely denying it. To save her, I have to draw out Iblis. What gives me hope is that she can't have submitted fully and completely like so many others have...'

'Others... in *England*, like Brigit?'

'Of course, the majority don't even know it.'

'Who the hell are they! Lunatics and perverts?' As Conti drew on his cigarette, an unpleasant vision of Squeers in the car park of the Green Man came to mind.

'Only a handful are what you'd call lunatics, most appear sane, possessed by money, or luxury goods, drugs and status. What they all have in common is that they believe their condition is "normal". Low-level "perfect" possession is much more common now than it was a hundred years ago. It thrives in a greedy epoch. Look into the eyes of every corporate whore and you'll see it.'

'But then wouldn't the whole world be going mad...'

'Isn't it? Possession in most carriers is a seamless, private affair compatible with the rot of dominant reality. That's why your wife's possession is different. In most cases Iblis does not want to kill, only exercise complete control through possession. But your wife is being physically destroyed because something in her cannot give consent or reciprocate. If people choose to live like objects then they can be occupied as objects, dumb unthinking vessels. For evil, your wife is a tempting challenge.'

'All of a sudden I can understand why me and Martin are safe.'

'You can?' the Rector stroked his moustache, 'Enlighten me.'

'Because we're a pair of cunts aren't we? Without souls to lose, we destroyed them ourselves. I don't see what's to stop me making a hostage of myself and trading Brigit out of her fix. A dud for one that works.'

The Rector shook his head ruefully. 'The Devil likes pacts but tends to not keep his end of the bargain, and besides, it wouldn't work because you don't truly believe in Jesus. You just don't care what happens to you.'

'Do you blame me, what do I have left to lose?' Conti flicked his cigarette stub out of the window. 'I look at Brigit and I don't see a single thing in her that I recognise as human, let alone the woman I loved. Before you arrived she, or "it" was pretending to be my old University Professor, and two days before that it was mimicking my first girlfriend! Of course I still care, but we could be trying to save a monster that rolled off a flying saucer for all I know about that *thing* in there. It's even changed what she looks like, you saw...'

'Hartley...'

'No, let me say this. You tell me all this time that Iblis was hiding in her, waiting for us to come to this hell house like a time bomb,' Conti exhaled like someone winded in the solar plexus, 'so...'

'Yes, it's an unholy trinity, Iblis, your wife and Tyger Tyger, each seeking a part of the other...'

'That's why it's worse than being told your wife was fucking another man, or had a secret life. Knowing this evil was inside her all along, stops me from trusting any of the good times we had, everything I loved about her is tainted, do you understand? I feel like a fucking fool for thinking I knew her, and for trusting what I thought and felt in *here*,' Conti thumped his Pierre Cardin shirt. 'Jesus, what am I trying to say?'

The Rector touched Conti's hand, 'Listen Hartley, good runs the surfaces, it has to otherwise they don't work, evil exists below them but that doesn't render the surfaces false or meaningless. Evil isn't any truer than good.'

'It seems more real to me than good; it has a life of its own, always waiting to be tapped into, participated in...'

'This is to do with its *irreducibility*, its effect can never be wholly explained by its cause. Our understanding always lags behind the deeds it inspires. We are at the point where material horror, and what you used to think of as the supernatural, have *merged*. Listen to me though; neither good nor evil have the final say on what is *real*. They're both in conflict, sustaining each other with no last word until all struggles cease. The monotheists call that "judgment day", but before that there's the apocalypse…'

The Rector winked and pointed up the corridor to Brigit's room, 'Let me do the talking, and remember, evil can't bear truth, where there's a lack of it, Iblis prospers, but the closer you move to truth, the weaker *he* will be. Trust the good times with your wife, remember her face, and you'll see it again.'

They found Brigit naked, standing between an upright mattress and the wall. She looked as if she had crawled out of a pyramid of bodies, only her long hair and the absence of a tattoo distinguishing her from the victims of the 20th century's most notorious genocide.

'Is it my bedtime already? You can't find me!'

'You've already slept,' said Conti, folding his arms. He felt like a boyfriend, incapable of accepting that a former partner has moved on, eager to coax one last sign that a fragment of their love has endured. 'We can't leave you alone any more. You'll die. So you're going to have to trust this man Brigit. I don't know what else can help you.'

'*Please* let me stay up longer!'

It was difficult to avoid coming to the conclusion, watching the crusts of scum encased round her mouth crumble apart, that the worst had already happened and that there was no one left to save. Quickly Conti checked himself, his pessimism succumbing to what the demon in Brigit wanted him to feel, if the Rector was to be believed.

'I have someone new to introduce to you Brigit.'

'Have you hidden my clothes, naughty, adulterous Hartley?'

'Just try and be calm, listen…'

'I want to Hartley, but the trouble is I can see through you! I'm not stupid trusting Brigit anymore! How can I listen to a man I no longer respect, I see your little dalliances and humbug for what it is, vain attempts to save your conscience, however well meant...'

'However I've hurt you Brigit, I didn't mean to, I never meant deliberate harm... I thought I could seperate things.'

The Rector tapped the knot on his tie twice. Conti took it as a signal that no more was required of him for the moment, the fight for Brigit's soul no longer a domestic matter.

'Sssshhhh!' sniggered Brigit jumping out from behind the mattress, the smell of freshly crushed road-kill wafting off her armpits, 'If Hartley can't explain himself, nor will his wifey!'

The Rector glared at her coldly, 'We could have this conversation without speaking but I'd rather hear you.'

'Not for free!' laughed Brigit knowingly, 'I don't put it about for nothing, do I Hartley? Isn't it wonderful, how the self-educated process information? Where did you find your telepathic friend? Selling joss sticks outside Brixton tube? At a Rock Against Racism gig, tee hee! The incontinent versus the impotent!'

The Rector sighed patiently, tapped a cigar against the shredded remains of the dressing table and spat on the floor. 'Who are you and what have you done to Brigit?'

'You've got to kill to care!' Brigit chortled, 'she's in here, humping darkies as we speak, heeee!'

'And who are you, since you're not Brigit?'

'I'm a lady girl if you know what I mean,' said Brigit, nudging the air, 'but you can start addressing me by real name whenever you like.'

'What is your real name?'

'Scabtape.'

'Is that so?'

'Screwtree.'

'Uh huh.'

'Screwtape and Scabtree, are both me!'

'Bullshit.'

'I don't have a name, priest, I'm a fucking idea,' the voice had grown low, angry and gruff, the colour of Brigit's eyes changing from brown to a yellowy red, 'Respect me, or you won't leave here the same as you came in.'

'That's very clever, changing the colour of your eyes to that of sunsets, they have a special significance for you, don't they?'

'You tell me, the music's too loud in here for me to hear.'

'You said you were an idea, what kind of idea?'

'One that fucks and doesn't kiss, you know the one.'

'I can't say I do, I don't trust visions or theories that make a virtue of lacking love.'

'Are you trying to make me, priest?'

'My name is Rector, you know it already. You still haven't told me your name.'

'I will not bow down to a mortal made out of dark clay and black mud. I was made from the fire of scorched air. I am the Creator!'

'You are a liar, you cannot make or create, only latch onto other lives like a parasite.'

'I am a killer. Those I cross pray for death.'

'Life chooses itself over all other options, even death.'

'Ambition in the back of a black car, you know what I mean? Your seed in one weaker than you, huh? You fuck?'

'I admire the shape of women as I admire all of God's creations. Answer my question, *what* are you?'

'Talking to you nigger is the spiritual equivalent of eating too many chocolates. Bitter dark ones.'

The Rector clicked his tongue and touched his cross. Brigit flinched.

'Crosses? You think I believe in the power of those.'

'Neither of us has to. All I need to do is think of it as good, like you do when you recite prayers back to front, trying to be evil. The meaning is in the intention we attribute to the object. If you have no use for truth, why should we?'

'Fuck your philosophising. *Slave.* You've made the wrong choice.'

The Rector bent over her so their faces were practically touching, 'I will talk and you will listen. Slave? To choose God is not to choose slavery or relief but heroic and unbearable freedom. Your master does not have all the best tunes. He is not more *interesting* than God. He wants you to forget that you are a human being who has been given a freewill in the likeness of God. I believe in the agony of free will. But you already know that.'

'Boring, boring.'

'Have you considered what it would be like to be expelled, disgraced, condemned, deprived, and defeated forever...like the one you serve, or perhaps the one you are?'

'What are you talking about, you strange little man?'

'The Ritual of Exorcism.'

'Is the reason you read from those stupid rituals because you know that the prayers you construct in your own words, spoken in your voice, would be too embarrassing to credit as meaningful? And shouldn't you have a woman of repute with you, if you are going by the book and exorcising a woman? I've never met a priest like you before.'

'Are you a woman?'

'Sometimes,' Brigit leered, 'where the wind is a raven, the trees are snakes, rocks are giant ants and the sky sticks its tongue out and sings songs in every room in the house, then, yes, I am a woman. This house priest, its songs are millions of years old. I am the sunset and the dusk... the atomic consecration of the angel of light...' Brigit paused and pointed to her crotch where a small trickle of blood had emerged. Sighing languidly, her pupils turned white and she let her head fall to one side.

The Rector snapped his fingers. Brigit came to with a sharp little shriek.

'I thought your "Body Without Organs" had no need of that

kind of Edgar Allen Poe mumbo jumbo.'

'No,' replied Brigit, her voice adopting Squeers' lisp, 'the "Body without Organs" was the process that bought me to him... Save me, save me! I dare you!'

'Rector, look at her face,' said Conti.

Brigit had begun to shudder and with it her features had grown pink, an unaffected prettiness replacing the haggard mask that possession had bequeathed her. Conti rushed up to her and grabbed his wife's contracting body, 'Look, she's changing back to how she was, you've done it...'

'Hartley, you hurt me by sleeping with all those women. How can I ever forgive you?' Brigit spoke tenderly.

'Rector, it's her voice!'

'Spit at her!' said the Rector, 'quickly, for your own sanity, spit at her face and the demon will be revealed!'

'Are you mad, look at her, she's recovering!'

'Don't be deceived. Do it.'

To trust his instincts and hold Brigit close to him, or to listen to a madman who had crashed in to his life that morning? A part of Conti could not believe that he could even ask the question, let alone answer as he was about to. Hocking up a mouthful of saliva, Conti exited it over his wife's imploring eyes. Guiltily he braced himself for the sight of Brigit's phlegm coated face.

Instead he saw what had kept hell burning through eternity ask him, 'Kiss me Hartley, am I not your wife?'

Whether he lost consciousness or not he did not know, but he was on the floor when he next heard the figure address him, 'How shall I talk, how would you like me to be now that you see me as I am? I taught Eve what she did not know, are you here for instruction also?'

'Is it real,' Conti asked, trying to control the trembling that had spread right through him, 'or are we being sold an illusion? Can you see this and live?'

Before them was a feminised man, so indeterminate as to

border on the beautiful, his naked body poised between genders. Playfully he pointed to his painted torso; its lewd existence a taboo his erect member dared the watchers to ignore.

'We're alive, aren't we?' replied the Rector, 'He's showing us what he thinks we expect to see. The Devil's playing the Devil.'

He laughed, 'I have fires for eyes. The adulterer and pantomime Moor! Would you have me speak in the voice of a parishioner you seduced Rector, or the woman whom you sought to torture in this very room? I see it in a single look of yours, all your doubts... God has never shown himself to you, but I have. Am I not a fallen Angel of Light?'

Collecting his wits, the Rector said quietly, 'If before this day we have forgotten you Lord, do not now forget us.'

'You flatter yourself! What is there to be gained by tiresome prayers that bore and intimidate you in equal measure? Or the Church with its bishops and popes, a revolting caricature of Christ's teachings! They never told you Adam walked out of the sea as a fish or the Gospels were written generations after Jesus' death, did they, Rector? Compare the pomp of the Vatican with the plain hills of Galilee!'

'Beautiful, and not a word too long, are you about to offer me the world?' asked the Rector, 'You have a reputation for empty gestures which precedes you.'

'Hear me Rector, I am truth, you are dogma, I am life, you are sleep, I am an angel who has seen the Lord, you are not even a slave. I survive science and atheism, meteorites and stars, geometry and metaphysics. I pour fire on a slave morality not strong enough to withstand the doubts of a 12-year-old. You have never known reverence or awe, only four walls to protect you from my voice, your voice Rector. And your Exorcisms! Laughable acts of petty heroism.'

'Iblis,' the Rector replied, 'if that is who you are, you have discovered my weakness, my arrogance and pride. All you say is true, but true *only* if my doubts and your voice, and not God, are the measure of things. I have learnt to overcome myself, as you have not. You believe my pride is as great as yours, but I allow you to knock me down with mine. You, though, will be destroyed by yours. I ask you again, what *are* you?'

The figure he was addressing had changed its appearance with each defiant word, so that by the time he had finished, the Rector was speaking to Brigit again, the apparition of "Iblis" fading onto the form of a broken woman on her knees.

'I'm having a very bad dream... I've hurt you Hartley but it's no worse than the hurt you're inflicting on me. Stop this and talk. You loved me, we *knew* each other,' begged Brigit.

'No,' replied the Rector, 'I cannot let you come and go as you please, or hide. You are no woman. Tell me, what are you?'

'She's my wife, my wife, Rector, I can feel the difference. You've won her back.'

'Get a grip man, have you forgotten what you just saw? You're being played again.'

Weeping loudly, Brigit had crawled under a blanket and drawn it over her ears, her frailty pitifully visible, 'Why? I'm your baby asking you for what sin I've been killed, why are you letting him do this to me, Hartley?'

'She's taken enough Rector, whatever was there; it's gone, at least for now. Look at her.'

'Can you take that risk?'

'I feel like I have to. We'll kill her otherwise.'

'Do you want to live like this for the rest of you life, scared every time you hear knocking or terrified to see that your wife has that devilish glint in her eye again? He'll keep returning. We have defeated your wife, not the demon. That means it wins.'

'Damn the demon and winning, I have my wife back, that's enough. You can carry on the war in heaven with some other guinea pig. For now we've beaten the thing, it's gone.'

'Listen to me,' said the Rector, his hand around Conti's neck, 'how long do you think before it's back, maybe not as a Devil but in another form, perhaps harder to detect but more dangerous? Who would stop it, do you think you could? We've done something just now Hartley, we've stared down the face of perfectly realised evil and survived. But it'll amount to nothing if we don't finish Iblis off. Otherwise Brigit would be vulnerable for the rest of her days and maybe you would be too. This is about wits and wills, and if we're outwitted there'll be no second act. Look at her Hartley and don't be fooled. Beneath that blanket is a brief respite, not your wife. Nothing could be more dangerous than leaving her like this.'

'Except perhaps leaving her to us?'

'Ah yes,' smiled the Rector, somewhat sadistically, 'Iblis wouldn't be playing the raped slave if he didn't find us a scary proposition.'

There was laughter from under the blanket, a pair of yellow eyes peeping out at them. Conti stared back, defiant, not afraid, at least not for himself, any more.

Book Three:

WEST END GIRLS

In accepting himself in this way without curiosity about God and without problems, Man is now nothing but an inert Automaton, generating boredom and madness, which all consciousness has abandoned, and which the still pure soul has fled, because it senses in advance the moment when this Automaton will give birth to the Beast and the Beast to an obscene Demon.

Antonin Artaud

Chapter Seven

One day later.

The Rector pulled the torn curtains together, the more ragged of the two nearly came off in his hand. He was dressed in a red and gold tracksuit, conveying an athletic air that its designers would have considered a free advertisement.

'Is it daytime,' asked Brigit feebly, 'Tell me Hartley, I've had such bad dreams.'

Saying nothing, the Rector wiped a lump of antiseptic cream over the dried cuts on Brigit's cheeks.

Brigit giggled coquettishly and then clenching her face like a fist she said, 'What's the use, all that will survive of me is hate, and that's not worth keeping. I've seen what goes on behind closed doors. Don't you remember the first time you heard someone talk behind your back? How you thought you could never return to social life again? Well I can't and no one can make me...'

'You're all alone now,' interrupted the Rector, 'and I think you know what that means.'

*

'He said no prayer I recognised, chanted nothing you'd hear in a church, there was no holy water or rituals. But he got somewhere with her,' said Conti to Martin, as the train neared London Waterloo, 'He knocked her front down. I believe in him, even if he hasn't told us everything.'

'I thought he was a prick at first,' said Martin wiping his nose on a flaky tissue, 'but even if he's making it up as he goes along, he still gets my vote. Usually if a guy does you a favour, you want to know what he gets in return. But the man's a hunter, he does it because he loves it.'

'I wouldn't have left him alone in that house with her if I didn't trust him, not that Brigit has any need for me, or wants me there.'

'Or any of us.'

'He said that once "Iblis" declares himself, then its control over Brigit fades. I think we saw him for a moment yesterday.' Conti grimaced, 'It was uncanny, real but not really, his face was beautiful, like I've always imagined a vision would be.'

'Don't overcomplicate things. It's the fucking *Devil*, man.'

'Sometimes I think so too. And then I think it might be something weirder than that. An ancient psychic virus that he's got to rid her of. And the reason why he uses all this religious stuff is because it's a method that works with us humans who've been bought up with it, not because it's *true*. If we were in Africa, The Rector would probably be conjuring up the names of the local spirits, and who knows what other strange Gods, but in Hampshire it's Christ and the Bible.'

'Sure,' Martin replied absently, 'Africans are bloody crazy. But believe what you like, when you were there, and you saw what you saw, you knew it was no damn mental virus. You know what this reminds me of? Just because we're a pair of idiots who talk crap and think like goofs doesn't mean real evil isn't amongst us and hell's not where we're going. That Rector has it right. It's in his hands now. I've tried to stop thinking about it and maybe it'll forget about me. That's what makes the world go round, man, knowing when to stick your head in the sand.'

Martin paused for effect and tried to smooth the crease out of what was meant to be a baggy suit, but was some sizes too small for him. Dressed in white linen and plastic imitation deck shoes, it was hard not to feel sorry for him, and it occurred to Conti that his brother-in-law was no safer than Brigit. They had all come into open contact with whatever it was now, and they had all heard Brigit's parting words, screamed down the steps, 'Wherever you shall go, I will follow...'

'So long as it goes, who cares where it comes from or who it follows...' murmured Chantal, her head resting on the window, 'It wouldn't like it here anyway. It isn't a city kind of monster.'

The rickety train carriage they were riding in already appeared too old for the landscape they passed; a loft conversion, neat semi circles of Barrett homes, retail trading estates and the odd midlevel office block, a world of come and go that had noisily replaced the one Conti knew. If the gap between town and country could be bridged so swiftly, then there was no barrier separating the problems they were leaving from those that lay ahead.

'I hate it,' Chantal said to herself, tucking her hand under Conti's thigh, her fingers honouring an old habit, 'the city is so new and depressing.'

'Compared to where we've come from?' said Martin, 'You've got to be kidding.'

'What do you mean, I like being locked in a room by Archer and treated like a little infant,' grinned Chantal, 'What more could a girl want?'

'What are you going to do in London?' asked Conti, still uncomfortable about the way Archer had confined Chantal.

'Selfridges is where they say you should go, then on to that club you were talking about. You?'

'There's an old lecturer of mine I want to look up. Brigit took on some aspects of this man's personality before the Rector arrived and I've had a feeling about him. He might be at the heart of a few loose ends. I thought it would be enlightening if he and I compared notes. He was a formidable teacher, or at least that's how he seemed to us at the time. Can you take Chantal shopping with you and I'll join you later on at the club. And don't lose your phone card.'

'Cool,' Martin nodded. 'Your professor, you were

mentioning... you believe he's connected somehow, otherwise why go and compare notes?'

'I thought you wanted to forget about it.'

'I have. I've forgotten. I'm only asking about him because I'm scared to shit you'll stir something up again for the rest of us!'

'He's the opposite of all this, but somehow, I sense, he may be tied up in it. Karel Mikes has no time at all for anything that only relies on *experience* for its truth. He believes in theory like a fanatic, he's a big ideas man like I used to kid myself to be.'

'You could have said the same about me. I believed in the theory of waking up in the morning and eating your cereal. Now I'd say yes to werewolves, the Abominable Snow Man and giant lizards,' said Martin tersely. 'All good, man, all good.'

'He's different,' Conti shook his head. 'He has entire books that tell you why it's impossible to believe in those things.'

'Books,' Martin snorted, 'whatever, man, but you must think he *knows* something otherwise why go... Like I told you, let it lie and leave it to the professional, you've suffered enough. And remember, all this shit was going on before we knew about it, the danger for us was tuning into its frequency. Time to tune back out.'

'You're right. I do want to know something and I think he can help me with whatever that is. But don't get me wrong, once this is over and your sister is better, that's it for me. I'll follow your advice and leave the hunt for Iblis's acolytes to the Rector.'

'Amen to that.'

'Yeah, amen,' said Conti, edging Chantal's hand away from his crotch. She bit her lip and held her fingers firmly where they were. The Rector had warned him of the mistake of loving two women at once, and how, if he could not commit, he risked losing them both to a fate worse than other men. It was a problem Conti was content to address another day, the sexual arousal that fear leaves behind was beginning to impose itself.

Martin watched, feeling no loyalty to his bed-bound sister,

only the self-pity and exclusion that follows a thwarted sense of entitlement, his identity shattered. He could never pretend to be an ordinary bloke again. It was hard for him to know what was left for him. Closing his eyes he tried to picture a chubby Asian prostitute he had embarrassed with a drunken, but sincere offer of marriage. The knowledge that she had rejected it, and not even slept with him, jerked him to wakefulness, his eyes catching Chantal's reptilian glare.

'They say the only thing that can harm a sleeping man is a memory,' she said cruelly, and dug her hand further into Conti's thigh.

The three sat in silence for the rest of the journey, as teenagers taking in different lessons from a party that had changed them forever might. Reality of a kind had returned, but they were no longer able to have faith in it. The Rector had told them that for the Exorcism to succeed they would have to leave. Its execution would be too harrowing for relatives to witness or be a party to. Judith had taken Emile to her aunt's and Archer had remained as his assistant. No one had thought of arguing with him after the night that had followed his first "interview", one so discomfiting that Conti did not think they could last another unless he was allowed to do as he wished. Which had been what the man from the hills had intended all along, Conti guessed, as the train came to a standstill and he breathed the same air that he had in the delivery ward 33 years earlier, its unwelcoming translucence the still point of a turning world.

To Archer's ears, the noise coming from Brigit's bedroom sounded like a married couple arguing, punctuated every few minutes by a herd of animals being chased off a cliff. All her life she had wanted those better off than her to know hardship just as she had, their lives untouched by even the faintest glimpse of the suffering she had known and endured. Was there something evil about holding to this desire, because in Brigit's possession it had been answered, and Archer still did not know whether she should feel guilty for harbouring it. It was normal for everyone to carry a little bit of ill will in them, and, she had thought, it was perfectly safe for them to do so too. But there was something in the quality of Brigit's screams that foretold of a moment when all such considerations would be laid aside and Archer would have to take responsibility for the house she served, and by implication, the purpose it stood for. If ever she had been in any doubt over what that was, and she had to admit that she never really had, Brigit's pleas for mercy seemed to say, 'Your time of reckoning is going to come.' 'Yes, but after yours,' said Archer answering her thought, 'after yours, my dear.'

*

For twenty-five years Karel Mikes had misled his students into believing that academia would tolerate difference in its ranks because it employed him. His status as the member of staff it was permissible to drink with owed much to his middle-European exuberance and little to his avowed aim of forming a revolutionary vanguard against the governors of the newly opened business school. A slight and impish man with no interest in his Chair of Sociology, but plenty in Romany dancing and bottom pinching, Mikes had constructed a series of lectures in which his life story was entwined with that of the century, his hopeful narrative ending with full communism and personal vindication.

Over the semesters, new students replaced the old, events unravelled, and privately Mikes acknowledged that relative harmlessness, denied to him in his formative years, was a fair price to pay for a venerable old age. After all, he reasoned, as a corrupter of young minds there was no dishonour in choosing influence over power, and the long view of history over the short. He could not have known that the majority of his students would end up in Interior Design not Utopia, but even if he had,

Conti thought, he would have said that history was full of futile gestures, no less noble for their uselessness.

Conti put his cigarette out against a bus stop and wondered whether Mikes had sold out in the fifteen years since he had last seen him, drunk at a fundraising event for striking dustmen. The signs were that his former hero had come to some kind of accommodation with normality. The languid Wimbledon street where Mikes lived exuded the sameness of a black hole on a never-ending Tuesday afternoon, the distant song of an ice cream van and rumble of stalled engines completing the preternatural effect. Whereas its residents saw timelessness and serenity, Conti felt the long reach of Capital slither round his ankles, the holding areas of the suburbs a soft prelude to the killing grounds of the Stock Exchange and the square mile of the City an Underground ride away. Time did not divide up into days here; it settled into depressions influenced by what happened elsewhere, its fears and those Conti entertained for himself bleeding into one another.

'Wherever you go I shall follow...'

An unannounced southerly wind blew past, reminding him of why he'd fled his cursed corner of Hampshire, its agony carried in specks of earth Brigit had walked over. An instinct towards self-preservation told him to disappear, but Conti knew that outer London could offer no more than a brief hiding place. The beast that moved between daylight and darkness, with no identifiable point of conversion had already followed him here. At its command trees leered at him one moment before standing benignly upright the next, cats crossed roads to avoid bad luck, and pigeons found somewhere else to defecate, damned initiates in the race to rescue Brigit from her diabolic fate.

Conti stopped at Mikes' front door, the short track leading up to it, neatly flanked by dwarf conifers and a pair of fun size British Telecom budgerigars. Part of him hoped that he had confused the address with the set of a television sit com, not wanting to sacrifice the hope that Mikes could still offer an outpost of reason against sorcery. The Radio Times surroundings, and Mikes' insistence that he would only offer his counsel on the condition that Conti had not voted for the SDP in the last election, certainly did nothing to alleviate his doubts. The old man would either have to dismiss Conti's testimony out of hand, or agree with it and show that they were *both* insane, or else appreciate the contradiction, thus forfeiting his role as an unlikely ally in the war against... the Devil?

Conti cringed to think of it. Trying to sell the idea of Iblis to a Marxist émigré was more than his silver tongue could manage. But it was Elmhurst's letter that had told him to come... If Iblis existed here then the horrors of Tyger Tyger could not be part of a shared delusion they had collectively undergone. If Mikes believed, then anyone would.

'Just say hello, take it from there,' decided Conti, 'it'll be worth it to see him again.' Briskly he walked to the door, noticed his eyes in the frosted window, hammered at the knocker, too loudly, he felt, and waited for the anti-climax.

The door opened slowly enough for Conti to see that Mikes had changed. Momentarily ignoring Conti, the old man glanced up and down the street, his grey comb-over dangling over his pince-nez, 'Is there anyone else with you? Answer me man, answer quickly!'

'Not that I know of, Dr Mikes.'

Mikes smiled showing surprisingly carnivorous teeth, 'The flower beneath the foot Conti! What we lack nowadays are proper ivory towers. Wimbledon, a borough without hope, ripe for alien invasion! We hoped for the best but it turned out as always. Come in quickly.'

The house smelled fresher than Mikes appearance suggested, the smattering of food round his collar and egg stained cuffs at odds with the aroma of air freshener and furniture spray, that hung in the air.

Though Conti had expected signs of demise, the timidity of Mikes' movements were not consistent with his voice, which if anything, was cunningly sure of itself.

'I apologise, though I don't have to,' said Mikes, lowering himself on to a mustard brown settee placed prominently in a room of the same colour. 'As you can see, things have changed. Since I retired, my wife is too frightened to open windows, old world folk superstition. Here, have some of these, she buys so many biscuits we have to store them in boxes in the garden.'

'Wife? I don't remember you ever mentioning a Mrs Mikes,' said Conti, the complete absence of books and a shelf of small portable televisions diverting his attention from Mikes' whiskery nose.

'Ahh, he who speaks with all the passion of ignorance.' Mikes pointed at the kitchen where a woman even older than he, her hair tied back in a bun, was making a great show of sweeping spotless tiles.

'I didn't feel there was any point in bringing intellectual attention to her. It would have had no impact on your education and besides, she's very shy, aren't you Ritzy? Come out, show yourself, however many years in this country and she still can't speak a damned word of English!'

Conti looked for a natural way of hiding his discomfort. Mikes' wife had eyes he had seen before, ones that did not belong to their owner but bore the mark of another.

The old woman put down her broom, curtsied in a parody of a greeting and, turning her long black skirt towards them like a curtain, vanished behind a plastic slide partition.

'How did you two first meet?'

'I raped her.'

'I beg your pardon!' exclaimed Conti nearly choking on his squashed fly biscuit.

'I raped her, or at least I held on like I was protecting her and waited until she was too tired to pull away. The prelude to the consummation of our first night together you might say,' Mikes flexed his elbow and winked. 'You Englishmen are too polite, though the gays are different I grant you. Your women don't respect you. They wonder what's wrong with their little men. We all know a little rough stuff is good for the soul. I had my way with Ritzy and haven't been unfaithful since. I got it all out of my system at once, so to speak. A man can be happy with a single woman all his life but he can't be sexually fulfilled by her unless she's capable of being several different people once the lights are out, if you follow me?' Mikes slapped his leg and laughed loudly, a shower of biscuit crumbs crash landing over his lap.

Conti wished he could leave at once. Mikes, who had evidently lost his marbles, might not even consider it rude. But an appalled fascination held him where he was. This was a man he had respected, but rarely understood. Now an understanding was there but the respect was not, leaving Conti sorry for them both. 'You're joking, aren't you?'

'Don't take it personally. Don't take it all! Old men and children are alike; they can get away with saying what they want, though whether that's what society wants to hear is a different matter.'

Conti relaxed slightly, 'You always did like to shock, didn't you Dr Mikes, and thinking about it, Women's Lib was never exactly your area of the Left.'

Mikes sighed good-naturedly and put his foot up on Conti's armrest, close to his arm. 'And your wife? You say you got married. Where is she? Afraid the old rogue would come in for a slice of the action, eh? No, of course I'm only joking with you. Ritzy is the only crackling for this old thruster!'

'My wife isn't in the best of health…'

'She needs to wrap up.'

'It's not that, she suffers from a rare type of mental health problem, though it's not as straightforward as that sounds…'

'Go on, no secrets between mentor and disciple!'

'Well, you could say that she's going through a big stage of unloving me at the moment, and not only me, but everything else too. It's been quite a testing time, very severe. Which reminds me, I can't remember if you've ever met her?'

'Disappointment, that's what ails her. Time has a way of demonstrating that we're not the people we wanted to be. The wrong decisions ruin lives. You've no need of a moral philosophy once you've grasped that. Buy her some chocolates, it'll cheer her up. Complicated problems often have simple causes and easy solutions.'

Conti paused, and then said it anyway, 'Dr Mikes, are you putting on an act?'

'What?' Mikes looked angry, 'what did you say?'

'I asked whether you still write?' Conti lied, the weight of lost illusions bearing heavily.

'Write you say? No, not since my last paper for "The Cheerful Nihilist" a few years back,' Mikes replied self-importantly, 'You probably read it at the time, if you still keep up, that is, the article is referenced all over the place these days, "Economics are only the method, the object is to change the Soul," a metaphysical take on Marx's materialism, you remember it of course?' Mikes paused solemnly, 'You don't? Well nor do I, ha ha ha! Even men of destiny aren't always on time! Ha ha!'

'What was it you said, that capitalist society respects its entertainers, but not its writers?' offered Conti, hoping he could lend Mikes' utterances a bone of dignity.

'Exactly, but they're not entertainers! Even intellectuals need a trip to the circus! Conti my boy, we were lied to but not about everything. Listen to what passes for opinion these days, talking heads not fit to wax Trotsky's moustache. "Human nature never changes" they say, but they're the first to agree that ideology is bankrupt because we live in a "completely different world!" These "realists", they're sons of bitches.'

'Yes.'

'Yes?'

'Yes,' repeated Conti, trying to get into the swing of things, 'it's sad but things will change for them like they changed for us. I've learnt not to get too used to anything.'

'Exactly! Reality is the narrowing of what is to come, with what is already here. But that's why I became a teacher, to take both sides of the quarrel. I'm for the Bolsheviks and Kronstadt, let the doers choose sides, I've decided to sit this one out. There's too much evil out there for us saints.'

Cautiously Conti responded, 'Evil? I don't remember you mentioning it like that before. You believe in it, evil, it's irreducibility?'

'No! I don't believe in anything at all now.'

'But wouldn't that precisely be the final victory of evil?'

'What nonsense are you talking about boy? Evil, whatever next? The law of God versus that of Man? Evil's just an expression for what men do, not a damned "thing". Listen. To get to my age and still think you're a general in the Spanish civil war, or that you could manage the national team of 1955 or get away with stealing next door's panties off the washing line, that's evil!'

Conti tried to change tack, 'You mentioned over the phone yesterday that you still remembered me...'

'Of course I remember you my boy!'

'Thank you, but you said your memory isn't what it used to be...'

'Tell me whose is?'

'No, of course, look, I don't mean to be impertinent but have you suffered from any serious amnesia recently, I don't mean dementia, more a rubbing away of periods or parts of your life? In a way that may have affected your personality perhaps?'

Mikes looked perplexed, then smiled darkly, 'no, not memory, you're barking up the wrong tree there boy. It's belief. That's what I lack today.'

'Belief in yourself you mean?'

'No! If I meant self-confidence I'd have said self-confidence! What I've lost is certainty and belief, and quite suddenly too, a month or so ago it all seemed to still be there in some capacity. And then nothing. I've sold all my books, stopped watching the news, given up completely on current affairs... ageing is what it is, or so Ritzy says. Half of me blames her, the things she's got involved in... I could tell you more, but I don't care enough to. It's all so recent, I'm not even sure I haven't imagined it, and tomorrow I'll wake up a militant again.'

'You don't think this built up slowly, gradual disenchantment? It's what a lot of people were waiting for, the final come down. The Left's been dropping by the wayside ever since the Tories were re-elected. '

'Ha! Nothing gradual about it, no way. You know, you shouldn't try and tell people what to think, it's an irritating habit I've noticed you've developed. Where was I?'

'Sudden change and loss of belief, Dr Mikes.'

'Ah yes, I was still an ardent Marxist who believed in the Communist future of mankind in January, then Ritzy gets involved with this man from the choir school and now look at me, I'm a bum who sits here growing lardy on biscuits and daytime television. Revolutions aren't made with double chins and arse fat.'

'What choir school man?'

'Belief,' said Mikes ignoring the question, 'it may have got you burnt at the stake or flayed alive but it was a mysterious thing that created beauty too... You have to want to believe, otherwise everything shows its flanks, is boiled down to its bare essentials and loses the sense in which it could be true.'

'You said that your wife...'

'Let's face it, if we had died before this crappy decade had begun, no one could say we were missing much, and now it's too late, the future is always with us.'

'Perhaps you need to be jolted out of it, a change of scene or engaging in another of those campaigns you were always organising.'

'No, those days are gone. I'm not great at spontaneity, Conti, oh no, writing and teaching are all about remembering that clever thing you wish you could have said at the time...'

'Me too, I suppose I dwell too much in the icy waters of calculation, to be spontaneous,' said Conti echoing Mike's way of pontificating. Out of one side of his eye he could see Ritzy spying on them, her black pupils following the flow of their mouths.

'No, all I believe in now,' continued Mikes, 'is that there is tenderness only in the coarsest demand, that no one should go hungry any more. My communist politics were no more than my revenge on humanity for possessing human nature, that's the true historical reality, not revolution. I don't know what you expected from this visit, but whatever it was I'm sure I haven't provided it. I tried to put on a little show to remind you of the old Mikes but you saw through me like I see through myself.'

'Maybe I had to,' agreed Conti too quickly, an uncomfortable tingling beginning behind his ears.

Mikes scowled, evidently not ready to be so hastily agreed with. 'You were never my favourite student actually, that's why I was slightly puzzled to hear from you. You were very far up yourself, you know. My favourite was Elmhurst, what happened to him?'

'He drove my car into a lorry several years ago. He was killed in it.'

'And why weren't you in there with him?'

'Because I was with his girlfriend at the time.'

'And what happened to her.'

'I married her. She's my wife. I asked you earlier but maybe you didn't hear me. Did you ever meet her?'

Mikes smiled. 'No, not with you.'

'But then with Tom?'

'And what if I did? Jealous are we? You talk of evil, take it from me. Evil revolves around what can no longer revolve around itself. It likes to replace things, goodness usually. So what of it, she carried the mark, the same as Ritzy.'

'What mark?

'I'm tired. Too much talking isn't good for me. It's time for you to go.'

Conti, brushing off Mikes' hostile tone, got up, the pain in his ears advancing in surges, 'Dr Mikes, please, you said that she carried a mark...'

Mikes grunted and waved his hand, 'Yes, a mark. You learn something new every day, eh? Man was made a rebel! Rebellion, good if you were not given enough, bad if you received more than you deserved in the first place.'

'You could help...' Mikes pushed Conti out to the tiny beige corridor, mid-sentence, following him predatorily. 'I don't see how,' he replied, 'I had high hopes for you and your whole generation when you were younger. Until I realised that all hope is the postponement of joy.'

Conti, resigned to gathering no more information, snapped, 'Frankly I'd rather postpone hope.'

Mikes shook with laughter and wrapped the side of the wall nearly knocking Ritzy down in the process. Screwing her face up she scuttled past him and waved a bony arm at Conti.

'Him!' she cried in perfect English, 'he runs from fire!'

'What?' Conti replied, cold spreading through his arms and chest, 'I apologise if I offended her in some way.'

'Hush boy,' said Mikes rudely, 'let Ritzy speak.'

Holding her hand protectively, Mikes urged his wife on, a salacious tint on his lips as the old woman hurriedly finished her accusation.

'Tell her I'm genuinely sorry for whatever it is.'

'Stop apologising.'

'See round his neck!' she pointed.

'What?'

Barging Conti out of the doorway, an elbow pressed artfully into his back, Mikes whispered, 'She says can't you see that there's a rope round your neck, the knot apparently is very, very thick.'

Without being given any time to answer, Mikes had pushed him out onto the street. Ritzy crouched hideously at his side yelling at him in her mother tongue.

'Move along, you've caused enough trouble here today.'

'Look, tell me what I've done…'

'You English,' Mikes shouted at Conti, who losing his balance fell backwards onto a dustbin, 'You're all the same, poofters, out for what you can get. You thought you could come here and seduce my wife! Well think again, a little birdie told me all about you, a bigger man than I is in your precious wife now, ha ha ha! Render unto him what is his!'

Conti winced, the screams in his ears worse than the elderly defective's laughter coming from outside. Raising two fingers he spat, 'You insane Nazi, don't you realise it's staked its claim in you too?'

'Claim? I claim *Iblis*! Don't you know the sound of a real man when you hear one?' his former tutor thundered ludicrously, pulling at his braces, 'because he knows all about you!'

So Mikes knew. Conti gazed skywards past the first pellets of rainfall, not too proud to search for relief in an obvious place. Above him hung a silent All-ness and beyond that an empty future to be filled with old gods or if he preferred, new realities. Turning his collar up and breaking into a trot, Conti skipped past a volley of twitching curtains to a cab that had stopped at the end of the road.

'All right there mate?' asked the driver.

'All depends on what you mean by "all right",' Conti replied dryly, the cacophony in his ears gently subsiding, 'The day has so many faces.'

The cab driver grinned, 'It's like that, eh? Where to?'

'The West End, teleport me.'

The cab driver laughed and pulled open the door, 'Bit of retail therapy, lovely jubbley.'

'God bless you,' said Conti, meaning it for once.

Chapter Eight

Archer was impressed with the way the Rector appeared to be taking his time. She felt that he had rushed into war the day before to show Conti, who had grown despondent, that it was still possible to be shocked into hope. Now that his point had been made the Rector had eased up, risen relatively late, dined on a breakfast of white wine, black pudding and marmalade, and even complimented Archer on her first aid skills.

'I must say,' she nearly sang, as she put down his mug of tea, 'that you are a very civilised gentleman. I knew a coloured person once, not very well I grant you, and he was nothing to write home about.'

'Really, where was he from?'

'Somewhere in Kent I think, though there could have been a bit of Chinese in there as well. He was a book keeper. Very foreign looking.'

'We come in all manner of guises. You place a lot of stock by locality, don't you?'

'It brings certain advantages.'

'Do you think the thing in this house cares where you come from?'

'Well, there's never been any trouble with those that were born here.'

'Perhaps that's because you have all come to some kind of accommodation with evil...'

Archer laughed boisterously, 'It's not us, but her upstairs that you should worry about. What have I ever done wrong?'

'Who said you had or that I was worrying about you! The reason I asked you to stay is because I know you to be a woman with a strong constitution.'

Archer rubbed her chin approvingly, a hair catching on her bandage. 'She was quiet last night, I didn't have to go in and tell her to pipe down once. Might be that you've taught her a lesson.'

'Most likely exhausted after all the attention we've given her.'

'Do you want to have another go at her once you've finished your tea? I'll say this, you've really got her on the back foot... I mean that *thing* in her on the back foot.'

'It's important to remember that it isn't her we're fighting.'

'Of course,' Archer conceded facetiously, 'once Mrs Conti is herself again I, for one, won't be bearing any grudges. It's rather like when somebody's had too much to drink isn't it? If they apologise the next morning then it's all right. Where's the harm in pulling their leg about it every now and then? So when do you reckon to another bash? I've never seen her look so scared, makes a change to see the boot on the other foot for a change.'

The Rector raised his hand, 'It can wait; it doesn't pay to indulge the beast, now that we've got the preliminaries out of the way.'

'I dare say you know best.'

'Experience, that's all.'

'Still.'

'Tell me Mrs Archer,' asked the Rector pleasantly, silent images of rioting on the portable television someone else's story, 'You've been here a long time, well before the Conti's arrival?'

'Oh yes, I go back donkeys years, over thirty at least.'

'And nothing like this...' the Rector pointed up at the ceiling, his tone still relaxed, 'has ever occurred before?'

'Not exactly.'

'That means no then?'

Archer looked away cautiously, 'I'm not stupid you know, I can tell what you're getting at. All these questions, about my being from here and you not.'

The Rector feigned a wounded expression, 'Perhaps you could tell me about the others. The other ones who came from somewhere else to live with you, with the house I mean.'

'Them.' Archer's countenance had paled considerably, 'I

suppose you could say there were *things* that happened. Some of the others who came would become unhappy here, very suddenly sometimes. One chap... an artist.'

'Do go on.'

'Well, he hanged himself,' Archer squirmed, 'and left a note saying a painting in his room made him do it.'

'Really...'

'Yes,' Archer pulled off her apron, her thumbs twitching, 'and another girl did herself in too, jumped out of a window because she was forced to sleep in a room she didn't like. And another fellow, his wife died in bed of shock, and he was awful sore because we never got to the bottom of what could have taken her by surprise so...'

The Rector raised his mug in a mock toast, 'Not a bad track record, and yet what interests me is that you've never been afraid to work here, or else I assume you'd have left.'

'I'm only a servant, why would anything be interested in interfering with me?'

'Does that mean your loyalty is to the house and not the owners?'

'As I say, I'm only a servant.'

'It sounds as though you think the presence in this house recognises class distinctions, which, if it's true, surprises me. Your husband, for instance, Judith told me last night that the end he met with was not exactly pleasant. Making deals with the Devil isn't a practice you come across every day.'

'She did, did she? Look here Rector, the kind of folk we're talking about are fast. We're slow, they see more than we do, but less of what matters. That's my take on people who come here thinking the world revolves around them. As for my husband, well he was bloody mad and everyone who met him knew it.'

'So they all had it coming then?'

'You're a sharp one, aren't you now! No, I won't have my words twisted round, though very clever you are at doing so.

They, and I mean those people who left, were plain ignorant of the way things are done round here, that's all, they couldn't adapt and fit in with what was already here.'

'Still, you can see how it looks to an outsider...all those people gone and you're still here. Unscathed. And all this information, which I expect has been yours to sit on from the start.'

'Anyway,' Archer blustered, her cheeks reddening, 'I've only mentioned the bad things that went on because you asked me. There were people who came to Tyger Tyger and took off bored, bored and angry, with nothing queer happening to them at all. Insensitive they were. There were a couple like that. Before the Contis in fact, they moved down the road to live closer to the Cathedral in the end, Townies truth be told. So it's not all doom and gloom. This place can be as dull as anywhere in the country.'

'But Mrs Conti *was* sensitive to what was already here, wasn't she?'

'Huh! If you ask me there was something wrong with that one when she arrived. The kind of things she ran in to, you find them in most places, tucked away under the stairs if you get my meaning. It takes one like her to get hooked, and once that happens you wish you'd never have looked in the first place.'

'This badness, what you say was already here. You've never "taken a look", or thought of asking yourself what it might be, even though you've made your life in its midst. I wonder why.'

'There are things here I'll never look at. Not if I'm under the same roof, country or world, I'll never look.'

'Why? This house has no allies. It's the vehicle through which a more powerful force enters the world. You may be right that it waits for the right person to secure its release, but you really believe turning a blind eye grants you security?'

Archer lifted a finger up to the ceiling, 'Asking myself silly questions about that that has no answer, and going poking my nose in things that aren't for me or any of us to know? Oh no, I may be a simple countrywoman but I'm no damned fool. Asking why, ha! I'll leave that to others! No I've never asked why. Mine's simply to do and die.'

'My very motto,' smiled the Rector, his finger running along the outline of his saucer, 'You're a woman after my own heart. Let's get started. If I can't finish this thing by tomorrow morning, I'll either be on my way, or dead and you're to tell Mr Conti to get in touch with the Catholics.'

'There'll be no need for that Rector,' joked Archer uneasily, 'I fully expect to see rainbows coming through by the end.'

'You'll see something,' said the Rector, his voice tightening, 'you'll see that thing you never asked to see, or looked for, or wondered the why of. And you'll see it broken, destitute and grovelling, so that if you're any kind of servant at all,' his voice playful again, 'you'll be searching for a new master.'

*

Brigit drew further into her bed. Iblis had shared too much of his secrets for her to ever feel at home in her life again. Her husband's infidelity, her brother's sexuality, even her son's helpless fear, these were what she could look forward to if the Rector succeeded in driving out her master.

His *eye* had enjoyed enlightening her, feeding sour news into her consciousness, when what Brigit had wanted was to under-stand the cosmos, not her petty little part of it. Now she was in danger of losing his trust. There had been no quick victory over the Rector, she had not been as strong as she thought.

The One that held power over her had sensed her weakness and sent other inhabitants of the Kingdom to her aid. The first of these spirits to enter Brigit was Lakwena from the Lower Nile, chanting in her native tongue. Brigit had allowed this ally to scream through her for hours. Lakwena spoke of bellowing hippos that had lost their limbs in a war against the people with two legs. These animals, that spoke Latin and 74 other dead languages, would destroy the Rector if he did not leave Tyger Tyger, Lawenka claimed.

The Rector had not been greatly impressed by this threat, in fact, he had laughed, patiently putting up with the noise and encouraging Brigit to reveal more. Over the course of the night Lakwena was joined by an American girl called Regan, several Koreans and Sister Morgan, a night nurse executed for eating a foetus.

The Rector was less surprised to encounter these spirits than Brigit was to experience them. Her Master had never said there were others like her before, keeping so much back when she thought he shared everything. More hurtfully, he had chosen to speak through her directly as she lost consciousness, once it was clear that she and his minions had been thrown into the fight in vain.

Brigit felt betrayed by this slight, knowing that it meant that she was no longer his favourite, only a base for his operations. To redeem herself she had to be purer and grant her Master something that it was only in a human's power to give. It was one thing to lose his trust but another all together to die unredeemed by the diabolic knowledge he had promised.

She licked her lips, there was one thing she could give him, a soul he had not even asked for, and in doing so earn the right to know as much about the Kingdom, as it already knew of her.

'Wherever you go I shall follow...'

This was what Martin remembered of London, its intolerance of failure, busy self-importance and contempt for indecision, all bathed in the ugliness of artificial light. Particularly, he sensed, in relation to those clumsy underachievers in search of a value higher than Mammon, lost in department stores they ought never to have heard of. Timorously he flinched as the shoppers rattled into him, his hopes trading places with reservations faster than competing bids before an auctioneer's hammer. Only Chantal's pert frame to his right could tread water within this consumer current, her rhythms dextrous enough to compliment the city's maniacal dance. Without hope, Martin eyed the yellow and brown carpet they were moored to, waves of customers moving closer to their goals as he wondered exactly why he had come here in search of his.

'It's a mistake, a store? More like Satan's Palace in London, people say this is cool. How? I don't see it. I feel sick.'

'It's anabasis Martin,' replied Chantal over the top of a two-headed pram that had rolled over his foot, 'Be patient and you'll click with it.'

It was the first time she had called him "Martin" rather than addressed him as a regrettable third presence, her lips pouting as they did when she spoke to Conti. Thus encouraged he replied, 'what the damned hell is "anabasis"?'

'The journey mankind makes from the shore to the inland regions, and leave hell out of this, I've had enough of it.'

'There's no hope for me, I can't swim and I have no sense of direction.' The flashing yellow lights had changed to violet, a switch that reminded Martin of dusk at Tyger Tyger, a portent that he found ominous. 'And am not likely to acquire one standing here like a sack of shit.'

Chantal laughed, not unkindly Martin thought, 'Go and explore,' he offered magnanimously, 'I'll stay and watch for Pirates.'

'You don't want to buy anything?' she was looking at him properly for once, her slim fingers fiddling with her junk jewellery, 'sometimes it's fun to just buy.'

'I only came to look,' he felt pathetic saying so, unversed in the ways of civilisation, 'no, what do they call it, I'm window shopping.'

'If you move from here I won't find you.'

'I'm fine here, move, stay, it's all the same to me. In fact, you know what, I'll see you at that club Conti's meeting us at. I'll wander round until then. In the open.'

He wanted to say something about Tyger Tyger but he was still too scared to, referring to what they had fled felt like inviting it back. 'Enjoy yourself. I'll see you later.'

Chantal waved her little finger playfully, convinced Martin's vagueness signalled an embarrassing excess of feeling he was trying to hide. Her observation, swiftly made and instantly forgotten, was partially true. Had she chosen to examine her own motivation she would have been drawn into a doorway from which she would never have emerged. Chantal's feelings were no more than what the hand guiding her allowed them to be, and her thoughts were barely perceptible at all. In their place was a confidence in the triumph of the present moment, reliant on nothing more substantial than her continuing ability to breathe. The "before" and "after" crucial in understanding who pulled her strings, was hidden away, Brigit's control of her mind was total.

'I won't be long, Martin,' she called over her shoulder.

As he watched Chantal glide into the throng, still distinct but already more like the others, Martin realised that there were certain things he was never going to be able to ask God's help for again. Instinct told him that it was only in God's power to answer honest prayers that sought good outcomes.

What Brigit wanted was evil which was why she had appealed to the Devil and yet he, her idiot brother had persisted in thinking God could help with filth. His night with the Archers had shown him the full horror of lust, the appalling mistake of obeying it and the way in which desire always led back to itself: never to people. The two servants had mothered him through a night of tears, the suggestion that this was not what they had expected of an "athlete" implicit in their condescension.

Martin grunted. It was always so, an aversion to sex preventing him from becoming fully adult or, loath, as he was to admit it, normal. The belief that he was sexually absurd explained his inability to masturbate over Chantal or become aroused over the magazines he had taken from Conti's well-stocked drawers. Much as he wished to, Martin had never found any woman physically enticing, even though he had been "in love", with one or another of them, every day since his thirteenth birthday.

With the impatience of a thwarted flasher, Martin tried to imagine the female shoppers brushing past him without their clothes on, the sounds they'd make as he entered their naked bodies, and the envious looks of the men who could only watch with admiration as he pleasured their wives and daughters, but it was no good. Even in the realm of fantasy he was a failure, incapable of taking his desires seriously because he could not feel them from the crotch up.

Succumbing to the inevitable, Martin peered up at the large poster advertising a perfume he had tried to ignore. In it two sailors, in tight pants cut high at the leg, were arm wrestling over a table emblazoned with the brand name.

Was it not enough that the curse of Tyger Tyger had virtually erased his libido? Would it not stop until it had forced him to accept he was gay? Men, it had to be acknowledged, touched the corporeal in him, but only when he entertained their physiques in the masturbatory abstract; actual flesh and blood males were too like guys for him to truly desire let alone want carnally. Which left him with his near sexless infatuation with girls.

Slowly the light he was stood under changed tone, a royal mauve marking the transition from late afternoon to night, as Martin noticed that he was walking further into the store. The path he had taken appeared to be spontaneous, though beneath the casual urge to browse he felt a colder hand guide him toward tight trousers and definitive conclusions. Many times, in his past life as "the Mighty Trunk", he wondered why he would stare dreamily, if discreetly, at the bar girls his teammates rode for sport. Pretending that it was alcohol, which interested him,

Martin had lived in fear of his ever more ludicrous crushes. This recollection posed a question he had long delayed answering. What if love, which he so readily lapsed into, was for the effete, and brute copulation the true domain of a category of male he would forever be excluded from? Unlike those studs with a passion for the real, who took their pleasure like steak dinners, he had wasted his thin virility on phantoms that disappeared the moment he sexualised them, when what he sought was so close at hand.

Martin stopped in his tracks, indifferent to the gangway he was blocking. The people coming the other way halted, something about his smile repelling them. Blind to the outline of his sister merging with and blackening his own shadow, Martin stumbled over to a mirror and embraced it. Like an author who has finally found the right title for a novel, he thumped the air with exaggerated joy. *He desired himself.* That was the point where his two irreconcilable aspects, lust and love, began and ended.

'Oh man,' he said suddenly, blood flowing back in that place he had all but given up on. It was his own body that he was allured by, the figure of a cricketer that looked very much like he did, only slimmer and with Saunders' voice as his ideal. Even this concession though, was more to do with the habit of giving desire a face, than any attraction to his former Captain. In attempting to reach others, Martin had broken from his one true love, and thus expelled himself from a paradise of self-regard and onanistic delirium. He licked his lips narcissistically and wondered why, without ever feeling comfortable around others, he had fed this unnecessary need for people, embracing naive notions of love and teamwork, selling short his serenity in the process. It was simple, he had never liked people and they had never truly taken the trouble to know him. Shaking his head, no longer bothered by the shoppers, Martin sighed, a pleasing symmetry emerging where before there had only been the grim excrescence of confusion.

'Wherever you go, I shall follow you…'

'I want to see you,' he said, addressing the ruddy face in the mirror.

'I can see you too!'

'Fuck you Brigit,' Martin laughed, dismissing the voice in his head, 'get back to your sick bed! You can't touch me now.' But Brigit could not be so easily dismissed, and nor was she just in his head, but really there with him, not to enjoy his moment but to destroy it. Her purple shadow, no more obvious that the lighting changes it hovered round the edges of, had stalked him all the way here, aware of how his journey would conclude even if he was not.

Boldly Martin strode over to a rack of jeans that had caught his attention, took down a pair and, encouraged by his daring, rubbed the denim in his hands. The trousers were at least two sizes too small, their legs inelegantly tapered to a leather bound crotch. These were his in a way another person could not be, the excitement akin to the capture of an animal he had hunted down. Spotting an isolated cubicle with a feral sharpness, he joined the current of bodies drifting over the floor, disembarking seamlessly. With the care of a felon securing a crime scene, Martin locked the door behind him and removed the belt from his linen suit, Brigit's presence confined in there with him, passing unnoticed. The pleasure he was feeling swelled rather than tingled, the ignorance of the voices outside lending a sordid complicity between their unknowing and his delight. Lying on his back, he squeezed the new slacks on, giggling at the panting gut that resisted the tight alien material with all its weight. With some effort, they were on, and leaning over the full-length mirror, Martin saw past the red splodges that covered his face, calcified eye bags, and chin hang, past even the new trousers to the centre of his being. He even saw past the other figure facing him in the mirror, mouthing the words, *'When you go brother you'll wish you'd been doing something else with your hands!'*

What he found in the mirror was a sight he never dared imagine, the unique and beautiful soul God had endowed all cricketers with. In haste, he undid himself and enjoyed his beauty. It was the most impulsive act of his life and felt delicious, his self hood erect not, as he supposed, in his hands, but in the claws that appeared behind him, holding his head under the waves, pulling him into a life more real than the one marked by a blasphemy natural to his species. His sister had given her master the last thing it was in her power to offer. There was nothing he could do to stop what happened next; all good things come to an end.

'I never loved you baby brother,' Brigit hissed, the mist congealing over Martin's falling body, 'no one ever has.'

'An ambulance for the entertainer!' laughed Brigit, opening her eyes in bed in Tyger Tyger.

There was silence in the empty room broken by the muffled sound of shoppers and the jingling of cash registers moving through the air like the noise from a distant television station, traces of the space her malign soul had just left.

'Is there a doctor in the house?' Brigit asked, labouring the point uneasily. 'Or a tiger in Tyger Tyger...' her voice dropped faintly off the walls and quite suddenly Brigit, Queen of Hell and daughter of the falling morning star, felt quite alone.

'I've given you my own brother! I made him your food!'

There was no answer.

'You're never alone in here,' she growled, imitating the manner of the One she sought.

'Master, come hither!'

This time there was no doubt, the voice Brigit heard was her own and not summoned from within the Kingdom. She coughed and ran a finger over a freshly formed scab. Had Iblis, abandoned her, forcing her to take responsibility for herself? Her association with him had certainly left her in a more exposed position than her devotion deserved. It was true her powers made most humans quake, but if trapped, they also marked her as a freak destined to spend her life subjected to electric shocks by men in white coats.

She cursed herself. Her doubts about her Master were too like those she had once entertained about God, the same dreary fear of being lied to showering her discoveries in cold worry. If something as great as consciousness could create itself without the need for God, then there was no need to believe that astral projection and psychic powers required the existence of the Devil. The Kingdom, which once appeared so large, had nearly been reduced to the size of a paranoid memory.

There were footsteps moving along the corridor, Archer's followed by the Rector. 'Why have you forsaken me,' Brigit groaned at once regretting her disbelief. There was another presence in the room. Her brother was sat at the end of her bed, dressed in a purple robe laughing, his lips smeared in rouge.

'You're killing me Brigit,' he giggled, 'really killing me. Look at you, wondering what I'm doing here. Am I a ghost or figment of your imagination? You should know; you killed me! You took my soul, as surely as your master took yours. But you shouldn't have asked him in a second time. It's the trick men and beasts play on you, getting you to miss us so you forget how *bad* it was!'

'You? He chose you?'

'Yes, I have entered the Kingdom. Thanks to you. And I will remain here unless you consent to having your soul saved by the Rector!'

'I...was meant to be the one...'

Brigit's temples stabbed as a pair of burning fists punched their way up through the bottom of her skull; opening like fiery flowers inside her. She could see nothing. He had left her so as to come back more complete and she had willed it.

'Wherever you go, I shall follow...'

Chantal put down the Lycra exercise pants and half turned to the crowd. Through the chaotic jumble of bodies a coarse voice called out to her again, her name rising over the heads of the passive mass like a whispered secret. From the blankly animated faces that surrounded her, it was clear that no one else heard the call, its echo ramifying to her alone. She could not remember when she had first known she was different, but she had guarded it, along with her other secrets, as a private pleasure to be kept not just from the world but also from herself. In the place of a naive and artistic nature, she had created a careless bike girl that slept with married men, smoked Winston's and didn't care about the future. To what extent her actual personality affected the assumed one was uncertain, as it had been so well hidden that Chantal did not know where to find it or even where to begin to look. The voice that called her did though, and in its alien urgency she grasped that her destiny and Brigit's were two parts of a related misfortune.

'Chantal!' Conti was out of breath and wired, the slowing of his steps anything but assured.

'You look different Hartley, from this morning,' her tone surprised her. It was tender. A tight and near paralysing happiness was stirring in her; it had always been there in Conti's presence, but never this acutely. Ignoring her usual instinct to suppress it, she allowed the feeling to rise to her lips, warming her cheeks and reddening her nose.

'Different but not bad,' she said.

'I know, I feel it. Different, I mean.'

His forehead bore freshly carved lines, which, though long in preparation, had broken onto his skin that afternoon. Having struggled to keep apace with his ideas, his subconscious had finally risen to his face, ennobling him in the process. Conti rubbed the sweat from his hairline. He was used to feeling emotion in agreeable bursts, but now his countenance displayed irreversible signs of cirrhosis of the soul, worry jutting off his brow like an uprooted limb.

'I have so much to tell you, it's crazy,' he said, 'lots of things make sense that didn't before, and even the things that don't... don't seem as bad. That sounds mad, I know, after what we've been through, but...'

Conti aligned his brain and voice so as to say more but the compulsion and resolve to do so was vanishing. A wistless discovery stood in the way of everything he wanted to say, its essence unsentimental and utterly of the moment. Chantal was staring trustingly into his eyes, nourishing the hope that this was the face she was waiting for, his old one too smooth for the minx in her to commune with. Now that the travails of Tyger Tyger had overcome his conviction that comfort and taste were the panacea of the universe, and humour and libido its handmaidens, there was nothing to stop his descent into seriousness unmitigated by irony. Years earlier, abandoning ideologies had been his way of demonstrating that making money and love expressed a greater truth than po-faced political abstractions. But this had proved to be "just an idea" too. Darker realities than those he could legislate for lurking beneath his shopping list, they had forced this return to belief, of what kind yet he could not say, but for this alone he was grateful. 'It's gone, what I wanted to say. But it'll come again.'

His relief at finding Chantal was greater than any doubts over her reliability as a soulmate. She smiled, his silence selling an idea of her back to herself. On either side of them people jostled past, Conti appearing like an overdressed estate agent and she a French lesbian for all he knew. He was not the same man who had voted for self-interest a year earlier, or four years before that. He did not just want to sleep with his neighbour, he wanted to take care of her too. 'We'll be all right.'

'Why do you say that?'

'Because I love you and I want everything to be all right.'

'Hartley!' Chantal blanched, her arms draped round his neck, a decade's worth of hard-earned independence exchanged for this moment, 'I love you, I love you, I love you,' she cried, her face pressed against his lowered cheek.

'I know,' he replied, sincerely immodest but taken aback, 'it just took a while for you to break.'

'You have to help me. I don't ever want to go there again, with her in that room, in that house. I forget everything, and something terrible happens to me whenever I do, I feel it. The Rector man has to cleanse me too.'

'He doesn't have to. Brigit is the one making everyone sick. When he cures her, we'll all be safe. Then we can leave and start somewhere else.'

'You and me?'

'And Brigit and Emile if no one else will have them.'

'If he saves her and you bring them, what use will you have for me?'

'The same use I had before she needed saving. And it isn't "use"; it's much more than that, it's always been more than that. We'll all go together. After what we've seen which of us will give a damn about unconventional family arrangements? Tramps like us can live anywhere.'

'But she'll always need saving.'

Conti drew Chantal further into him, muffling her words in his coat, his cock hardening unbearably against her perfect smallness. Neither noticed in their embrace the commotion growing around the dressing rooms or the stretcher ushering away a body, a blanket drawn up over its plump face.

Chapter Nine

The Rector took the room in quickly, Archer dutifully taking her place within the grooves of the battered mahogany shelving, her face ageless and maidenly in the dull pink light. Round the kaleidoscope of broken windows evening was blowing in, its colours and scents alluding to dusks that presaged living witnesses, the inorganic strain in the Rector's blood sharpening in the chill air.

'Human meanings? They came centuries after the *force* I first fell through,' Brigit croaked, 'Beautiful night, isn't it. Oh I read you well, the weather and I are old, old, old. Older than you gloaters, coming to tell me you told me so,' her accent had morphed into that of an elderly eastern European, each word delivered with pain and difficulty. 'Prehistory, feel it trickling in. Call me the perceptive one, children, I was here when the planets were uninhabited and young.'

'Though for how much longer I wonder?'

Brigit spat a clot of black phlegm into her hand and wiped it over her face. 'Moisturising. Drying up. I asked for help but none came.'

In the detritus, the Rector noticed a purple robe wrapped across the foot of her bed, soot and ink smeared over it in an attempt to blend the garment in with its surroundings.

'There is a watcher over every soul,' Brigit sighed, examining the cuts in her hands; her sore ridden body slumped against a cushion that barely supported her. 'I swore by the declining day that my watcher had gone away... but he hadn't, no, he had...not.'

'Even by your low standards you're looking terrible, Brigit. A vampire with blood poisoning isn't the kind of image that impresses a dapper fellow like Iblis.'

'I didn't think you wanted to talk to *me*,' she replied quietly, 'I thought great Iblis is who you sought.'

'I'll deal with him when I feel like it, for the moment I feel sorry for you. You've suffered enough to be rewarded with a little reality.'

'Have you come to give me my pronounced orgasm without end yet? You know I've a minkle like a mole's eye!'

'You're tiring yourself needlessly.'

Brigit let out a sharp groan, rolled onto her front and spread her buttocks apart, revealing a sore button, 'You've been in here today,' she growled, 'while I slept, Incubus!'

'I can see that it won't take much to upset you this evening,' said the Rector dryly. 'You don't have long to become human again. Are you beginning to feel ill used? I doubt whether you can even tell. Your trouble is that you don't know very much about your Master. He's as scared of me as you are.'

'He warned me. Of your coming, of your lies.' Brigit's voice dropped several octaves, 'Lieeees!'

'Save it please,' said the Rector reproachfully, 'you don't have the power to act up any more. Iblis is lost, more frightened of killing you than you are of dying. He knows the closer he comes to destroying your body, the nearer he is to destroying himself. Real victory for him is the ability to control you as a mouthpiece, not the physical annihilation of the subject. His physical presence in you is quite literally that of a large maggot in your intestine, he has no larger material embodiment he can call his own; he is nothing without the survival of the host he is embedded in. He's like a human, liking life – but on his terms, eternity brings him too close to God, whom he is terrified of.'

'And you, aren't you like a human too?'

The Rector smiled, 'No, old, like you.'

'*Meeee*? Old! That's no way to speak to a woman. To a *lady* of my age!'

'She's barely 32,' sniffed Archer.

'That may be Mrs Conti's age, but Iblis is so old that he was in the first Tyrannosaurus Rex that toyed with its prey, finding it more fun to play with it, than simply eat it as nature intended it to.'

'You are not what you seem, Rector,' said Brigit trying to control the surging in her voice, 'He is not what he seems old woman... The black man is not what he says he is,' Brigit clasped her neck. On the wall opposite, a shimmering globe of light, immaterial but eerily embodied, was moving towards her.

Archer's hands went limp. A tuneless organ march, like a caricature of church music, filled her ears, and an image of her wedding day crossed her inner eye. Firmly she tried to pull away from the awful noise welling inside her, her body suffering an electric allergy to the light on the wall. Though it was far less grotesque than what had come before, the globe's strangeness lay in its status as the product of an utterly inhuman intelligence. More unnervingly, the Rector appeared to be coordinating the devices jerky progress with his eye, like a child playing with the sun's rays through a magnifying glass.

'I'm not feeling too good, Rector...'

'It's all right Mrs Archer, don't worry.'

With haphazard purpose, the light settled on its objective, Brigit's eyes, affecting an unpleasant metamorphosis. Archer edged further in against the bookcase, pleased to disassociate herself from what she saw. Brigit's body had remained the same but her face was an ugly old man's, shuddering angrily under their gaze. It was her dead husband of 14 years since, Malcolm Archer.

'Remember me, two score years and ten, walked up the aisle with you so that fat sow daughter of yours didn't grow up a bastard!'

Archer cleared her throat and whispered a prayer, her quiet voice steady amidst the hum of the light circling her husband's sick image.

'Ignore "him", it's a mask designed to divert us,' said the Rector.

The superimposition of the old man, Malcolm, stared lecher-ously at his former wife, tutting unpleasantly under his breath, 'Lord, what I could tell you about her. The mud she stored with the cobwebs. The hay she made when the sun went down...The cocks she stewed for nothing.'

'You aren't my husband,' Archer said, 'though you're like him. He tried to find weaker people to pick on too. And he had the same bad luck.'

The face flickered out like a stubbed out candle, the darkening room beset by the smell that always rose with Brigit's anger. 'Funny fuckers,' her shadowy figure chuckled.

'You sound ready for last rites.'

'Delivered by a Moor? Never!'

The Rector spat at the shadow.

Whereas the day before, the same act heralded the appearance of a beautiful, if insidious, Angel, the Rector now watched a mound of leathery skin with yellow eyes, bowed legs and a hump emerge in Brigit's place. Iblis in all his glory had been trans-formed into a troglodyte Buddha.

Gone was the sculpted grace and bright red lips, instead a pint sized hermaphrodite with indiscernible genitalia and a small voice squeaked, 'Ahh nice of you to wait until I slipped into something more comfortable.'

'From He to She-man reptile, you appear to have forgotten what you were before,' the Rector had taken off his cross, and was toying with it, 'If I didn't know better I'd think you were trying to confuse me...'

'Unencumbered by the little people, breast to breast with the cosmos and still all these questions of identity!'

'I've seen him before in this house! That horrible face appearing at the window, peering behind curtains,' Archer blurted out. 'I always thought I were seeing things, little green men.'

'You were, it was this monster's idea of being playful and

marking out territory,' the Rector replied, 'but the bogeyman has the sweats. It's wearing this filthy costume to save what's left of its energy because it knows it will have to move house. It relied on your fear and with it your acquiescence. In the open it's nothing, just another facet of its master's deceptive intelligence.'

'It doesn't look real to me, or made of anything, like a Cheshire cat.'

Although partially absorbed in Brigit's flesh, the apparitions translucent skin hung over her like a hallucinatory costume, lurching forward as it spoke, its helium inflected voice chiming, 'Only your love can make me real, make me good, save this woman, only love...'

'Avoid eye contact with it,' said The Rector, 'think of it as the side effect of a drug or the product of too many sleepless nights.'

'Eye contact with it? I should just as well make eye contact with a compost heap,' Archer replied haughtily.

'Call yourself a Christian?' the apparition laughed, its jelly body incapable of staying still, 'You look at me as though I were a hideous growth. Do mercy and charity only apply to your own species?'

The Rector grabbed the purple robe off the mattress, 'From whom did you steal this?' he asked, raising the garment above his head like a captured flag.

Deep in its compressed face a greedy little hole opened in an imitation of a smile, 'You know what I am and you know what that is. The cloth in your hand is a symbolic artefact. It has rendered a million men mad and launched a thousand futile wars. It is the torn curtain of delusion, worn by the inmate of every asylum ever built. Even you have worn it from time to time. Render back to Caesar what is his, give me back my gift to the world...'

'And then you'd have me believe that you'd leave this woman and go back to bothering cats? I don't think so, answer my questions plainly and simply, without recourse to speeches or history lessons. What are you?'

The shimmering light above Brigit had blackened into a shadow, the apparition's face now bottle green and anything but playful. 'I am the many colours of an angry sun, wild bright blood flows in my veins. Purple is the royal colour, that robe was given to me by God!'

'You should consult a mirror,' said Archer, 'you look like a mouldering turd!'

'The woman you've made your hostage,' said the Rector silencing Archer with a raised hand, 'is why we're talking. You chose her, not her, you...'

'She came to me!'

'Because you tricked her.'

'I make war on her and her seed, she who would keep the commandments of Christ!'

'Enough!' the Rector snapped, 'you know full well the woman your Master chose was an atheist, don't take me for a naïve young Parson who uses The Cross like a yoyo. I care about her because she lives. I require nothing else. Extraneous sacrilegious posturing, and my humouring it, was yesterday's game.'

'You deny your religion even as I'm ready to dignify you as my enemy?'

'I deny everything that prevents me from understanding and expelling the one you serve,' the Rector's voice was tight with feeling, but not, Archer thought, so serious that she could not imagine him laughing off the whole spectacle moments later.

In a voice as high as a dog whistle, the apparition screeched, 'What human dust shall spring up behind me as I speed on my reckless way! What women shall I fling carelessly into the pit in the wake of my magnificent onset! Even in this form I am a brilliance your eyes cannot bear, a perpetual fire, burning perpetual fire!'

'Delusion, you're the blue ice dropped from the rest room of a plane, *freezing* cold.'

'Lies again!'

'You're freezing cold, that's why you are that disgusting colour. In a human you appear as person because you steal their heat, their memories and their lives. Outside one, you're just an abrasion on stone. Hell isn't hot, it's cold, like the storage you're kept in to remind you of your separateness from living things. It's why you *need* the species you profess to hate.'

'You mock my appearance but I could stand before you as the biblical beast of seven heads if I so wished, with ten horns and upon them ten crowns and upon my crowns the name of blasphemy...' with each boast the image of the squat figure grew smaller, its evaporating presence sucked through Brigit's skin like molecules of sweat moving the wrong way. Once more the figure of her frail body rose over that of her "guest", its weakness inspiring neither compassion nor restraint in the Rector.

'It's a primordial jealousy that motivates you,' he said standing over the bed. 'Nothing in humankind stands alone. Look at the woman whose mind you sat in,' he grabbed Brigit's face and held it under the shadow on the ceiling. 'She is part of the world just as her skin is part of her, the sun is in her blood and the earth her feet, her soul the cosmos, and her genes her family. Nothing of this woman is alone except her mind. The one place you could enter, so as to isolate her being and make the rest of her alone too, as alone as you yourself are.'

There was a pause broken by the sound of the downstairs television switching itself on loudly, followed by the other television sets in the house, the weird chatter between the channels like animals unable to agree on a single course.

Brigit bent her legs up protectively, squashed bile from the fetid mattress plastered over her bony knees. Imploringly she looked into the Rector's eyes, almost in the hope that she would find someone else in his place.

'She's back,' said Archer, 'that's Mrs Conti all right.'

Grasping her head away from the tight bundle she had

retreated into, the Rector resembled a preacher about to administer baptism, 'Brigit, royal blood is purple, it oozes, it's dark. You've been sold a pup, yours is fungal. He wants you to kill for him and you'll be given nothing in return. Without you he is an empty idea in need of sustenance, you have his power...'

'I...need him still.'

'You never have.'

'I...'

Brigit's eyes flickered, changing from yellow to green, their appearance natural but somehow more terrible for it. Slowly and with malice she said, 'I see a lake of fire burning with brimstone, neither from or towards anywhere, I am happy there so long as I know she is unhappy here. The more you understand the less I am. I can't let you have her...' on the last word her head flopped back, hanging precariously off the Rectors arm.

It was as if Brigit was waiting for the final command or reprieve. One by one the lights came on in the room and in an electrical rush the atmosphere changed from the weird to the elementally dangerous.

The Rector let go of her. Her Master was with them, not the conversationalist he had come as before, but desperate and malevolent, the shadow of a man.

Grabbing the Rector's leg in a furious clinch, Brigit sat bolt upright and screamed, first in French and then in English,

'Dance upon my sparks! I am the French girl!'

Before he had time to restrain her she snatched the crucifix from his hand and, swallowing it whole, she grunted, 'Now your Kingdom will meet mine.'

Little about the nightclub was as Conti had remembered it. The bright carnival entrance had been replaced with a fake portcullis, the disco chick at the door for a bouncer dressed as a vampire, and the glittery sign for "Rapture" was usurped by one for "The Pit", spelled out in neon cobweb lettering. Once inside a narrow tunnel covered in plastic ivy led on to a chrome dance floor hidden in dry ice, the low ceiling coated with dark velvet drapes, rubber vines and plastic spiders. The overall effect was of a National Trust site taken over by adolescent necromancers, the ambience too much like a comical Tyger Tyger for Conti's liking.

'Apologies,' he said, his voice barely audible over the PA system, 'I don't know what's happened to this place since I was here last. Bela Lugosi must have bought out the management.'

'Nice funky sounds,' said Chantal with affectionate sarcasm. An assortment of Kensington Market Goths were bat dancing to an industrial buzz saw and its gruff vocal accompaniment, their moves mimicking a gypsy's over a crystal ball or a troop of rock climbers in search of rope. 'They're hilarious,' said Chantal, 'they remind me of the Muppets.'

'Muppets or masturbators, we're stuck here for the duration. I told Martin this is where we'd meet him. But with a name change, God knows how he'll find it.'

Taking their place in a coffin shaped chair, Conti wandered over to the bar conspicuously, returning with two noxious looking cocktails, 'Best to think of these as magic potions or toothpaste. Cheers.'

Chantal slurped hers down in one, licking the sticky remnants off the top of the wide brimmed glass. 'It's funny,' she said.

'Our being here?'

'No, you. How you came to be what you are, from whoever you were before. Thinking of you dancing in a place like this years ago, when you thought it was cool. And that Cathedral school still a far away mistake in your future.'

'That's funny?'

'Funny because you didn't know what you would become, you were still ignorant of your own outcome. I wonder who you were then, and what it felt like to be you. Did you want to wear suits and marry a freak with money ... to become a country squire who lived through affairs and dry remarks to middle class parents, was that what you wanted?'

'Why ask me now?'

'Because I've never been interested in anyone before, not me, not you, no one.'

'I...' Conti reddened a little, the strobe light he was sat under turning the cheek that faced Chantal a spotted purple, 'I know what I told people I wanted, but I knew I could never have it, that it wasn't *possible* to have it, so I don't know whether it counts.'

'Are you too embarrassed to tell me what it was?'

Conti pulled out a cigarette and looked at it, 'What I wanted for Christmas was the withering away of the State, with perhaps a distinguished literary career and a harem of adoring fans thrown in. My smaller wish, though far more pathetic in hindsight, was for a kind of liberal socialist Buddhist utopia, too tiny to be annexed by a bigger country, where I and a group of 30 or so hand picked friends could occupy an island, growing our own food and creating shelter, putting our social theories to the test, a sort of cool version of the boy scouts.'

'That really doesn't sound like you.'

'It wasn't me. I was missing television and electric guitars before we'd even decided how we'd find the place, and as for the first "wish", enough said. I might also have dared think that love was important.'

'So nothing survives of those feelings you had.'

'No, not *nothing*...'

'What then?

Conti hesitated, 'A great desire for the opposite of whatever "common sense" is. You know, that if life can appear out of nothing, then...'

'Go on.'

'Well what's there to say that something as incredible as our being here can't happen again, after we die, or maybe *in* life, right in the middle, at its most depressing and normal. Sometimes I think Brigit is our proof that life can still be revelatory,' Conti looked round the club. 'I even feel it in a shit-hole like this, that our lives were meant to be extreme, lived outside of habit, past all the selves we're bound by. Self worship, the elevation of a limitation, I've ruined myself with it, and the worst thing about it is I'm not the only one, I've become typical.'

Chantal drew as close as she could without actually joining Conti in his clothes, 'That's the way I feel too,' she decided, 'especially when I'm in a shit-hole like this.'

Conti cleared his throat and put the cigarette down without lighting it, 'My mistake was to confuse a sense of wonder with thinking I could have anything I wanted. To stop thinking about life, and just think of myself.'

'I call it your "eggs" moment.'

'You call it my what?'

'"Eggs", with me upstairs and your wife downstairs and your eggs made just as you like them, all of us second best but still special, and you able to exist in an infinite sequence of perfect situations without any comeback or fuss. You still want it, but it's impossible. We all have to give something up.'

'I don't know how to answer that.'

'Clever people can be sexy when they just listen.'

The music had changed and the dance floor cleared. A laconic synthesizer track began, the voice of a well-spoken man talking over the top in an English parody of rap.

'Let's dance.'

'To this?'

'Why not?' said Chantal, trying to pull Conti up by his sleeve.

'Not now, you can if you like.'

Chantal giggled flirtatiously, rolling her eyes round in circles with mock abandon. Taking a couple of steps back on to an elevated part of the floor, she ran her hands over her hips and ground her bottom slowly, too slowly even for the uneven music, her small hips straining at the sides of her jeans.

Conti groaned; the pubescent fear that all women were

whores, especially those he loved, was all too apparent. 'She's doing this for herself, and not to attract attention,' he said to no one, as Chantal closed her eyes and mimed a sex act with her mouth and hand.

'Oh Chantal…'

Dizzily she stumbled to one side, catching the heel of another dancer. There was something askew in her movements and Conti took to his feet in an attempt to steady her.

'Are you okay,' he asked, his voice drowned by the songs chorus.

Chantal, who had been floating on ether seconds before, felt the speed of her heart accelerate and the music give way to a piercing voice. It was not coming from the club but inside her and there was little she could say to prevent it from exploding. A shower of sparks fizzled about her face, as Conti's eyes and those of the mascara caked boy who had caught her body froze in a pirouette of fire.

She knew what would follow, the fall, the inevitable darkness and the remembered knowledge that there would be no afterlife. But it did not happen like that, in the darkness where she fell there was a twinkling, as though she were laid on her back watching a night sky, the sparks vanishing under a glorious constellation of stars. The murderous intent that had tried to kill her was killing itself. Conti's plea for mercy over the closing bars of the song was loud enough to have sent death back from whence it came.

'Someone call an ambulance,' shouted Conti, 'I think she's had a heart attack!'

'Iblis son of the Morning, take this unworthy girl as my last sacrifice…'

'Whatever you're attempting isn't working Brigit.'

The Shadow of Death would not come to her; Iblis could not find a way past the Rector. Time moving backwards was Brigit's undoing; she had not become the French girl or had the slut dance upon her sparks. Instead she had moved through Chantal's consciousness and out into the cold London night, her dark half dissolving above Regent Street, far from her essence and that of her impatient master.

The effort of bringing Chantal to the Kingdom, a girl whose soul she thought she mastered, had delivered her prostrate to the Rector. 'Merde, veux-tu m'emporter dans ta chute? O mon cher Belzebuth, je t' adore!'

'You're still here, though weaker than before and nearer death,' replied the Rector. 'Talk in English if you can at all.' His voice as milky as hers was shot, 'I know you are ready.'

Brigit blinked. The Rector had changed colour appearing biblically white to her, his clothing, hair and skin, like a hide worn over his blackness.

'Forget all evasions, it's very late now. You are on your own.'

'You are not an apostle. You cast devils out with their power,' she muttered faintly, 'What are you? You serve strange gods.'

'He isn't protecting you, you are hiding him.'

'You, you know him...' Brigit gave out a wet cough, 'I'll do whatever you want. If you take me to the Kingdom with you.'

'It's not the sort of place to take a woman. And how can you be sure you're not already there, Brigit?'

'He's hungry. If we were there he could eat. To satisfy hunger the food must be destroyed. What I am for me, I am not for him. I am the only food here. Take us.'

Slowly the Rector removed a small book from his jacket and began to read from it, quietly and with purpose. From the sound of his words it was not at all clear, to Archer, that what he read was from the Bible or a religious text. Nevertheless his low incantation was soothing and in peaceful but sudden stages, she fell, the wooden throne carved in to the bookcase she was leant against catching her sleeping body. Afterwards, when Archer woke, she could hear the Rector's voice, and would continue to hear his voice until the night she watched Tyger Tyger burn down, six years hence.

'People,' said Brigit, 'you can't love them. You're doing this because you hate me. What do you owe them? I make you what you are, I give you what you do... you owe me safe passage to the Kingdom.'

'How do you know you're not already there, Brigit?'

'How could I be? The Kingdom holds answers, this place just *is*.' Each word was costing Brigit too much; she was down to her last few sentences and no more.

The Rector continued to read, every third syllable rising slightly, a definite rhythm emerging, like the sound of an incoming tide.

Exhaustedly Brigit choked back her tears, an estuary of brown mucus rolling out of her mouth like piles of discarded clay, 'Stop, stop it. It's heresy to deny the difference between the eater and eaten...'

'The eater isn't your master or you his food, and besides, heresy is for believers,' said the Rector. 'In nature the higher wave overturns the weaker, but has no more claim of superiority than one part of the ocean has over another.'

'The movement of water in water, I remember,' Brigit mumbled, 'Don't leave me here, I know nothing in the water, I can't remember him... I can't find him. If I'm not food I drown.'

'You've nothing to remember or find. You've worked too hard. Unknowability suits you better than all this naming. Naming granted you sovereignty over things but gave you the pain of becoming something. Return to the deep nothing of ignorance, give up pretending. Let go and I promise you'll experience the deep enlightenment that only those that have come back from possession can. You're *close*.'

'I can't. If I leave him, I leave me.'

Brigit gasped, a spirited airlessness was filling her body in reverse proportion to her attempts to remain grounded. Slowly she let go, firm ripples of energy travelling from her shuddering cranium down to the base of her spine and tingling feet.

'I see a still white sky emerge from behind black waves, and light everywhere. Rector,' she called, 'am I in eternity?'

Her body had levitated, every suffering particle of it, off the bed, as she always knew it could, but not towards the Kingdom, extinction or any other fate speculation had prepared her for.

'Have I become a principle? Such strange theology priest...whereof Jesus, the ritual of exorcism...' she stopped talking, an ecstatic trembling tore through her, 'What has happened to all the prayers!'

And there she hovered, neither an end nor the means to one, but a digit cast over the shoals of continual being.

'Good,' said the Rector, 'we are nearly done.'

*

The Rector walked around her, praying wildly and sweetly and like madness. Upside down, Brigit observed the ceremony. She felt as close to the Rector's commands as a wolf does to its claws, his words a refining fire, the very act of obeying his will no more alien to her than acknowledging her own nature.

When she moved to speak it was his voice she heard address her, 'Remember,' he seemed to say, 'I've met people like you, but you will never know another one like me. You came all this way without knowing what you came for, or how to go back. The glory of the world lies in being able to see it, your insanity searched for complex proof, but goodness was already the precondition of your pointless quest. Good is, evil is not. Which of the two has earned the greater right to be thought of as the truth of our condition is not your concern.'

'There is... evil in you.'

'You are right. I collect it,' he said, stroking her crooked neck, 'and very occasionally, I find it interesting.'

'It kills...'

'No. I have been possessed many hundreds of times before and drunk myself sober on it, you've done it only this once. You wanted what I did, a world past this one, and you discovered in its place a force utterly unworthy of your exertions. He has lied to you, even about what he was. You have entered the Kingdom, Brigit, it was never denied to you, what you saw was its truth. It is nothing.'

Brigit's chest rose slightly; the knot in her loosening towards an alignment with the self she abandoned that Spring afternoon, the same voice she heard then threatening,

'*You cannot leave the Kingdom.*'

'I must!' she screamed.

'*You are ours.*'

'Leave me...'

The Rector was at her ear, 'Brigit, Iblis is a sportsman who understands cunning matched with cunning; many have enjoyed his deals and cheated him. Do what thou wilt shall be the whole of the law is his way. Copy him.'

'They won't let me go!'

'Leave the Kingdom.'

'How?'

'By giving him to me.'

'But what will happen to me?'

The Rector passed one hand over her, the other supporting her bottom, which felt fuller than before. The lines on Brigit's skin softened and patches of freckles rose over her nose and forehead as they would under the sun. The filth on her body was dropping away, carried off in the breeze, her sores and scabs were separating like sand to reveal clean, toned flesh.

'He can't follow you if you leave of your own free will.'

'It's vanishing...'

The eye whose control she had fallen under blinked. Then it closed. Vast waters poured from one end of her to the other, the

Kingdom swilling on a sea of waste trapped low in her womb.

The Rector tapped her feet, 'Excrete Brigit, feel it fall from you.'

'It's burning inside me.'

'Push.'

With no small effort, her face straining as though giving birth to a brick wall, Brigit released a tiny red sliver, no longer than a worm, out of her womb into the Rector's waiting mouth.

'*He is who he says I am...*' the words came from everywhere, the voice unmistakably the one Iblis had spoken through at the height of his power, '*do not let him have me...*'

Brigit dropped to the floor like a giant leaf. The Rector, wiping his lips greedily, drew a figure of eight over her with his index finger and made a low whistling sound. Then he shook her hands, flicked a sachet of sugar over her and muttered another incantation.

'I'm not going to take him all. Only the maggot, only the soul.'

Brigit listened, unsure of whether it had all happened or was about to, the Kingdom fading like the dreams of the night before, ignorance the parent that would protect for now. The room had filled with colour and fresh air, probably no more than what would normally be regarded as natural though for Brigit, nothing less than a miracle.

'Am I me again?'

'You are you.'

With a sleepy eye she watched Archer get up and become part of the bookcase, or rather grow out of it, her head a circular cavity, the composition and structure of her body obeying some territorial imperative of the house, its wooden bosom completed by two perfectly delineated breasts.

'Oh,' said Brigit.

She remembered everything; she could forgive no one, least of all herself, but it did not matter, her perspective was now too wide to take account of anything so small as her life.

'Enlightenment!' she laughed. 'Hmmm, yes...the hills are moving to and fro, the carousel is full of light. Strange gods are watching over me.'

Brigit could say no more. The Rector's hand was in her mouth.

Conti watched the afflicted come and go from the arched hospital window, its gothic finishing befitting a secular temple of medicine. Light years away the stars were merging into the first shards of dawn, the view of Paddington he surveyed not limited by past association, but enlarged by the celestial spread above it.

The physical sensation he had carried in him since Brigit's possession began; which he'd experienced as a panic above his bowel, was no longer there. Gone was the spirit of heaviness, tired irony, and forbearance that afforded him gravity, all banished, leaving him on the sunnier side of doubt.

For the first time since his teens he felt that he had risen above the levels of an average human being.

Throughout Brigit's possession the man who fell in love with her and who would always be hers, simply because the past belongs to whoever was there, had wilted. No area of his life had remained unexamined. But tonight the pain had stopped, as swiftly as a light switched off at the mains. With his hand pressed to the glass, Conti wished he could leave the building and go outside, like a prisoner released from jail or a boy at the start of a holiday, the infinitude of an eternal present his reward for years spent inside.

Chantal was still alive. His faith in the absurd state of affairs that no one could do anything about, which he had begun to think of as God, was strong. As Chantal had been carried away he had even promised that if she lived (and Conti had trouble believing this even now) he would attempt to *spread the Lord's message and do his work*. In the time it took for Chantal to collapse and the paramedic to pronounce her alive, a change had occurred. Brigit's possession, he sensed, had ended and with it his pain.

The relief he felt was matched by the knowledge that his love for Brigit, qualified as it was in the past, had attained a selflessness it had never risen to in happier times. He had never had to earn Brigit's love before. Whether he had done enough to earn it in her possession was immaterial, it was not a detail he could expect her to care about now. Conti had always found it difficult to think of love separately from its circumstances, whether that involved Emile, Brigit's dowry or the guilt he felt in allowing her to fall in love with him. To his amazement, this bundle of factors had worked the other way too, and his love for her had continued in spite of repulsion, disgust and fear, a binding agent that he never sought to question, or seek approval of.

A jumbo jet passed overhead and for once, Conti did not secretly desire to be on it. He would never forget that irreducible evil existed, though so too did absolute good, the tragedy being that it had taken a direct encounter with both in their purest forms for him to believe in them.

Possession's terrible reward was a mixed harvest of survival and existential disappointment, the unknown having to be turned to for help, his own efforts at containment having proved altogether inadequate.

With all the generosity he could muster, he hoped that Brigit had found the enlightenment she sought in the Rector's exorcism, having failed to find it in their marriage or the Kingdom. His guess was that her health and sanity had come too late for them as a couple. She would never love him again, the insights offered by her possession, portrayed the man he was in too accurate a light. But Chantal, rescued from the threshold of death, loved him selfishly whether she woke or not, this love was now the highest value; every other emotion felt dishonest somehow.

Moving away from the window, Conti felt his knees weaken,

the impulse to spend an hour in the company of a bacon sandwich and the sports pages of a tabloid, took over. Unhurriedly he shuffled towards the hospital cafeteria, confident that his new resolutions would be waiting for him on his return.

Hearing at last the deepest silence, the Rector threw the cross he had retrieved from Brigit's throat over the side of the balcony. It landed in a dewy puddle of feathers, a flock of rooks having earlier fought over the space for a worm.

The Rector looked at Brigit, her body bulging with life, as work well done, peacefully asleep if not quite out of harms way. Lightly he pressed her stomach, checking for the last traces of possession, his touch causing her to hiccup slightly. With a gentle rumble, her chest palpated and she let out a deep burp. The remains of Iblis belched into a new day to configure again, beyond God's reach or man's concern for him.

'Crikey,' yawned Archer stretching her arms, 'I can't believe I fell asleep during all that. God knows I must have needed to though...' she stopped.

The one she was addressing had already begun the long route back to the hills, confined spaces, like houses or skin, never able to hold him for very long.

*

Tyger Tyger was sold as cheaply as it was bought. The Archers' formal association with the building ended two days later when Judith tried to kill herself, and did not desist from her suicide attempts until her mother began a fire in the basement, six years later, destroying most of the structure of the house.

By that time, several owners had passed through, the last of which, a record executive who had bought the building without viewing it, and left as soon as he had, transformed the basement into a recording studio. This quickly fell to disuse, strange voices

214

and screams making it onto the final edits of adult orientated rock ballads.

These shrieks were the same ones that Conti and Chantal were to hear as they sometimes made love on their barge, and Emile perceived from time to time, at warehouse parties and raves.

Only Brigit strode on unscathed by fear, visiting the burnt out wreck on her infrequent visits to England with the Iranian budget airline tycoon she married. There she would notice the old evil waiting in the ruins for a little human sympathy to tease it back to life, and laugh nervously, her enlightenment coloured by the world she had returned to and the strange gods that would never allow her to forget.

ACKNOWLEDMENTS

Having never written a novel based around a memorable nightmare before, I thought it prudent to seek the counsel of more help than usual. Ian Hartshorne, Matteo Mandarini, Nina Power and Flora Stubbs all aided with a draft that turned out, to my surprise, to be the first and not finished article. Thank you also to Eugenie Furniss, Cathryn Summerhayes and Alice Ellerby at William Morris for attempting to engage publishers and their marketing departments with a literary horror story. My gratitude also to Mat Osman and Sarah Bartell for designing by far the best cover of any of my books, and Lucy Castro, my Mother and Father and John Hunt for their encouragement and belief.

Contemporary culture has eliminated both the concept of the public and the figure of the intellectual. Former public spaces – both physical and cultural – are now either derelict or colonized by advertising. A cretinous anti-intellectualism presides, cheerled by expensively educated hacks in the pay of multinational corporations who reassure their bored readers that there is no need to rouse themselves from their interpassive stupor. The informal censorship internalized and propagated by the cultural workers of late capitalism generates a banal conformity that the propaganda chiefs of Stalinism could only ever have dreamt of imposing. Zero Books knows that another kind of discourse – intellectual without being academic, popular without being populist – is not only possible: it is already flourishing, in the regions beyond the striplit malls of so-called mass media and the neurotically bureaucratic halls of the academy. Zero is committed to the idea of publishing as a making public of the intellectual. It is convinced that in the unthinking, blandly consensual culture in which we live, critical and engaged theoretical reflection is more important than ever before.